# playing with matches

Lit Lovers
Book Five

## ciara blume

# acknowledgments

Thanks to all my friends and family who have bolstered and supported me over the past year of writing a ridiculous number of words.

Leane Vandeman, I cannot write about the topic of reality TV without thinking of you and smiling. Forgive me please for the extreme liberties and leaps of logic in my story sculpting. It might not be realistic, but it's good TV. And by that, I mean it's probably fiction.

To all the beta readers, ARC readers, newsletter subscribers, and fans, I am so grateful for your time, your feedback, and your faith in me.

I'm so grateful for Anya Kagan of Touchstone Editing and Michelle Price, my "Peaches Resort" pal and pinch-hitting proofer extraordinaire, who have made both my story and my words better and more readable.

Brian, what can I say? We made it! You deserve a medal for your patience and support.

Finally I'd also like to thank all the little old ladies at the Heritage Pointe beading club, with whom I've spent two years of Tuesdays stringing beads, swapping stories, making something out of nothing, and laughing. I've learned so much more than I've taught in those sessions.

# prologue: isla

. . .

*Six Months Ago*

"GOOD MORNING, ISLA," Emily Romano's beautiful smiling face pops up on the Zoom screen. Her hazel eyes are twinkling, and her curls are hanging loose around her face. It's nighttime in Washington State, and her living room is bathed in warm lamplight. She turns the laptop around so that I can get a peek at the other people in the room. I'm a special guest for this week's episode of the *Lit Lovers* podcast, which Emily co-hosts. She's been trying to get me on the show to talk about my romance novels since we met in Rome a few months ago.

"What time is it there again?" I ask, too lazy to do the backward math. It's a little before 7am in Rome. My apartment feels chilly and damp, and I clutch my cup of tea against my chest to warm myself. The weather forecast was good for today. I'll probably take a long walk past the Pantheon if it pans out.

"It's a little before 10 pm here," Emily says. "Thanks for agreeing to meet with us so early. Next time we'll meet in person, right?"

Emily's been after me to come visit her this summer, which seems like a good plan. If I sublet my apartment to tourists in August, it will cover much of my rent for the year.

"Ten's a bit late; aren't you all tired?" I ask, trying to get a better look at the assembled podcast crew that Emily's told me so much about. They don't seem sleepy though. They seem like they've just stepped away from a fun night out. There's a couple of bottles of beer sitting open on the side table and a bowl of chips.

"It's a great time to record - there's not a lot of noise outside, and we're all still wide awake," Emily says. "Love that wrap, by the way!" she comments on my electric blue, embroidered silk kimono visible at the bottom of the screen.

"It's actually my bathrobe," I admit. "But it's a fancy vintage one, so I thought it would do!"

"Hi, Isla!" a curvy brunette in a close-fitting pink and orange-striped sweater waves from the couch. I recognize her from posts on Emily's Instagram account. "I'm Alexis. I'm the one who dragged Emily onto the *Lit Lovers* podcast. I'm so excited to meet you! I can't wait to hear more about your books."

"This is Chelsea," Emily turns the screen to face a willowy blonde woman who is writing in a notebook. She looks up and waves. Chelsea is the younger sister of the *Lit Lovers* podcast founder, Jackson Porter.

The podcast started as a bit of a joke - the two siblings and their friends love to dish about romantic films and books. Chelsea likes her romance sweet, and Jackson, who prefers logic to emotion, thinks it's all ridiculous. Alexis is unabashed about her penchant for smut, and Emily serves as the referee.

"Hi, Isla!" Chelsea says. "I'm such a big fan of your series! We're still chatting about matchmaking, right?" Chelsea asks.

"Fine with me," I stifle a yawn and sip my favorite imported smoked Earl Grey tea. You wouldn't think that bergamot and fire mix, but sometimes things surprise you.

"We're just waiting a moment for my brother, Jackson," Chelsea explains. "We were all out at a bar earlier, and one of his students had a bit too much to drink. Jackson gave him a lift home. He should be here any–"

"I'm here, I'm here! Calm down." I see the heavy wooden door at the far end of the room swing open. A tall, slim man comes in, brushing snowflakes off his coat. He carefully places what appears to be an axe on the coffee table and pulls a set of earbuds out of his pocket. "Is that her?" he asks, gesturing at the screen as he approaches. He's squinting suspiciously at me, as if I'm a screensaver and not a real live person waiting on the other side of the camera, albeit halfway around the world. "She's so young. And a redhead. I was expecting a little old lady."

*Ummmmm.....*

"Nice to meet you, Jackson," I say.

"Jesus," he says, startling like I just jumped out from behind a wardrobe shouting *boo*! "I didn't think you were *on* yet. You must have frozen. I thought I was looking at a photo."

"Sorry to scare you. Was that an axe you just put on the coffee table?" I ask, fascinated. "I've heard about lumberjacks living in the Pacific Northwest, but I didn't think people actually walked around with axes."

"Jackson, a lumberjack?" Alexis snorts and doubles over laughing, hugging herself. "Isla's *funny*. I like her. Cute British accent, too."

"It's a throwing axe," Emily lifts the computer and walks across the room with it, ostensibly looking for a good place to set it while we record the episode. The room behind her, along with the people in it, sways for a few seconds. I look away and stir some organic local honey into my tea while she gets everything settled. "Sorry, Isla. Just give me a sec. I told you about that place we like to go. The Grumpy Stump? They sponsor the podcast, and we generally like to go there on Wednesdays."

"That's Jackson's lucky axe," Chelsea says. "He calls it the Cupid Special. Uses it to con people into signing up for his dating app. If they lose a round, they have to become his guinea pigs."

"I am not conning people. My app provides a legitimate service," Jackson protests. "There's a waitlist to get on the beta."

"I still don't get the whole concept of you being an axe-throwing Cupid." Chelsea's brow is furrowed. "It seems a little bloody and violent. And isn't the whole point of your app to avoid the drama?"

"Yes, that's the whole point, Chels. My app hits the target every time so nobody has to get hurt." Jackson sounds exasperated.

Emily places the laptop on some sort of raised shelf or ledge, so I am looking down at everyone and steps back. "You're on the mantel, Isla. I think you can see everyone now, right?" Emily places her earbud in her ear. "And speaking of Cupid, happy Valentine's Day!"

I can see the whole crew now. Emily twists her long locks into a makeshift bun and takes a seat in a leather wingback chair towards the center of the room, facing the mantel where I've been stuck. I can see that Emily is wearing a chunky woolen knit jumper, which I suspect is her handiwork. She reaches for a colorfully crocheted afghan that was draped on the back of the chair, wrapping it around her shoulders. I can just barely make out the firelight reflected in the vase on the coffee table in front of her. The axe, covered with a leather sheath, is laying beside the vase.

Chelsea and Alexis are both sprawled out on deep brown leather sofas on either side of Emily, each draped in yet more afghans. The sofas are facing each other, but both women are turned sideways so they can face me. The room looks so Western and cozy that I kind of wish I were there in person for this.

"Nice roses," I say, admiring the giant deep red blooms.

"Aren't they?" Emily's smile extends to the corners of her eyes. "And you should smell them," she closes her eyes and inhales dreamily. "My guy did well."

"Whatever." Jackson takes his place in the empty armchair beside Emily. "You do know that the red roses are a remnant from the pagan blood rituals that were part of the origin of Valentine's Day?"

"There's no real evidence that Lupercalia and Valentine's Day are directly connected," I reply. "It's probably more of a coincidence related to the dates and not a direct cultural link."

Jackson glances up at me, looking a bit surprised to hear me mention the ancient pagan event. I see his face properly now. His hair is a tawny, streaked brown. Shiny and thick. He has high cheekbones. Excellently arched brows, if a bit haughty. And a straight, classic Patrician nose. It's hard to tell what his jawline is like under all that facial hair though. I'm guessing he hasn't grown it to hide a weak jaw. His eyes look dark and smoky in the firelight. Something is pleasing about his face. It's unusually symmetrical and balanced. He's got such a classical look that he could be a marble bust in one of the many architectural gardens here in Rome.

For a moment, I like him. Then he has to ruin it by speaking. "So, Isla, you've heard of Lupercalia," he says, all cocked, locked, and loaded, ready to mansplain. "Did you read about it on Wikipedia?"

"I live in Rome," I say, pointing out the sunrise behind me. "The day is dawning on the city where the pagan ritual happened. Plus, I've studied it. I have a degree in anthropology."

"Right…interesting," Jackson drawls dismissively. I don't think he's listening to me. He is looking down now, reviewing his notes. He lifts a copy of my book and fans the pages, then wrinkles his nose as if he's unintentionally stirred up something smelly and unpleasant. "Well, we should probably get this session done and in the bag. I have an early class tomorrow and an even earlier meeting with my investors. What's the trope of the week, Chels?"

"Matchmaking," Chelsea says.

"Okay then, everyone's all mic'd up here. You all know the drill. Isla, I'm going to hit record in a moment and do the intro - then we can all just sit back and have a conversation. Thirty minutes tops. Alexis, try not to say anything too scandalous this time. I'm still getting emails about your graphic rundown of BDSM terms from the last episode."

"Sheesh. People are such prudes." Alexis rolls her eyes. "Most of that stuff is common knowledge."

He stands, walks over, and leans into the computer screen to hit record. I catch a flash of a neck chain and a small green medallion of some kind tucked into his collar, resting in the hollow of his throat. Jackson squints at me again. His whole face fills my screen. "I really did think you'd be older. Plus, I didn't picture you as a redhead," he shakes his head and shrugs like he's shaking off a bad idea. "Here we go."

As soon as Jackson is seated again, he launches into the introductions and thanks his sponsors. Then Chelsea announces the trope of the week.

"We thought it would be fun to talk about matchmaking this week since that is Isla Fairfax's specialty," Chelsea says. "We are so lucky to have the bestselling author with us this week. Her series, *The Mystic Matchmaker*, is a must for anyone who is a fan of this trope. Want to tell us a little more about it, Isla?"

I take a breath before speaking. Even though I'm used to the pitch and have written nine books, I still get nervous every time I have to give it.

"*The Mystic Matchmaker* series is about a gifted psychic who, with the help of friendly ghosts and spirits, can psychically find the perfect matches for even the most difficult singles. The only catch is that she's cursed and can't find love for herself."

*Just like me.* I take a sip of my tea, before going on, which isn't necessary, thanks to Chelsea.

"The matchmaker can't find love for herself... *until she makes one hundred true love matches*!" Chelsea breathes out excitedly. "And the last book ended on the ninety-ninth match! We're all dying to see what happens in the final book of the series!"

*We sure are. All I have to do is write it.*

"I guess that remains to be seen," I smile enigmatically.

"So, Lupercalia!" Jackson announces, apropos of nothing. He leans forward. "Tomorrow is Valentine's Day and we're chatting about matchmaking, so it makes sense to talk about the ancient bloody rituals that took place on this very same date in Rome, the very city where Isla resides. Many would argue that Valentine's Day is just a pallid, cleansed, and commercialized version of Lupercalia."

"Actually there's never been a direct link established between the two events, but sure, let's explore that if you like," I say. I can see the firelight gleaming in Jackson's eyes as he gazes up at my face on the screen on the mantle. I imagine from his point of view it must look like the fire is licking at my feet. I'm literally in the hot seat.

"What the heck is Lupercali-fragilistic-whatnot?" Alexis sits up and toys with the tassel on the corner of her afghan.

"Well, Isla, apparently you're quite the scholar. You want to take this?" Jackson says. There's an edge in his voice. A reserve. He's like a father who's handed the butter knife to his toddler and asked him to cut the bread. He's willing to stand back while the child makes the motions but intends to finish the job himself.

"Why don't you share your knowledge first, since you seem so anxious to chat about it?" I suggest.

"What does any of this have to do with matchmaking?" Chelsea shakes her head impatiently, looking from her brother to me. I can see the resemblance in their bone structure, but Chelsea is finer-featured and fairer. Her hair cascades in soft, highlighted-blond waves over her shoulders.

"We're getting to that," Jackson says. "Fine, I'll explain. Lupercalia was a pagan ritual that involved the slaying of multiple goats and possibly a dog."

"Gross!" Alexis exclaims. "That's horrible."

"I agree," I say. "That part does seem awful. But it's important to remember that ritual sacrifices were not uncommon at the time. Goat sacrifices were done to ensure male fertility, and the dog was an offering to the she-wolf who raised the infant twins Romulus and Remus, who were the founders of Rome."

"But all that was already ancient history by the time the festival of Lupercalia peaked," Jackson interrupts. "This annual bloody ritual sacrifice would kick off two days of feasting and coupling. The young virile men would run naked through the city, strutting their stuff, whipping willing women with leather thongs cut from the hides of the sacrificed goats."

"Oh my," Alexis sits up, whipping the tassel back and forth. "This is going in an interesting direction. Do tell me more about the naked dudes with the whips?" She raises her eyebrows hopefully.

"Ummmm….." Chelsea pauses, looking alarmed. "Seriously guys. I didn't think we were talking about that stuff again this week?"

Jackson is still staring at me with a whiff of challenge about him. His chin is jutted out and the corner of his mouth is quirked up. "Do correct me if I'm wrong. Am I getting my facts right, Professor Fairfax?"

"Isla," Emily tentatively breaks the tension, "do people in Rome still celebrate this festival?"

"As far as I know, there are no ritual sacrifices, and I have yet to see any public nudity since I've lived here," I explain. "But of course there are still some people who honor pagan traditions."

"Interesting. Are you one of those people, Isla? You seem to be really into all the woo-woo crap…" Jackson tilts his head at me.

"Guys! What the heck does any of this have to do with *matchmaking*?" Chelsea gripes.

Jackson leans back, arms folded, smiling vaguely, still waiting to see if I'll respond to his provocation.

"We should back up and explain to your listeners that public nudity was not the norm in Rome at the time," I explain. "It was a pretty wild thing for them, too. And the men who participated as the Luperci priests were not like priests in any sense you might picture nowadays. These were young, virile, marriageable men. This was an opportunity for them to show off, to show the world what they had," I explained.

"To flaunt their package!" Alexis nods appreciatively. "I like it."

"Sounds like a really awful frat party," Chelsea rolls her eyes.

"I don't think I care for the whipping the women part," Emily frowns doubtfully.

"The whipping part wasn't meant to inflict pain," I say. "At least, we don't think that was the point. It was more of a playful act. The mosaics depict the young women deliberately baring their breasts, hoping to be 'whipped' by one of the priests. This was supposed to ensure their future fertility. They thought it was a good thing."

"Kind of like having beads chucked at you during Mardi Gras!" Alexis's eyes are sparkling now. "So everyone was running around naked, drinking and feasting, for two whole days, and then what?"

"Then the Church got involved," Jackson says. "And the flower and chocolate industry took over. That's the blood and guts of it all now. But of course, some depraved people are still into whips." He casts a judgmental look at Alexis.

"Match. Making. Can we circle back to the trope of the week?" Chelsea is getting frustrated now.

"Absolutely. The ritual was also believed to include a ceremony where the priests drew the names of young women out of jars," I say.

"At random! Can you imagine?!" Jackson snorts.

"To what end?" Chelsea asks.

"That's what she said," Alexis snorts. Chelsea tosses a pillow at her.

"To the end of having wild sex for the next two days," I say, gazing back at Jackson who is still staring intently at me, one eyebrow raised. "Wild, wanton, drunken, festival sex."

He leans forward. "And there you have it, Folks. The original Tinder date mechanism. Name in a jar! So romantic, no?" His voice is dripping with sarcasm.

"Actually…" I lean towards my screen. "It might have been. It turns out the majority of those matches stuck. The couples generally remained together for the following year, and by all accounts, many of them ended up falling in love and getting married. The ritual itself was considered a great and powerful blessing. Enough that everyone involved considered themselves touched by the divine."

I lean back and take a small sip of my tea. The rare winter sun is just starting to spill through my window, and I luxuriate in it, stretching and bathing. Now I've got the urge to stroll past Palatine Hill and go looking for the Lupercal cave, where they actually performed the sacrifices long ago. The thought gives me goosebumps.

"Damn you look like you're on fire, Woman," Alexis says. "I'm sold on that magic. I wish I was in Rome right now. Maybe I'd finally find someone for myself there."

"Ugh, I guess there is something weirdly romantic about it," Chelsea concedes.

"Are you women all freaking kidding me?" Jackson's eyes bug out. "We're talking bloody animal sacrifices and drunken orgies."

"And a belief in something divine," I narrow my eyes at him. "Don't you believe in magic, Jackson?"

"No, Isla. I don't. I believe in *logic*." His brow is furrowed and he is clenching and unclenching a fist. "I think what we've just been talking about is a perfect illustration of why. I mean, I enjoy wild festival sex as much as the next guy. But what you've just described as 'divine' and 'magical,' sounds a lot more like a big shitty mess to me."

# jackson

. . .

*"There's a reason so many love stories start with an awesome meet-cute. It's like a chemical reaction. All the right ingredients have to be there at the right moment, and poof! Alchemy!"*

*~ Isla Fairfax, Playing with Matches Confessionals*

I'M SITTING in the car with the windows down, fighting off a headache while I take a call with my investors. It's hot and humid, even in Ephron. The dog days of summer are setting in.

The app just isn't performing, they say. They talk about the "issues" in the soberly hushed and clinical terms that doctors use when they discuss erectile dysfunction with a patient. Not that I've ever had that issue. But it's the same tone as a med commercial. *Talk to your doctor if you've experienced negative reviews and an unacceptable churn rate.*

"There are still things that can be done," Geoff, the venture capitalist says. "Marketing. Although we don't have a lot of budget to put into a big campaign. But there's grassroots stuff if you'd be willing. But we need to act fast."

"Hit me," I say. I'm not going to give up just yet. I've been working on my algorithm-driven dating app for the better part of a decade. It's not about the money; I don't need more of that. It's about making a difference. It's about opening up new and enlightened ways for informed, would-be couplers to make optimized matches. It's about preventing the kind of train-wreck relationships that my parents had. Love is over-rated. It makes people do crazy, toxic shit. Security is where it's at. If you're looking to make a long-term investment in a life partner, an AI-enhanced match is a smart way to go.

"So…" Geoff pauses. "Have you ever considered being on a reality show about dating?"

"As what?" I ask. I already have an inkling where Geoff's going. My friend Dean, who's a bit of a Hollywood who's who mentioned that one of his LA contacts asked about me and was interested in having me on his Summer of Love reality TV special. *My best friend Dean, who's also my future brother-in-law.* I'm still not used to the idea.

Geoff obviously thinks that as a data guy, reality TV wouldn't be my thing. But my podcast co-hosts and I often discuss what happens on shows like *The Bachelor* and *Love Island.* Studying the tropes and behavior patterns exhibited on these shows has helped me train and perfect my algorithms. By the end of the third episode of most dating shows, I can predict who will end up together with greater than sixty-seven percent accuracy - just by scraping public data from the contestants' Instagram profiles.

"I mean, I'd consider hosting a dating show, if that's what you're thinking," I say. I could see myself providing wise counsel and hope to the heartbroken contestants. Explaining to them that there's a better way.

"Yeah. That's not exactly what they were thinking, Jackson," Geoff says.

"Well, I hope you weren't thinking I'd sign up as a contestant," I snort. "There's no way. No way in hell."

"Relax, Jackson," Geoff says. "Nothing so demeaning. A production company reached out. There's a new show filming at one of our partner properties next month. Short format - it's a three-episode special, and it's coming together quickly. They're looking for experts and some software to feature. It seems right up your alley. Matchmaking 2.0. They're pitting old-fashioned ideas about setting people up against newer, better, data-driven models."

"Interesting concept," I consider this, a small thrill coursing through me. This could be a great thing. "What's it called?"

"It's called *Playing with Matches*," Geoff says.

My heart sinks. "Playing with Matches" is also the name of the one, and only, hit single my father's band had back in the 80s. Of all the stupid things to call the show.

"Listen, if you're free to fly down to LA tomorrow, we can get you in with the producer before lunch. They are anxious to meet with you."

"You think doing this will make a difference?" I ask. On the one hand, I think it sounds like a tailor-made opportunity. But something about the name is giving me pause. I hadn't thought about my dad in a while, but Dean and Chelsea finally getting together has stirred stuff up recently. Stuff I'd rather not sift through. I shake off my misgivings.

"I think that this might be our best option. We can't afford to pour any more budget into ads, but if this show is giving you a shout-out over the Labor Day holiday weekend when it's set to air? Dude, this is a national primetime audience. It could bring the app back from the dead. Think of it as the blue pill."

"Fine," I reluctantly capitulate. "I'll at least hear them out. What have we got to lose?"

"Our shirts," Geoff says. I can hear the stress in his voice. "We're not all as independently wealthy as you, Jackson."

After this long and uncomfortable call, I'm running late for my meeting with Emily and her writer friend Isla who's here in town visiting for the week. Emily's been talking about Isla's visit for weeks. She's so excited to introduce us in person. But I've just been so damned busy dealing with issues related to the app release. I don't even really have time for this coffee date, but I know Chelsea and Emily won't let me live it down if I don't show up, smile, and nod. Chelsea has already texted me twice, forbidding me to talk about any pagan rituals.

Not a problem. I'm still thinking about my conversation with Geoff when I race towards the corner booth where my sister, Emily, and Isla are waiting. But those thoughts fly straight out of my head and into the ether the moment when I first see Isla Fairfax.

Perhaps it's her fluorescent yellow sweater. Or maybe it's the unapologetic combo of flaming-red hair and hot pink glasses framing bold, blue eyes. She's not a normal human being. She's a neon tetra. She's electric.

I blink a few times, trying to get my eyeballs to adjust. I feel like I need sunglasses to look at her.

"Sorry I'm late," I mumble.

"Better late than never," Emily smiles.

"You remember Isla Fairfax, Jackson? She wrote *The Mystic Matchmaker* Series," Chelsea reminds me. "I recall you said you *loved* that series." My sister smiles sweetly at me, all the while staring at me with squinted eyes. She's pissed that I'm late even if Emily and Isla aren't.

Loved would be a strong word. I do appreciate the solid plot structure and whimsy of the series. She's a decent writer. I'll give her that. Even if her wardrobe choices are a bit over-whelming. I take a seat next to my sister.

"Yup. I remember her," I say, making eye contact with both of the other women in the booth. "Lupercalia." Then I dive into the black-and-white ocular security of the diner menu, pretending to peruse it, even though I know I'm just going to order my usual black coffee.

I can't help stealing another quick sideways look at the psychedelic author though. Her pale blue eyes have thick, golden-tipped lashes. Her freckles make her look slightly younger than she actually is. She's probably in her early thir-ties, I'm guessing.

"I'm back!" announces a curly-haired blonde in a pink barista apron. Kenna, the barista who likes to call herself a "coffee witch," comes over to our table. She's holding a silver carafe of coffee. "Refills? Or can I make anything special for you guys?"

"I didn't know you were away," Emily says, waving away her offer of coffee. "Nothing for me, thanks. I know you said to try the mocha macchiato the other day, but I'm afraid it just wasn't *me*. I'm holding out for a London Fog when your latte machine is fixed."

"Oh, I can whip you up a London Fog with the frother, I don't need to use the coffee machine for that," Kenna offers cheer-ily. "It's no problem, and it's on me."

"I'd love one of your special, custom drinks, too," says Isla. I forgot how British she is. Or maybe I hadn't even noticed when we were recording the podcast. It's funny how someone speaking on a screen strikes you so differently than someone speaking in person. Her very proper accent actually reminds me of a fully grown up version of Veruca Salt from *Charlie and the Chocolate Factory*. I'm suddenly picturing her in a thigh-baring, bum-skimming, red mini-dress, mid-tantrum, petulantly stomping her foot and demanding, "I want it NOW!" while ripping my shirt off.

*That's not an appropriate thought, Jackson. Too colorful.*

I immediately wish my mind hadn't wandered there. I'm annoyingly horny, and it's not like I can do anything about it tonight. I have to be up so early tomorrow to make the flight to LA. There's no time to swipe right on a competitor's app this evening. I scowl into my water glass. Fortunately, Isla can't read my mind. She can't possibly know what I was just picturing.

Isla turns to the woman holding the coffee pitcher. "You must be Kenna. I've heard all about your magical, psychic drink-matching abilities."

*Magical, psychic, drink-matching abilities?*

I snort. More like magical upselling skills.

"She isn't always right," I pipe up. "Case in point - Emily's macchiato."

"Anyone can have an off day," Isla peers over her oversized glasses, looking reproachfully at me. A thick, wavy red strand of hair falls across her face, and she puckers her strawberry-pink lips to blow it away. Oh shit. Now there's a sexy, punk rock librarian vibe happening. I find myself wondering what color underwear she has on. She turns toward Kenna.

"I'm Isla, by the way. Emily and I met in Rome." She reaches out to grab Kenna's hand and holds it, staring at her wide-eyed and expectantly. "Tell me, are you getting any kind of read on me?"

Kenna might not be getting a read on Isla, but I most definitely am. Full-on, fruity nut-cake. Yet I am oddly tempted to sniff and taste her, just like the kids licking the wallpaper in the *Charlie and the Chocolate Factory* film. Would her snozzberries taste like snozzberries?

"You're… apricot tea with honey, frothed oat milk, and a ginger shot," Kenna grins as she makes her proclamation.

"That is so uncanny!" Isla lets her hand go and claps like a delighted child. "Now I cannot think of anything I would rather drink more."

"Power of suggestion," I roll my eyes. I bet that's one of the priciest drinks on the menu.

"Just for that, I'm not offering to make anything special for you, Dr. Spock." Kenna retorts. The town barista is not my biggest fan. "How's the ol' dating app going?" She looks at me with disdain, almost like she knows something about how badly the app is doing. Which she couldn't.

"It's out on the market now," I say. "Still testing, but we'll see. I can give you a code if you'd like to get in on the beta."

"Kenna doesn't need your app or your axe," Isla smiles mischievously. "Cupid's arrow has already struck this one." She winks conspiratorially at me, and somehow this small, random, intimate gesture makes my heart jump. I don't know this stranger well enough to have an inside joke with her. So what's with the dopamine surge? As I follow Isla's gaze to Kenna, I cannot help but spot the massive hickey on Kenna's neck. An actual hickey - junior high school style.

I see the exact moment that Kenna figures out what we are all staring at, reflected in the shiny mirror-like surface of the coffee pot. Blushing red as a beet, Kenna makes excuses and rushes off abruptly, mumbling about fixing drinks.

"Poor girl," Isla chews her lip. "I hope I didn't embarrass her. I can just tell she's in love. I'm definitely getting a vibe that it's something serious."

"Let me guess, you read hickey shapes like entrails?" I smirk, stirring some raw sugar into my coffee, for a change. I don't usually indulge, but something's definitely off today. Maybe my blood sugar is running low.

Isla blinks slowly at me, her wide, blue eyes sympathetic and patient. "Excuse me?" She turns toward Emily for clarification. "What is he talking about?"

"I'm talking about the blue butterfly she was sporting on her neck flesh," I clarify. "The hickey. The leech marks. Dracula's love stamp. Whatever you wanna call it. Looks like our girl has reeled in a regular lamprey eel this time."

"Jeez, Jackson. That's so rude! Even for *you*," Chelsea exclaims, coloring.

"She had a hickey?" Isla tilts her head considering.

Seriously? How had she missed it? I thought that both of us realizing that Kenna had recently gotten some was the whole point of our little inside joke. But apparently I was wrong.

"Are you kidding me?" I ask. I can feel the tiny, pulsing, tap tap taps of a tension headache beating a drum in the distance. I gotta get home and pack. I'm not sure I can stand much more staring into the bright light that is Isla. I'm already seeing spots.

"No, I didn't notice her hickey, but now that you mention it, it *is* interesting that it was butterfly-shaped. Butterflies are powerful symbols of transformation, hope, and faith. They are a good omen and portend love. Haven't you ever heard the term 'butterflies in your stomach?'"

"That butterfly flew the coop," I laugh. "And I don't do butterflies."

*I'm lying, though I don't want to admit it to myself.*

I had a whole kaleidoscope of butterflies fluttering in my guts a few months ago. It happened when I walked into the Grumpy Stump axe-throwing bar and caught Dean Riley kissing my little sister. They said they were pretending, pranking me. But I knew. I just knew without a doubt, then and there, that they were made for each other. I knew it even before I ran their profiles through my app.

I still have no logical explanation for that. I can only chalk it up to knowing them both so well. I must have internalized the algorithm. It's possible that I'd already been running the data on a subconscious level.

"You are in rare form," Emily shakes her head disapprovingly at me. "Don't pay him any mind, Isla. He's always a grump, but he's not usually this bad. Did you wake up on the wrong side of the bed today, Jackson?"

"Or maybe you found a lizard in your sheets?" says Chelsea, rudely referencing my childhood phobia. I ignore her.

*Emily's right. I know I'm being a dick, but I can't seem to make it stop.*

I shake my head. "I'm working on a headache. Do you mind if we take a raincheck on coffee? I've got some out-of-town meetings tomorrow. Maybe we can all meet up later this week?"

"I'm afraid not," Isla is watching me, guardedly. "I'm leaving tomorrow. I'm visiting with my editor in California, and I also have a few meetings and events to attend."

"But hopefully you'll be back in the fall?" Emily says. "It's glorious here when the leaves are changing."

"I'll try," Isla smiles warmly at Emily. "I'd love to see the leaves, but more importantly I'd love to see more of you and Blaze. I always knew you two were *destined* to be together."

*Destiny. Ugh.*

"On that note," I toss a bill on the table, trying not to flinch as I glance back at Isla, "I hope you enjoy the rest of your travels stateside, Isla. Meeting you has been brilliant. Perhaps our paths will cross again." I slide to the edge of the circular booth and stand to go.

Isla holds out her hand palm down, and I take it a little reluctantly. I'd rather just get out of here. Is this a European thing? Palm down? I'm not sure whether she expects me to shake it or what? Am I supposed to kiss it?

*Fuck, this is awkward.*

Isla has neon purple fingernails, and she's wearing a large opal ring that's shooting iridescent sparks at me. Maybe I'm supposed to kiss the ring? No, that's royalty. But there is something vaguely regal about her. *Fuck it.* I bend forward, holding her hand firmly and raising it to my lips. Isla's eyes don't stray from mine. Twin blue beams pulse over me, like the shiny blue beacons on top of a patrol car that's about to pull me over. No turning back now.

I pause before I plant the lightest, most feathery kiss across her snozzberry-scented knuckles.

And that's when I feel them. Fucking blue butterflies. Not just in my stomach. I can feel them all the way down in my goddamned balls, too.

# isla

. . .

*"The odds that you will marry someone who can't figure out the right way to load the dishwasher are far higher than the odds that you will find your soulmate. I say, plan accordingly."*

*~ Jackson Porter, Playing with Matches Confessionals.*

"I'M SORRY," my agent shifts a pile of folders to the other side of her desk. "I wish I had better news."

"Oh well," I exhale. "I wasn't holding my breath."

"Tissue?" Sylvia, my agent, holds out the box with a practiced air and a steady bicep. It's obvious that her tissue arm gets more of a workout than her cork-popping thumb.

"That's okay. I'm okay. Really." I stand and walk to the window, blinking back tears as I stare out at the cityscape. The LA skyline is fuzzy and hazy, either from the marine layer or smog. And the palm trees look suspiciously fake, like set dressing. No matter how many times I've come here, I've still not managed to look at the palm trees and accept them as a natural part of the landscape.

Sylvia places the box back on her desk. "Movie deals are overrated, Isla. Half the time they buy the rights and never make the movie."

"I know," I concede wistfully.

"Let's talk about the reality TV show instead. You're so fun, Isla. Everyone is going to love you. Your adorable British accent and your whole quirky psychic act… and who knows, maybe you'll meet someone special yourself?"

"I think I'm actually supposed to be the one setting the couples up," I say.

So much for this conversation passing the Bechdel test.

I have been writing women's fiction novels for close to ten years now, and yet this is where the conversations always seem to drift. Even with my agent. Maybe it's because I write romantic fiction? Would people be less openly concerned about my single status if I were an archeologist or a city planner? It's not like I don't have a social life. I just haven't ever seen any of the relationships sticking. And then there's the Fairfax curse - a truth even stranger than the fictional account of *The Mystic Matchmaker*.

Despite what my agent clearly thinks, I'm not desperate to meet someone. Not now and possibly not ever. I refuse to marry anyone just for the sake of getting married. I'm content doing what I do. My books make people happy.

Writing is really the only career I've had since uni. It hasn't even occurred to me to do anything else with my anthropology degree. I've always looked at my education as training in how to do background research for my novels.

Or as my parents like to call them, "Isla's wild and wacky imaginings."

At least my father has read a couple of my books. They are too tame for my mum. "Isla, I have an idea for you," she's always saying. Said ideas usually involve a threesome (or more), a murder, and someone dying via autoerotic asphyxiation. My mum's books, were she inclined to sit down long enough to pen them, would absolutely get a movie deal. She would look impeccable at the premiere, a rented man on each arm. And she would be on the cover of magazines and at the top of bestseller lists. Until she got bored. And then she'd take up another pastime. Something expensive and pointless that I'd end up paying the bill for eventually.

I didn't choose to be a writer, any more than I chose to be psychic. Both things just sort of happened to me – like my red hair. These traits are the manifestation of a particular brand of spiritual and creative sensitivity that's been bundled into my DNA, bound to and intertwined with the fabled Fairfax curse. I'm hardly the first in the family to possess the sight. Although it's been known to skip over the male generations. It missed my father and grandfather, jumping directly from my paternal great-grandmother to me.

Sometimes, I just know things. I might be sitting at a take-away lunch in the market, minding my own business, and eating a beautiful chip butty while I scroll through social. Then suddenly I will "see" a vase full of flowers in my mind's eye. There it is - plain as day, like a photo. In that brief flash of a moment, I will also know that the man sitting at the next table was the one who bought the flowers and set them on his dying mother's nightstand when he visited her this morning. Then poof! The vision evaporates, leaving me wondering whether I imagined it, ate some bad chips, or really felt *something*.

It's almost always something.

It can be overwhelming at times, knowing things you're not supposed to know. Things you didn't ask to know or even *want* to know. They just show up on the switchboard of your senses, like radio signals from a foreign tower.

Once upon a time, I would have been in real danger of being burned as a witch.

Legend has it that the Fairfax curse goes back to my tenth great-grandfather's first wife, who was accused of witchcraft. The family was wealthy enough to buy her safe passage abroad. But once she was spirited away, they abandoned her. They left her in the West Indies to live out her days alone while her husband returned to England to make a more advantageous second marriage.

The witch-wife waited in vain for her beloved husband to return. When he did not and news of his second wife eventually reached her, the witch was broken-hearted. She cursed my ancestor and all his progeny, warning she would not be forgotten so easily. Henceforth, no Fairfax man could ever truly love another woman. And no Fairfax woman or bride could truly be loved.

The red hair, creativity, and second sight that seem to pop up every few generations were the witch's parting gifts.

Of course, my father has always insisted this is foolish nonsense. He asserts that no such witch ever existed, except in his crazy grandmother's tall tales.

Anything I ever thought I intuited as a child was swiftly dismissed by my parents as a figment of my overly-active imagination. But I know better. I don't claim to understand it all. But I believe there is some truth to the stories.

When I was a child, there were "incidents." For example, there was a time I told my mum's friend that her recently deceased husband liked to watch her swimming laps in her backyard pool. I was four. We were having a proper tea party in the Diamond Jubilee Tea Salon at Fortnum & Mason, but I could barely eat my pastel-colored petit fours or drink my sugary strawberry tea.

I'd had the distinct sense that there was a strange man, sitting next to the piano player. He was there, but not there. Just sitting on the bench, slightly overlapping with the musician, and watching us drink our tea. And then suddenly he was beside me, speaking softly but insistently in my ear. "Tell her about the pool," he said. "And please tell her the red bikini suits her."

"What I don't get," I'd overheard my mum whispering to my father later that night, "is how she knew about the red bikini, let alone that Petra had put in the lap pool?"

"Oh, she just has a wild imagination," my father said. "Gets it from my side, I fear. You know what a crackpot my nan is."

When we went to see my great-grandmother at the care home, I'd shyly tell her about my visions. She hadn't dismissed me. She'd taken me seriously, and she'd encouraged me to write all my visions down. "It makes the ghosts rest easier. They just want to be acknowledged, so they can move on," she'd explained.

My stories made Granny Fairfax smile, and I'd loved that. It made me feel less alone.

Once, I'd asked my granny how to lift the curse, but she'd sighed deeply before telling me that only the sound of a returning lover's sacred horn blown over the water has the power to travel across the centuries. Granny had shrugged as if this formula was an even greater mystery than the most complex equation in my maths class. The sound had to be a signal, shared by two lovers, deeply in love. Also, it had to be loud - loud enough to rouse the witch from her eternal slumber where she still waits for her lover's return.

"Were she to hear that sound," Granny insisted, "she would finally be able to rest in peace."

"Has anyone tried a trumpet?" I'd asked hopefully.

"Trumpets, trombones, you name it. I once made a suitor serenade me with a full brass band," my spry great-grandmother had laughed. "But clearly he didn't love me enough. Or the brass wasn't sacred. Who knows? All I know is we're still cursed. I'm sorry, Child."

I started writing *The Mystic Matchmaker* series shortly after she passed. She was 103 and had outlived her own children. She was the inspiration for my series.

Unlike me, my fictional matchmaker has a simple, explicit way to release her family curse. All it takes is one hundred true love matches, then the curse will be lifted. Perhaps when I started writing it, I thought my writing could somehow break the curse. Then I wouldn't have to be alone, or worse, doomed to a loveless marriage like my parents.

Ten years later, I now realize that was just wishful thinking. There are no horns blowing for me on either side of the Atlantic. And even if there were, it wouldn't matter. I couldn't return the sentiment. I have never actually been in love.

To be fair, my parents' platonic relationship doesn't seem to bother them all that much.

"Do you know what the divorce rate is, Isla? We're just lucky to be good enough friends to put up with each other's foibles." So my mum's argument goes.

While not in love with each other, my parents do share a grand passion. They are both committed to frittering away whatever's left of the Fairfax family fortune on ridiculous ventures. Everything from miniature horse farming to selling NFTs of said horses. It cannot go on forever, and it doesn't take a psychic to see that. My parents are out of money. I'd promised Granny Fairfax I'd do my best to hold on to the family estate, and it's taking all of my literary creativity to do so.

Lately, it doesn't seem like that's enough.

I watch as a jet breaks through the clouds above, making its final descent into LAX, and depositing dozens of people at the doorsteps of their dreams. Dreams that hardly ever come true.

What am I even doing here? Americans don't want my books. They'll never do well enough in this market to save the estate. I shouldn't have even gotten my hopes up about the film option.

"So you're definitely doing the television show?" my agent asks. She uses a letter opener to pop the tab of a flavored soda water can, lest she damage her nails.

"That's the plan," I gesture with my palms up. "It's my next stop."

"Good," she sighs. She opens her mouth, and I get the sense she wants to say something, but she thinks better of it. She sticks the end of the letter opener in it instead, biting down on it as if she's fighting a battle between prying her mouth open and keeping it shut.

That's fine. I already know what she wants to say. What she is thinking.

*"Boo hoo, Isla Fairfax didn't sell the movie rights to her little ghost romance series. The one who really deserves the tissues is me. I'm the one who won't be getting the commission. How am I going to pay for a facelift now? Who is going to want to work with me when I'm an old hag? Who is going to love me? I need a drink. Just one shot. As soon as Isla leaves."*

Her thoughts are coming in loud and clear. Almost as loud and clear as Jackson Porter's naughty Veruca Salt fantasy at the Diner yesterday. At least that had been vaguely amusing. Oddly arousing, too. It's a rare gift when the knowing of things you're not supposed to know doesn't totally creep you out or piss you off.

My abilities can make it hard to stay friends with people. I've learned techniques to block it out, but it requires a lot of energy when the people around me are feeling things intensely. Energy I don't have to spare today.

But then another voice intrudes. A disembodied one. My skin prickles with electricity, and I can feel the fuzzy hairs on the back of my neck standing up straight.

*"Don't listen to her, Honey."*

It's been a while since I've sensed a ghost. Her voice sounds kind. She has a funny accent. Brooklyn?

*"Syl's just bitter because she thinks nobody loves her. She doesn't even realize that the lawyer who works one floor down has been trying to work up the courage to ask her out for the last year. He waits outside every day so he can take the elevator with her."*

The second voice seems to be emanating from a silver picture frame facing away from me on the desk. The air above the frame looks wavy and unfocused. Like heat waves or a mirage. I take a deep breath.

"Sylvia," I ask. "Do you believe in the sort of stuff that I write? That ghosts are real, and there's more to this world than meets the eye?"

I feel a feverish shiver pass through me and recognize that the spirit is already fleeing. She's said all she wants to say.

"I don't know," Sylvia sighs. "I guess deep down we all want to believe. But who knows? Who really knows?"

"Well," I say as I gather my bag and belongings. "I've got to prepare for my meeting at Goodfellow Productions, but do me a favor. Skip the vodka shot. And you know the nice lawyer who takes the elevator with you every day? Ask him out to lunch. Somewhere nice. And charge it to me."

Her mouth drops open. "How did you know?"

I walk to the desk and pick up the silver picture frame. When I flip it around I see that the photo is of a much younger Sylvia standing with an older woman. The two are unmistakably related.

Sylvia raises one brow at me and glances at the picture frame in my hand then back at me again. Once again, I know what she's thinking.

*"Did you get that from my ma? Did she give you a message for me? Is she here right now? Can you help me speak to her?"*

If only I could. My visions don't work the way visions work for psychics in the movies and on TV shows. I have no control. It's not like I hold someone's hands and achieve a mind meld. I cannot dial up the spirit world on my landline. I've tried using Ouija boards. They only seem to attract pervs and weirdo ghosts like a bad subreddit sinkhole full of blockable trolls. Never again. My gift can be quite maddening. It only gives little snatches of static-y songs as if they are wafting out the windows of a car that's speeding by.

"I just had a feeling," I say. "A hunch. I rode up here with the lawyer, and he asked if I was meeting with you." I shrug. "Also, I see the bottle of vodka over there. You glanced at it twice while we were chatting. We've all had those days. I'm sorry to be the stressful client."

It's all true. Every last word. I had ridden up to Sylvia's office with the lawyer from downstairs. He had asked about her. His whole face had softened when he said her name. There's a bottle of Tito's on the console by the window, and it's only half full.

Now that the moment has passed, I doubt myself. Perhaps I've convinced myself Sylvia's mom was speaking to me.

*I want there to be a point to all of this.*

It's wishful thinking. Like the endless planeloads of people landing at LAX with stars in their eyes. If I make a match today, it won't get me a movie deal, and it won't somehow help pay down the Fairfax curse. Will it?

*No. But it couldn't hurt.*

I refuse to believe that everything is all ones and zeros like Jackson Porter seems to think with his ridiculous app. Maybe we're all cursed, chasing after romantic dreams that don't actually exist. But better to live with hope and mystery and butterflies in your stomach.

Meeting Jackson Porter in person has really knocked me off center. Ones and zeros cannot explain the way the booth spun out for me when that jerk kissed the back of my hand.

# jackson

. . .



*"I just get a feel for people. I'm an empath. I'm that weird chick who sees people's auras and feels their souls. It's really hard to fool me. If you know, you know."*

*Isla Fairfax, Playing With Matches Confessionals*

MY UBER DRIVER is pale and paunchy, middle-aged, and not real talky, which is fine with me. He's dressed all in black and listening to 80s music. "Playing with Matches" comes on the radio. The driver taps the steering wheel and hums along. Nobody remembers the name of my dad's band or specifically recalls my father, but absolutely everyone knows this stupid song he wrote and recorded.

> In this game of love, we play with no rules,
> We're lost in the passion, like two desperate
> fools,
> But when the smoke clears, will we still remain,
> Or will we be ashes, consumed by the flame?

"Hey man, can you turn that off?" I ask. Just hearing the opening chords puts me on edge. If it stays on till the chorus, it's going to be an earworm. I won't be able to shake it for the rest of the day.

"Not a fan?" the man says, glancing in the rearview mirror to look at me. His watery gray eyes are a little bloodshot, and for half a second my heart spasms. I feel a little squeeze, like a hiccup. But the sensation is gone, as fast as he changes the radio station to something more current.

I can't even recall the exact color of my father's eyes anymore. Blue? Green? Gray? Bloodshot. Always bloodshot. The red canceled everything else out. It's been so many years since we've heard from him. We don't even know for sure if he's still alive. Though I'd like to think we'd know if he were dead. Wouldn't we?

My dad was a pop star for all of ten seconds in the 80s. And then I was born. And then he became a drunk, and it fucked up our family. *The end.*

I gaze out the window at the endless strip mall scenery that characterizes this part of LA. Tan cement and relentlessly bright blue skies. The first time I came to LA, I could hardly take off my sunglasses. I felt like some sort of Pacific Northwest vampire, hissing in the overly-bright daylight, twitching at the neon-colored billboards. Isla colors.

*Why am I still thinking about her?*

I can't seem to get her out of my head. Her colors have stained blume. I'm picking them out of the landscape like I'm trying to subconsciously match paint chips. There's the neon yellow of her sweater over there on a road work sign. A pink dress, the color of her glasses, hanging in front of a shop billows and catches the breeze like a flag, waving to capture my attention.

It's around 11 am when I arrive at Goodfellow Productions. The parking lot is packed with cars wedged-in and double-stacked like a game of Tetris. A tired attendant in a plastic lawn chair looks up from whatever he's watching on his phone to see if he's going to need to collect the keys, but when he sees the Uber decal on the windshield, he gets right back to his program.

"Okay then. Thanks. Have a good one," my driver says, barely waiting for my door to close before zooming off to his next pickup. I feel a small pang of guilt about not making small talk. Why hadn't I bothered to ask him to tell me anything about himself? What if that had been my dad? And what if that was the last time I'd ever see him?

*What a ridiculous thought.*

The Uber driver couldn't have been my dad. He's just some guy who's around my dad's age. The thing that's bugging me is realizing I wouldn't even know my old man if I did happen to see him somewhere. That bugs me a little. A lot. Would he look like me?

Last time I saw him, he wasn't too much older than I am now, but he wasn't healthy. He'd looked like he was in his sixties.

*Shake it off, Jackson,* I tell myself, shaking out my limbs one at a time. Right arm. Left arm.

Dean's dad used to always say that when we were Scouts. He was super sporty, more coach than Scoutmaster, but he'd always say in his gruff voice, "Shake it off, Gents!" We'd all get super silly and shake ourselves out.

Next, I do my legs. Then I finish with a neck roll, shoulder shimmy, and a few jumps. The parking lot attendant looks up to check me out, then goes back to watching his show, unfazed. It's LA. I'm sure he's seen stranger stuff.

I turn to face the building I'm about to enter, only just noticing it's glass. All glass. Wall-to-wall windows. Which means everyone on the inside just had a front-row seat to the shake show.

Oh well. I shrug it off. I'm a rich tech guy. I'm supposed to be a weirdo. I've got nothing to hide or be ashamed of, physically or otherwise. I'm in the best shape of my life. I've been hitting the gym every single day in the months leading up to the app launch. Exercise has been the only thing keeping me sane since my two best friends moved back to Ephron and both immediately got engaged.

I just don't get it. I don't get them. Even though the gang's back together, I've never felt more alone.

"I'm here to see Rob Goodfellow," I say to the receptionist. She's a white girl with dreadlocks and a thrift store chic vibe. She barely looks up from her game screen. "Rob's in a meeting; he'll be right with you."

Animal Crossing, I see when she sets it down for a moment to type something into the computer.

"You can have a seat," she says to me.

Rob is the "show daddy" for *Playing With Matches*, and the one who allegedly has been dying to talk to me. I tried to learn more about the show on the way down here, but there's not much info out there. All I know is that it's a three-night special, slated as part of the grand finale to the "Summer of Love" lineup on a major network. Filming is being rushed. It's all coming together at the very last minute. Probably because they are subbing in for another show that was mysteriously canceled.

Dean, who went to UCLA with Rob, was able to fill me in a bit more. Rob founded Goodfellow Productions a decade ago, and he's produced a bunch of super successful reality shows. Everyone says he has a magic touch.

"Just be careful," Dean had warned me. "He's a chameleon. He's great at what he does but he's got a rep for being a bit of a trickster."

I shudder at the lizard reference. Can't stand them. But if any of that's true, I have yet to see any evidence of it. I haven't found anything overtly negative about Rob online. If anything, people seem to adore him. He has a couple of Emmys and a large collection of sports memorabilia, some of which he's donated to charitable causes. He's made several "most eligible bachelor" lists and has won multiple awards for being a "pioneer" and "visionary" of reality-based programming. I feel like I'm in good hands, but I'm reserving judgment till we have our face-to-face chat. I want to be sure we're all on the same page, and I need to hear more about Rob's vision for the show.

The lobby doesn't offer up many clues. Cement floor. Shag rug. Modern leather sofa that's more for looks than comfort. Glass table, complete with a two-year-old issue of *Variety* magazine. Standard stuff. The receptionist is chewing gum. She blows a bubble, and I jump when it pops, loudly.

Why am I so on edge? Is it the investors? They're really pressuring me to do this show, no matter what. I'm not even sure I have a choice in the matter. I hate feeling railroaded.

"Jackson! There you are! Man of the hour!" Rob jogs into the lobby from the hallway, smiling enthusiastically. He's wearing lightweight, black sporty tech pants and a simple, green microfiber athletic top. High-end European athletic trainers complete the picture. His well-groomed hand is already outstretched to shake mine. I jump to my feet and grasp it. His grip is firm.

Then he completely surprises me, pulling me in for a hearty impromptu bro hug and a slap on the back.

"Man, I know you don't know me from Odin, but I just gotta give you a hug and say thank you, from the bottom of my heart," Rob's smile is infectious. I cannot help it. I'm instantly grinning goofily, too. It's one of those awkward good-faith smiles where you have no clue why you're doing it, your brain is still struggling to come up to speed, but your face believes it's worth it, the reason is coming.

"Okaaaay," I say awkwardly.

I size Rob up as he pulls back. He's a little shorter than me. Wiry. Super tan, like he spends his weekends on the water. Green eyes and thick strawberry blond hair. There's something youthful and slightly feral about him. Like a sporty Peter Pan. He could be a Lost Boy.

Rob waves his left hand back and forth in front of me, like a bride showing off her engagement ring, and I note the wide gold band.

"Met my wife through your app, Dude," he says, shaking his head reverently. "Never thought I'd get married. But here we are, and it's all because of YOU!" He points at me. "Come on back to my office," he pauses. "You need water? Green juice? Butter coffee? Did Casey offer you water?"

"He didn't look thirsty," Casey blows another bubble and continues to play with her virtual pets.

"I'm good," I say.

Rob's office is decorated similarly to the reception area, but there is crap everywhere. Movie and show posters and random sports memorabilia. Cereal boxes. A bobblehead that looks just like him.

He moves a box of *Playing With Matches*-emblazoned water bottles off a seat so I can sit down, then grabs one and tosses it to me.

"So Jack," he says.

"Jackson," I correct him, smiling politely. Jack, Jackie, Jax, I've never been partial to the usual nicknames people come up with for me.

"Sorry, JackSON," Rob amends, stroking his chin. "I think I need to tell you off the bat that this show is a *passion project* for me. I'm in a place I never thought I would be. In love, married to the woman of my dreams. Hell. I'm about to be a dad. I am just so happy. And I owe it all to YOU. So as far as I'm concerned, if you don't want to do this show with me, then I don't want to do this show." He leans forward, squeezes my forearm, and gazes intensely and imploringly into my eyes.

"It's you and me, Man. We're gonna show the world what's possible with the new tech that's out there. If a simple guy like me can find his happy-ever-after due to the brilliant app that you've brought to the market, then anyone can."

"Wow," I'm not sure what to say. "That's quite the pitch."

He leans back in his chair, playing with the gold ring, spinning it on his finger.

"All true. Tania and I probably never would have gotten together if it wasn't for your technology."

"How long have you been married?" I ask.

"Not long, a couple of months."

"And you actually met your wife through AI Swiper?" I ask. Why hadn't anyone told me about this before I took the meeting? Our teams are supposed to be tracking success stories like this. Certainly, our PR firm would want to know about this.

"Yeah, that's one of the reasons I was so determined to have you on the show. I've been on it since the first beta," Rob shakes his head with affirmation and admiration. "Two words: Life. Changing."

"What about your wife?"

"Oh yeah, that's a funny story. Her mom signed her up for the beta. Tania didn't even know till we matched and her mom told her."

"Hmmm…." I frown and pinch my brow wishing he hadn't just told me that. "That's just the sort of thing that can mess with the data. It's kind of important that the profiles are completed by the customer."

"Oh, uh… yeah she did the quiz and all that stuff. Her mom just didn't tell her what it was for." Rob waves a hand again. "Anyways, Jackson," he rocks back in his chair again. "I realize it's a huge ask for you to join the cast at the last minute like this. We can't really pay you much, but what we *can* do is feature your app on the show and make you our CLITO."

I swallow. Is he joking? *Did he just say 'clit oh'?*

"Excuse me?" I blink.

"Chief Love Intelligence Technology Officer," Rob rattles off the title quickly.

"Yeah… I'm not so sure about that," I say, raising my brows at him. "Clit Oh? Sound a little like something else?"

Rob considers this for a moment. "Oh!" he says. "Ohhhhh…." he bites his lip. "Well, damn. You're right, and you know what? Give yourself any title you see fit. Hell, call yourself 'The Love God.' I'd be down with that. I know how powerful

AI Swiper is and what a gift your app is. The point is, Jackson, we need your tech on the show." Rob slaps a hand down on the table to emphasize his point. "We need you. Much more than you need us. Without you, this show can't happen. And if it doesn't happen, I don't know what I'm going to tell my new wife and unborn child. This isn't just about TV. It's about *family*. Making a difference."

"How so?" I ask, a bit overwhelmed by his passion.

"Everyone knows that dating agencies and traditional methods of matchmaking are utter bullshit, right? You can't win. It's either religion, economics, or politics forcing us to make decisions and marry people we don't really love." Rob looks to me for agreement, and I shrug and nod. "And God help the folks who leap before they look when they 'fall in love.'" Rob does air quotes. "Our libido screws with our heads, clouds our vision, and fucks up our lives. Most of us aren't smart enough to make good choices for ourselves, are we? Just look at the divorce rate!"

I notice that he is tearing up, actually tearing up, and I'm touched. He really gets it. All the reasons why I've poured so much effort into my app. I can't recall when I've worked with someone so passionate in the past. I hate to admit it, but it's inspiring. I feel the last of my misgivings about the show melting away. Dean was wrong about Rob. Rob's a straight shooter.

Rob wipes his eyes self-consciously.

"I'm sorry, Man. I told myself I wasn't going to get emotional today. I'm just so excited to finally meet you in person."

"That's fine," I say. "I know my team has already licensed our tech for the production. I'm just not sure what it is you want *me* to do on the show. Like do I have to be physically there?"

"Abso-fucking-lutely!" Rob leans forward, excitedly, elbows resting on his knees. "Peaches Resort, Jackson. We're filming at one of the top luxury resorts in the Caribbean. A week in Paradise, making dreams come true. God, sometimes I really love my job!"

"Okay," I say slowly, thinking about the implications. I've seen the ads for Peaches, and while it does look nice, it's still in the tropics. I'm a bug magnet. And I don't want to even think about the lizards. I'll just have to suck it up and pack plenty of mosquito repellant. "When would I need to be there?"

"Pretty soon. We'll need you down there in just over a week. Everything will be comped of course. Flights, room, etc. We'll put you up in a private suite. You can even bring a plus one if you want. Do you have a plus one? Anyone special in your life?" He waggles his brows at me, speculatively.

"Not at the moment," I shake my head. "I'm more about keeping it simple."

"Well," Rob smiles knowingly, "you're probably doing the right thing. No shortage of peaches at Peaches, if you catch my drift. And when they know you're with a TV production…" He exhales through pursed lips and shakes his head. "Of course, those days are all in my past, but you, my friend, are free as a bird!"

"So what is it I'd do?"

"Not a hell of a lot other than enjoy yourself and rest on your laurels," Rob snorts. "I mean, you've got a full-on cast credit but you don't have to be on camera too much. We mostly want you there to comment on the technology, answer questions, attend parties and gatherings, and maybe opine in a few interviews. Everyone loves experts who can opine…."

"Right," I say, knowing where this is going. "So basically you want me to shoot the shit and dumb the tech down for the viewers?"

"Yes!" Rob laughs and fist bumps me. "Dude, I knew we would get along. I gotta tell you I have been listening to that *Lit Lovers* podcast of yours, and that was the clincher. You are funny, Jackson. You're the secret sauce that we need to make this show a hit. Loved the Lupercalia episode. And what do you think of the show title? I understand you've got some kind of a family connection with the show's theme song?" Rob holds up a finger as he glances down at his phone, distracted. He fires off a quick response to a message before I can respond.

*They're using my dad's band's old song as the theme song for the show?* Mother. Fucker.

"Give me a min?" Rob says. "I gotta make a quick call." He excuses himself and slips out into the hallway.

While I'm waiting, I check my own phone. Geoff texted me ten minutes ago.

> You're doing the show, right?

> I'm still here, talking to them

> OK but I'm just saying, you're doing the show

> Is that a question or a statement?

> It's a statement. If you don't do the show, I think most of the investors are gonna bail.

I sigh. It's not like I can't self-fund the app, but I don't like being that exposed. I've worked damn hard to get the kind of security I never had growing up.

Rob comes back into the room. "You hungry, Jackson? What say we grab some tacos for lunch to celebrate this partnership, and afterward I'll introduce you to the rest of the team?"

"Sounds like we have a deal," I slip my phone back into my pocket and stand to shake his hand again. I don't really have a choice, and it's the logical thing to do. I was going to do it regardless. But now that I've met Rob, I actually believe some good is going to come of this.

I just have to figure out how to get the stupid song out of my head.

> Playing with matches, burning up the night,
> Walking on the edge, but it feels so right,
> Flickering flames of passion, we can't contain,
> We're lost in the heat, playing dangerous games.

# isla

. . .

*"People lie all the time. You can't trust a thing they say about them-selves. But you can't lie to an AI Engine. Santa's got nothing on my app."*

*~Jackson Porter, Playing With Matches Confessionals*

I WOLF down a quick lunch at the food court in the shopping mall next to my agent's office tower before calling for a car to take me to Goodfellow Productions. The seating area is evenly divided between harried mothers shaking strollers to keep their babies asleep and harried office workers guzzling coffee to keep themselves awake. I'm not sure where I fit, so instead of sitting down, I eat standing up at a cocktail table by the windows. I'm treated to a view of the cars whizzing by on the freeway below. The great mystery of LA traffic is how it's always moving until you're in it.

Once I'm in the Uber, barely inching along on the I-10, I reply to my editor's insistent texts about my now overdue manuscript. What better time to address it? If only the twin miseries of traffic and unpleasant conversation will somehow cancel each other out.

My editor tends to nag me like she's my mum. Except my mum has never nagged me about the things normal mums nag about. My mum texts me reminders to get waxed. She sends suggestions about booking boudoir sessions while my boobs are still perky. That's my mum. Always looking out for me.

When am I going to see those chapters Isla?

I'm working on it

That's not what I asked. You need to finish this book by October. You're down to less than two months and I have not seen Chapter One!

I'm hoping to have plenty of time to get everything together for you when I get to the islands.

That's what I keep telling myself, anyways.

Wonderful. The show should really help with sales. The publisher will be pleased. It might buy you another chance.

Another chance for what?

Sylvia didn't tell you they canceled the fall book tour?

No. My agent probably didn't want to double up on the bad news. But it's not a shock. None of the bookstores I've stopped into while I've been in the US have had a single copy of my books.

Not enough orders?

Sad face.

I guess my books don't align as well with the American market.

They are such repressed pervs over there. Have you considered spicing things up in this last one? Maybe adding some animal shifters to the mix?

No.

At the very least, some professional athletes and mob bosses? Maybe a former athlete alphahole who is a billionaire mob boss?

Eggplant Emoji. Gun Emoji. Hockey Emoji.

Aliens?

Eggplant Alien Eggplant Alien Eggplant Easter Island Guy.

*Easter Island Guy?*

Here we go again. I put the phone on silent. I know my editor means well, but I'm not entirely sure she's joking. Either way, she doesn't understand my process. It's not like I wander through the supermarket, pulling story elements off the shelf and tossing them into my basket like ingredients for a lasagna. I don't go home and measure things out, following a recipe.

The stories choose me. They flow through me, pumped by my heart, mixed into my blood. Coming up with stories has never been a problem for me before. I usually have to scramble to keep up with my main character. I normally feel less like an author and more like a court stenographer, chasing down her story as if I'm following her in real-time.

*The Mystic Matchmaker* series makes me see romantic possibilities everywhere I go. I see the invisible forces that pull on people. People are like magnets waiting to snap together. Like dominos lined up to fall. One tiny little shove is all it takes to set things in motion. *Usually.*

But at the moment I'm blocked. I've hit my first dry spell at what feels like the worst possible time, just when I'm supposed to write the finale to my decade-long series. Where has my mojo gone? How can I gather the creativity to resolve my character's curse, knowing I'll probably never be able to lift my own?

*Maybe you'll meet someone… .*

Sylvia's words echo, chafing me like a heat rash.

May as well get all the difficult conversations out of the way while I'm stuck in traffic. I dial my parents back in England for a quick catch-up call. First the editor and now them. Look at me, being an adult.

"Isla darling is that you?" my mum picks up on the first ring. "How's Rome? I do hope you're not too hot."

"I'm still in the States, currently in Los Angeles, Mum," I sigh. "Remember I told you I sublet the apartment for August?" I've told her multiple times, but she still keeps forgetting. It isn't dementia. She's just that self-absorbed.

"Oh right. Such a pity, Darling. I don't know how you can stand letting strangers rent your place."

"They're not strangers, Mum. They're friends of friends, and it is not a pity. The summer sublet pays the rent for almost the entire year."

"Really? But still. Strangers in your home. Is it really worth it?" She pauses her monologue, probably deciding that thinking about money is beneath her. She brings the conversation back to her comfort zone, speaking about herself and how I can help her. "So Darling, there's a problem with the plumbing in the en-suite in the west wing. I'm afraid there's been a small flood, and we've had to turn off the water. Do you think you could call someone to come and look at it?"

"Wasn't the plumber just there at the house last month, Mum?" I ask. Cutting my parents' housekeeper's hours and taking over paying their bills for them is just one of many of the recent cost-cutting measures I've tried to avoid having to sell the estate. I've just paid an enormous plumbing bill, presumably for some kind of plumbing overhaul.

"Oh no, Dear. The plumber wasn't at the *house*. He was at the barn. We installed state-of-the-art showers and a jacuzzi for bathing the mini Shetland ponies."

My driver lays on the horn and gestures rudely at another driver as he guns the engine and swerves into the HOV lane. We're finally moving again.

"Why on earth do the horses need a jacuzzi?" I am sure my eyes are bugging out as I grip the armrest.

"The ponies love it, Isla. I wish you could see them! It's so good for their nerves!" my mum says.

"Okay, well I'm not sure what to say, Mum. I won't be getting another advance till I turn in the manuscript for this next book."

"I suppose I could sell another one of Granny Fairfax's dreadful paintings. There's a few more up in the attic," my mum sighs.

"No!" I object, feeling a sharp pang of loss at the very thought of letting another piece of my inheritance go. "Don't do that. Please? Just hang on for a bit? I am going to a meeting right now to see about being on this reality show. It's filming in the Caribbean next week, and I'll be going down there for the shoot. I'm hoping to finish the manuscript at the same time."

"But Isla, where do you expect your father and me to bathe in the meanwhile?"

"The barn?" I suggest, hopefully.

"Perhaps we should go stay at a hotel," my mum sighs. "Lucky you getting to go to a resort! And what's this about a reality show? That seems interesting. What's it about?"

"It's a dating show," I say.

"Oh, how exciting! Are they going to find someone for you at last?"

"No Mum, I'm a consultant. I'm not there to get set up. I'm helping make the matches," I explain. "I'm the romance author and matchmaking expert. Because of my books?" I remind her.

"Pity," she sighs. "You seem so uptight. I think you could really benefit from a good shagging."

"Mum!" I protest. "We've been here before. If I need your advice about my sexual health and well-being, I will seek it out."

"I'm just saying it couldn't hurt," she sniffs. "What's the point of this show, anyways? They can't be serious. Aren't all the shows ultimately about getting laid?"

"No, Mum. This one is about finding your soulmate."

"Ah. That drivel again." I can hear the eye roll. "Well if it helps to sell your books and gets me a new bidet...."

"Not everyone is like you and Daddy," I retort. "Some people still believe in true love."

"Sure they do," she says. "And there's height-restricted rides, lovely costumes, and fairy bubble wands waiting for them at Disneyland."

"*I* believe in true love," I argue. "Even if our family curse means I won't ever get to experience it for myself. I am honored to have been asked to help other people seek it out."

"Oh Isla, again with the Fairfax curse. There is no curse, Darling. It's just a story, and you're using it as an excuse. And I think it's lovely that you're such a romantic. But at some point, you have to stop with these whimsical ideas, grow up, and be *practical*."

*Says the woman with a barn jacuzzi.*

"What exactly is it I'm not being practical about?"

"Well, taking care of your father and me, for one thing. And protecting your inheritance. You're going to have to marry well if you want to keep the estate in the family, Isla. Has that ever even occurred to you?" My mum lectures me haughtily, as if she's been lifted straight from the pages of a Jane Austen novel.

"Right, Mum," I say, biting back all the things I'd love to say to her. Things like, *How about you get a job* and *Horses don't need hot tubs.* "I'll give you a call later and let you know how it goes with the show. In the meantime, maybe you and Daddy should stay in the apartment in the East Wing. We haven't really got the budget for a hotel right now."

"Fine," she sighs. "I don't know who I would have gotten to take care of the horses if we tried to get away anyways. It's impossible to find good help these days."

After I hang up, I use the rollerball applicator in my purse to apply some lavender and mint essential oil to my pulse points. I do a short breathing ritual, attempting to quiet my mind. It involves focusing all my attention on my breath work.

*In and out. In and –*

"Motherfucking-son-of-a-motherfucker!" The driver curses and hits the brakes, causing me to slam into the back of the passenger seat.

THE RECEPTIONIST at Goodfellow Productions offers me some Fiji water before she resumes ignoring me. Otherwise, the office seems quiet. I take a seat on the white leather IKEA sofa in the lobby. Most of the team must be out to lunch. A tall thin young woman in tailored cream pants and a matching fitted jacket strolls by speaking perfect Italian into the phone.

"Si, si, Marco," the woman is saying. "We will have every-thing set up for you. Don't worry about anything. I will take care of it." She sees me and waves. Turning towards me, she wraps up the call. "I have to go now. I'll call you back later, and we can go over your wardrobe requests."

"Buongiorno," I smile and hold out a hand to greet her. "I'm Isla."

"I thought so!" she replies in English, smiling broadly and shaking my hand. "I've heard about you. I'm Rory, the assistant producer for *Playing with Matches*." Rory perches against the end of the sofa taking stock of me. "Love that dress; is it silk?" she adds, in a perfect American accent. She seems a bit young to have such a big job. Younger than me, for sure.

"Yes, it is," I smooth my skirt. "I dyed it myself in a natural dyeing workshop I took in Rome. I love the vibrations turquoise has."

"Wow. I'd make a mess if I tried to dye my own clothes. It'd be like the sad little summer camp shirts I used to make, only sadder. You're so creative! You really are the whole package," Rory gazes at me appreciatively.

"So I understand you met our host Marco last winter in Italy?" Rory mentions. "I was so excited to land him for this project - he was the star of an Italian show I was working on. Pazzi per Amore?"

"I'm familiar with it," I reply in a complimentary tone, sensing Rory's need to be acknowledged. "It was a fun show."

Rory preens at the praise.

I don't bring up the fact that some people in Italy called the show "Pazzi per Cazzi," which translates roughly to "crazy for dick." The show placed a dozen hyped-up romance readers in a house with Marco, the world's sexiest cover model. They'd had to compete for the chance to re-enact select scenes from the books he's posed for, in the hopes of becoming his real-life leading lady. It was a cute concept. But the contestants were really over the top, and rumors abounded that none of them were really there for the "right reasons" - especially Marco. He hadn't stayed with the winner for more than a week post-production.

"The show did really well," Rory polishes her phone screen on the sleeve of her pristine jacket. "Anyways, Marco is the one who mentioned your books to me and pointed me to your website."

"*Marco* pointed you to me?" I'm surprised. I'd only met the man once, briefly, at a book signing when he ripped off his shirt and jumped on a table. I'd promptly ducked out the side door.

"Yes, he was so impressed with you, and so are we. What can I say? I'm hooked on your series, Isla! The books are so juicy. I'm so excited that you're actually here, in the flesh! And I know that Rob, the executive producer and creator of this project, also can't wait to meet you."

Rory stands and waves to someone she has spied coming down the corridor. "Oh cool. Here's Rob now," she points to the man gliding towards us.

Rob is medium height and reasonably fit. He's wearing a simple white cotton shirt and loose-fitting, natural linen trousers. I can't help noticing he's wearing a Baltic amber bracelet and a simple, but tasteful, yin / yang necklace. He has the gait of someone who practices yoga, a sort of purposeful and perfectly balanced heel-to-toe stride. Lastly, I note the eco-friendly gym shoes he is wearing. I just read an article about how the company that makes them donates two pairs to charity for every pair sold.

"We'll have to chat more later. I've got a million questions for you!" Rory pats my arm and takes off just as Rob stops in front of me.

He's really not at all what I expected. First of all, I was not expecting Rob to be a fellow ginger. He could be my cousin with his strawberry-tinged hair and freckled complexion. Secondly, he exudes a zen sort of calm. I'm instantly put at ease by his warm smile.

"Isla!" Rob steeples his hands before inclining his head at me. "Woman of the hour! Namaste. Welcome. We are so honored to have someone as sensitive and special as you here in our offices."

He is practically crackling with warmth and excitement. I can't help but respond to his positive energy.

I stand to shake his hand, but he doesn't offer his. Instead he stops in his tracks, grinning at me as he takes me in.

"Thank you for inviting me to be on the show," I bounce on my heels and shove my hands in my pockets to still them.

"We are honored to have you here." Rob stands and grins at me for another moment before speaking again. "It's such a lovely day; it would be a shame to stay indoors for our meeting. Why don't we head out to the garden to chat?" he suggests, gesturing towards the double glass doors at the end of the hallway.

As I follow him down the hallway and out onto the patio, I cannot help but notice the way he is breathing. Slowly, deeply. Intentionally. He pauses in front of the doors, taking a deeper breath in, followed by a long, slow exhale that feels anticipatory.

"You're in for a treat, Isla. It's such a special space we've created out here. I like to take a moment to release all negativity and set my intentions before I go out. And I like to leave my shoes indoors. The meditation garden is paved with imported pea gravel that has a very high crystal content. It's incredibly grounding. You're welcome to leave your shoes on, of course. But I also invite you to take them off, if you'd like to indulge in a little earthing with me."

"Of course," I kick off my sandals, excited at the prospect. "I've never earthed in crystal gravel before, but I am certainly game!"

"No time like the present," Rob affirms. He pushes open the door and reaches back a hand to pull me through. "Welcome to the Peace Garden!"

Being British, I expect my gardens to have roses and vine-covered arbors. At the very least, I expect plants. But there are no plants in this garden. The only source of the color green is the oxidation on the copper infinity fountain that lines one wall of the small courtyard.

The other three walls are covered in sculptures made from twisted steel. At the center of the space, two large bench-height slabs of weathered marble flank a large bronze gong. It's an entirely urban space. One that feels man-made instead of natural. Yet, despite the lack of plants, I have to agree that Rob's garden is a lovely place to sit and reflect quietly. The sound of the water is soothing, and the sun feels just lovely on my shoulders.

"Mind if I sit?" I gesture at the marble slab.

"Not at all, make yourself comfortable," Rob waves at the bench. "The slabs are optimally placed to enjoy the benefits of a cleansing sound bath when the gong is struck. Wait for it...."

Rob lifts a wooden mallet and strikes the gong. The entire space immediately fills with the low, resonant hum. It fills my chest. Rob settles himself cross-legged on the opposite slab with his palms up in mudra gesture, eyes closed.

"The gong is tuned to the heart chakra. A nice ritual to start our meeting, don't you think?" Rob peeks at me through one eye. "These soundwaves fill me with so much gratitude. I'm grateful you took the time to come here today, Isla."

"I'm glad to be here, too," I say, meaning it. For the first time since my agent mentioned the opportunity to me, I feel like this might be a good thing. A great thing even.

"Again?" Rob motions to the gong and I nod my acquiescence.

Rob hits the gong again and we both stretch out prone on our stones, letting the good vibrations wash over us. I close my eyes and open my heart, receiving the sound until it finally fades fully and vanishes.

"There," Rob says, sitting up. I follow suit. "Now I feel ready to talk. Although I have to say that the azure light you are emanating is extremely distracting. I don't think I've ever actually met someone with such a blue aura. Have you always had it?"

I feel myself blushing. It's not the first time I've been told my aura is indigo or blue . And I know it's unusual.

"It comes with the psychic stuff," I say. "Most people don't see it."

Most people don't see *or* believe in auras. I'm surprised to learn Rob does both. I'm not getting any stray reads on what he may be thinking, but that's no surprise. If he's like me, he would have learned how to protect his own thoughts years ago. People who live in neighborhoods with glass houses learn to put up blinds.

"If I needed actual proof that you come by your gifts as naturally as your title character," Rob looks around and gestures to the empty space around me. "Here it is."

"Did you need proof?" I ask, curious. "I was under the impression you wanted me because of the matchmaker character in my books, not because you thought I was a psychic."

"Well, yes, but I had my suspicions. My family line traces back to the same part of the UK as yours and I've heard some of the local legends about the Fairfax curse," Rob admits. " Your series inspired me to dig in a little deeper. Fascinating stories. But honestly, the reason your books are so believable is *because* you're the real deal, Isla."

"Rob Goodfellow," I mock gasp and clutch my chest, daring to tease him. "Are you telling me you believe in magic?"

"I mean…yes?" He shrugs. "If the crystal slipper fits. You have a rare and special gift. I know you don't always believe it."

I get goosebumps. Did he just read *my* mind?

"It can be hard to believe in magic, Rob," I confess. "Even when it's your own. Especially when it's your own."

"I get it," Rob nods emphatically. "Believe me, I do. But I think that's what people want in these uncertain times. More magic. It's what we all *need*."

We both sit silently for a moment before I ask a question.

"I don't understand exactly what it is that you want from me," I say. "I'm not sure the way the matches happen in my books would work on a reality show. Not to mention the fact that the matches in my books are all *fictional*. The stakes are quite a bit lower than they would be in real life."

"I don't know," Rob waves away my concerns. "Real or imaginary, what I'm curious about is how you, or rather the mystic matchmaker, knows who to put together. What's the methodology behind all the stories?" Rob asks.

"I'm not sure I can explain that part," I wrinkle my nose. "It just comes to me, and I just know."

"So THAT," Rob snaps his fingers. "That is what I am talking about. That is why I have faith in you. You have the ancient wisdom and magic that this show needs. You ARE that magic, Isla." He laughs triumphantly. "I *knew* you had it flowing through your veins. I just knew it! It's not just in the stories you write."

Rob jumps to his feet and paces around the garden, wiggling his toes in the crystal-infused pebbles as he takes each step.

"I think I have to tell you now that this show is a passion project for me. I've always known that there are great and mystical unseen forces around us. There are reasons why some of us belong together or maybe don't. And those forces cannot be explained with ones and zeros. They cannot be quantified or calculated. They can only be felt by special gifted individuals, such as yourself."

Rob pauses in front of me, leaning forward slightly as he speaks. He's actually a little breathless, passion and conviction radiating from him as he speaks. He bites his lip and sighs.

"Listen, I've sown some wild oats in my time. Nobody could call me a monk. I wanted to believe in the idea of soulmates and the power of true love, but," he shrugs, seeming lost for words. "Then I found your stories, Isla. And guess what?"

"What?" I ask.

"Your books spoke to me. I became a little obsessed. After reading your books, I finally had the courage to open my heart. I trusted the universe to lead me to love. And it did. I found my soulmate, Isla. All because you sparked that belief in me."

He holds up his hand to show me his ring.

"So when Rory and Marco also suggested you for the show? I nearly passed out. There are no coincidences. It was serendipity. Synchronicity. Part of the grand plan! It had to be you. You ARE the show. If you don't want to do this show, I don't want to do this show!"

I shake my head in disbelief. "Wow, that's really weird. I don't have a lot of male readers. How did you find my books if you don't mind my asking?"

"My mom and my sister are huge fans. My granny was, too. I started reading the series when I was visiting her in Cornwall for Christmas a couple of years ago. I particularly appreciate the way that the mystic matchmaker works to undo centuries-old feuds and right past wrongs with her matches. We tore through all nine books by Valentine's Day. Speaking of which - I loved your take on Lupercalia on the *Lit Lovers* episode you did!"

"You listened to that?" I ask.

"Of course. And while I certainly don't condone animal cruelty, I think the world would be a better place if more people were open to the possibility of the divine nature of love. It's just a miracle, isn't it?" I can't help but notice the tear in Rob's eye as he twists his wedding ring on his finger. "If you don't want to do this show, I don't want to do this show. But I certainly hope you do. For the sake of the couples we have lined up, and for the sake of the world. Think how many lives we could change with that message of hope."

"Okay," I say, suddenly feeling a bit breathless, as well. "But how do you see it working? What would I be doing?"

"We'd want you to weigh in, right away, on the singles we've selected and matches we've made - see if you have a feeling about any of them," Rob says. "And of course, we'd want you there to oversee the dates and help plan the couple's outings. We'd essentially want you to work the same sort of magic you do in your books, only in real life."

"But my books are fiction," I say. "I've had some luck setting up friends but I'm not sure I can get the same kind of results as the mystic matchmaker in real life."

"People want to believe, Isla. Your books give people hope. That's more than half the battle. Everyone wants to *believe*."

# jackson

*"I absolutely believe in soulmates. But I don't think it's as simple as stumbling on your perfect match and boom, you click and fit. When worlds collide, your shape changes. You grow together."*

*~Isla Fairfax, Playing with Matches Confessionals*

"SO THE ALGORITHM can tell when people are lying?" Rory, the assistant producer, is quizzing me in the conference room. I'm back at Goodfellow Productions after grabbing a quick lunch with Rory and Rob at a nearby Mexican place. Rob is taking another meeting while Rory and I go over some of the details of the show.

I'm in a much better mood now that I've got a belly full of seafood tacos. My team has given me the full green light to go ahead with everything. The contract is already being reviewed by our legal staff. I glance down at the most recent messages from Geoff on my phone.

> You're really doing it? Fantastic! The exposure is going to be epic!

The message is punctuated by hearts, shooting stars, and starry-eyed emojis.

Geoff's uncharacteristic use of emojis suggests he's a little giddy, as well as starstruck.

> I told you I'd do it.

Why is he acting so surprised?

> Yeah, none of us believed you.

*Whatever.*

I slip my phone back into my pocket.

"Most people aren't deliberately trying to deceive the algorithm," I explain to Rory. "Usually they are also lying to themselves. The assessments are really good at catching people when they aren't being truthful. And we all lie. We lie about our diets, our fitness levels, and what we like to do in our spare time. Everyone wants to present a sort of idealized version of themselves on their dating profile. But do you want to hear a secret?"

I lean across the table, thinking that Rory smells nice. Sweet. Is it vanilla? She's flirting with me. But she's so young. I have the distinct feeling that anything I did with her wouldn't make me feel better about being the last man standing in my close friend group. It would make me feel a little dirty. Sad. And ultimately, more alone.

I don't know why I'm so loath to try my software on myself. I should be looking for someone compatible to share my life with. Someone to shop for couches with and binge whole seasons of TV shows with. The only thing we'd fight over is whose turn it was to choose the take-out dinners. Maybe we could get a dog and start an ironic Instagram account for it. I'm well into my thirties. It's time to settle down already.

It's the settling part I'm having a problem with though. The idea of waking up to the same person every day for the rest of my life? No surprises? No more possibilities? Plus, I really don't want to give up hot sex. A part of me is really disappointed in myself. I really thought that once my frontal lobe gelled a bit more I'd be less of a horndog and more practical. I don't want to end up alone. And yet, given the choice between hot sex and someone to choose sofa upholstery with, I choose hot sex. Every time.

Nevermind, that most of the hot sex I've had in the last year or so hasn't been all that hot. It's all starting to feel a bit washed out and unsatisfying. Missing the secret spice. I can't flip the cap on whatever that is, or I would. I would shake it all over my "love" life like my beloved hot sauce on my tacos. I'm not even sure exactly what's missing. Everything just seems so pallid. The same.

That's probably why Isla Fairfax made me trip harder than a tomcat huffing catnip. That woman is saucy. The fantasies keep recurring.

"What?" Rory leans towards me and bites her lip a little suggestively.

"Huh?" I blush, realizing my train of thought has jumped the tracks again. This seems to happen every time I think about Isla.

"You were telling me a secret about people's dating profiles," Rory smirks, licks her lips, and unbuttons her off-white jacket to reveal a pale pink camisole underneath. At lunch, she ordered a salad and then ate it without dressing because she didn't want to risk dripping anything on her white suit.

*That is so not happening.*

"Right," I nod, backing it up a smidge and sliding back into the conversation neatly like I'm coaxing a zipper to behave. "The secret that almost nobody realizes is that most people shy away from perfect dating profiles. They don't trust them. When a profile is too glossy and good, it doesn't get as many matches. Deep down we all want to find people who share our same level of shortcomings and our penchants for weird junk food. What's the point of matching with someone who's gonna make you feel crappy about yourself? Ideally, we're all hoping to find ourselves a mate with our same kinks."

"Is this your way of telling me you're kinky?" Rory teases.

*I have always had a thing for redheads.*

The thought pops into my head, unbidden and irrelevant, as Rory is blonde.

"Nerds are all kinky, Kiddo," I say, lobbing back the volley without any force.

"Ha!" Rory smiles coyly and swivels in her rolling seat. With a shove, she propels herself back and away from the table. She reaches for a magazine on the desk and then rolls gracefully back to the table like she is performing a ballet on office chair wheels.

"So tell me, what do you call your *thing*?" she murmurs, leafing through the magazine.

"My thing?" I glance down at my crotch, reflexively. Rory catches me looking and meets my eye as I look back up. She laughs and folds back the magazine page to a photo of me from an interview I did last year. *Thirty-five Tech Moguls under Thirty-five.*

"Not *that thing*," she smirks.

I shift uncomfortably.

Rory taps the magazine. "I was actually wondering if you have a name for the Algorithm. Like do you call it 'Al' or 'Tony or something? You didn't mention it in the article."

"What makes you think my algorithm is Italian?" I tease.

"I guess I just get some serious Mafia vibes. Like nobody's messing with Tony. He's got your number."

Suddenly, the door to the conference room swings open, and Rob bursts in. He's changed into some kind of white-looking guru suit. And right behind him is the last person I'm expecting to see in this office.

"Jackson?" Isla Fairfax stops in her tracks. She is staring at me, eyes wide. She looks almost as confused as I feel. "What are *you* doing here?"

# isla

. . .



*"Dating apps don't work for people looking for long term relationships because they are about getting laid. Nobody is honest. Everyone is selling something."*

*~ Jackson Porter, Playing With Matches Confessionals*

**WE'VE BEEN TRAPPED** in the windowless meeting room with the casting director for three hours, and we're running out of time to make decisions. The production team has to act fast to get everyone on site in just over a week.

"I promised Rob I'd text him our final picks by end-of-day," she says.

She slides a folder in front of Jackson and me. There's a photo of a pretty blonde woman stapled on the outside. "How about Chloe and Darwin? I like her. She seems sweet."

The casting director looks at me hopefully, but unfortunately, I see through her phony smile. She's tired. Phoning it in. She doesn't really give a shit who we pick, just so long as we get it over with already so she can get home and read her cozy mystery novel. I feel for her, but she's going to have to be patient. I need to get this right.

"According to their responses on the app, Chloe and Darwin are an eighty-five percent match." The casting director slaps down a second folder. The photo on this one shows a bulked-up man who obviously spends all his free time at a gym. His hair is short and so is his neck, but he has kind eyes.

The selfie-style photos are not enough for me to get a read on either one of them.

"Done deal," Jackson says. "Those are excellent odds."

"I'm going to need a little bit more than that to sign off on them," I say, sliding the first folder toward myself to take a closer look at Chloe.

I flip the folder open, reviewing her bio.

*Name:* Chloe
*Age:* 29
*Location:* Columbus. Ohio
*Occupation:* Neonatal nurse at a children's hospital
*Hobbies:* Biking, hiking, volunteer work

According to her interview, she's dated a ton of guys but hasn't found anyone who shares her passion for social justice and activism. She's looking for a life partner who's up for adventure. Her ideal partner is someone who's flexible, spontaneous, and physically fit.

"We have the videos they submitted, too," the casting director says. "If you'd like me to pull them up."

"Maybe in a bit." I open Darwin's folder and place their photos side by side. Then I close my eyes.

"Are you freaking kidding me?" Jackson snorts. "What's the point of putting their pictures side by side if you're not even going to *look* at them?"

"Shhh!" I hold up a finger without opening my eyes.

"What are you doing?" he asks, clicking his pen impatiently.

"I'm getting a feeling about them. I need to focus," I say, struggling to keep the couple in my mind's eye. It's not easy in the small room with Jackson Porter sitting so close to me. I can smell his distractingly spicy scent. Something totally mass-market and probably synthetic, but on him, it smells hot. Irritatingly so, as I really am not a fan of non-natural products.

He won't stop ribbing me. Or clicking that damn pen. It's like he's deliberately trying to throw me off my game. I can't let it get to me.

Rob took me aside and explained why we need him here. It makes perfect sense. As a storyteller, I know the drill. There's no tension without opposition. If we don't demonstrate the obvious flaws in Jackson's matchmaking methods, we can't make a case for mine.

"Next thing you'll be pulling a tarot card to choose," Jackson says.

I open one eye. "Now that's not a terrible idea," I say, reaching into my bag for my deck.

"Holy shit. You have got to be kidding me. I was joking!" Jackson exclaims.

"Nevertheless, tarot cards are a great resource. They are a great tool for tapping into our natural instincts," I say.

I pull the World card for Chloe. Interesting! And then I pull a Tower reversed for Darwin. That's all I need to know. The two of them are on very different journeys at this time. They'd only hold each other back from being who they're meant to be as individuals.

"Pass on these two," I say.

"What?!" Jackson is incredulous. "That's ridiculous. Those cards have no meaning."

"Maybe not to you, but for me, they confirm my general feeling. I just don't see these two together. They aren't meant for one another. It won't work."

"I disagree," Jackson folds his arms. "Look at this. They agree on almost everything, from toilet paper alignment to car radio habits."

"Well then," I laugh. "They must be perfect for one another. Nothing's sexier than someone who puts the toilet paper roll on the right way."

"You laugh, but that's a greater indicator of relationship longevity than religion," Jackson insists.

"Guys," the casting director scolds us, "you need to stop bickering. We need to wrap this up. We don't have any more time. And we're all supposed to be on the same team here. We all have the same goals, right? Helping these young people meet the love of their lives? If I could make a suggestion, how about you each pick one couple, and I pick the third."

"Deal!" Jackson holds out his hand to shake hers. "I'm good with these two."

"There's no way. Chloe is an old soul, and Darwin is brand new," I argue.

"Hey, I get my pick, you get yours," Jackson shrugs. "Take your pick."

"Okay then, fine. I want her," I point to a folder that Jackson shoved aside at the start of our negotiations. The woman in the photo is a busty brunette with bee-stung lips and insanely long, thick lash extensions. Her eyes are an unnatural shade of teal, and I'm pretty sure she's had a nose job and is incapable of showing emotion from the brows up. But I love who she has matched with, even though they are the weakest of all the couples the casting agent has shown us.

**Name:** *Lacey*
**Age:** *27*
**Location:** *Tampa*
**Occupation:** *Cosmetologist*
**Hobbies:** *Attending music festivals, traveling, photography*

"Lacey?" Jackson snorts. "No way. She's a liar."

"How do you know that?" I ask.

"She filled in the same answer on every question. All threes. Neutral choices on everything. It's the kind of answer someone gives when they want to hedge their bets and have the best chance of matching. But it's also a major tell. Nobody is that neutral about everything." Jackson frowns, "She's not here for the right reasons, Isla. She's looking for insta-fame."

"Maybe she really doesn't care about her toilet roll," I shrug, reaching for the stack of male candidates. I pick up the pile of folders, fanning them out, and wave my hand back and forth over the top of them till I sense the one I'm looking for. I pluck it out of the pile.

"Ryker," I say pointing to the Australian hottie who bills himself as a global digital nomad. " I want Ryker and Lacey."

"Now I know you're nuts. He's almost as bad as she is," Jackson shakes his head. "I don't even know how these two total fame-seekers snuck past you." He chastises the casting director. "I don't see it. What was their compatibility ratio?"

The casting director pulls up a spreadsheet on her laptop. "Hmm… Thirty-seven percent?"

"Yeah," Jackson smirks. "Good luck with that, Isla."

"They'll be great together," I say, feeling quite sure of it now that I've laid them out on the table alongside Chloe and Darwin. "Ryker needs a Wendy-type, and Lacey needs a Peter Pan-type."

"Great," the casting agent says. "We're almost done. For the third couple I choose–"

"We have to keep Paula!" I shout, snagging the petite Asian girl's folder from the stack.

"I insist we use Owen," Jackson snatches a folder with the photo of a tall, dark, and handsome older man in full fire-fighter gear.

We turn to face each other, heads down and tilted like two rams about to clash horns. And then our eyes meet. Something sparks. Jackson smiles. I nod. We both laugh.

"Wait, what?" the casting agent, who is now positive we are both crazy, asks. "What's so funny?"

"Paula and Owen," we both say simultaneously. We're still making eye contact, and it's still buzzing. There's a vibration in the air not unlike the gong from the garden. Except it's hitting me a bit lower. The buzzing is happening below the belt. The butterflies in my belly are waking up.

The casting agent exhales with relief and looks between the two of us. "Did my ears deceive me, or did you two just *agree* on something?"

"Oh my God, we did, didn't we?" I laugh, placing Paula's folder onto the pile of keepers.

"Who knew it was even possible?" Jackson adds Owen's.

"Out of curiosity," I hold his gaze, "what made you choose these two?"

"Just the numbers," Jackson says confidently. "That's all that matters. These two are even more compatible than Chloe and Darwin."

"So it doesn't matter to you that she's legally blind and that he's an ex firefighter?" I ask.

"Nope."

"You're not interested in the fact that she likes to read and he volunteers at the library? Or that they both love the color blue and want to have three kids?"

"Wait, what? Where in their files does it say that?" The casting director leafs through the paperwork.

"It doesn't," Jackson says. "But even if it did, it wouldn't sway me. None of that stuff is all that important, it turns out."

"Bullshit," I challenge. "It would totally be important to me."

"I fail to see why, when you could simply close your eyes and pull a tarot card," Jackson retorts.

"I didn't need to pull a tarot card to get a feel about these two," I answer. "They just make sense."

The casting director scoops up the pile of folders containing our picks and pulls on her cardigan. "If it's all the same to you two, I'm going to head out now. I just texted Rob, and I've got some calls to make. I wish you both the best of luck with the show."

"Thanks," Jackson waves. "But I don't need luck, I've got science."

"Right," she agrees and pauses before scooting out the door, "I hope it all works out for you two."

# jackson

. . .

*"No, I've never used a hookup app. Those things will clog up your emotional arteries."*

*~ Isla Fairfax, Playing With Matches Confessionals*

**THE MINUTE** the casting director leaves, Isla and I burst into nervous laughter.

"Well that was a trip," I say while putting my laptop back in my carry-on bag. It's too late to fly home tonight. I had my assistant switch it to the morning and book a room near the airport.

"How long have you known about the show?"

"They just asked me to do it a couple of weeks ago," Isla says. "How about you?"

"Same," I say. "My friend Dean mentioned Rob called him last month, and then someone reached out to my software team."

"They reached out to my agent," Isla offers. "I really had no idea what to expect, but she seems to think it will be good for book sales." She shrugs noncommittally, but I note the tension in her shoulders and wonder if the stakes are higher for her than she's admitting.

"Such a shame, we could have flown down together this morning if we'd known," I say.

"Maybe," Isla says. "But I actually flew in late last night. I had an early meeting with my agent before coming over here. I'm completely knackered." Isla admits. "I'm just glad the selection process is done."

"May the best man win," I hold out my hand to shake.

Isla cocks her head at me. "But it's not supposed to be a *competition*, is it?"

"Isn't it?" I raise my eyebrows, thinking about what Rob said to me when he pulled me aside. We need the juxtaposition of old vs new to highlight how much more effective my methods are. Plus, her readers are the target market for the show. And my app. They might like reading escapist fantasies, but they have to live in the real world. I just hope she doesn't come off looking like too much of an ass at the end of it all.

"You know what?" I pull my unshook hand back. "You're right. It doesn't matter whose methods prove most effective. We're both doing this because we want to see those people happily matched, so what does it matter how it happens?"

"I'm so glad you said that. I totally agree," Isla smiles and finally holds out her hand to shake mine. Her hand feels warm, soft, and small in mine. I turn it over and pass my thumb over the large opal in her ring, half expecting it to throw sparks at me, like I'd imagined it doing yesterday.

The stone is lit with neon pink, orange, yellow, and blue fire beneath the milky surface. I wonder if it's her birthstone. It seems so *her*. Mysterious and bright at the same time. "I'm relieved this didn't get more adversarial." Isla squeezes my hand, and we release each other.

"Me, too," I agree. "And I'm satisfied with our choices."

Two out of the three of those potential couples have great odds, based on my software. So what if that one couple hasn't got a prayer? I consider today a win. "I thought the casting director was going to start smacking our hands with a ruler," I say. "Think she'll watch the show?"

"No way," Isla says. "I think she's more likely to watch the Westminster Kennel Club show in its entirety."

"Seriously," I chuckle, "she couldn't get out of here fast enough."

"I *was* being serious," Isla smirks. "She's a dog person, not a people person. She should be casting canines instead of people."

"You got all that from sitting in the room with her all afternoon?" I ask, spinning myself around on my seat, enjoying the release after the tension of the last few hours.

"No, I got that from her Corgi tote bag and the amount of dog fur on her pants. Amongst other things," Isla smiles enigmatically.

"Okay, Madame Fairfax," I say, playfully, "what's *my* fortune then? Read my tarot cards or whatever it is you do." I wave an invisible magic wand at her.

A shadow crosses her face. "No can do, Jackson. That's not how it works. I'm not a fortune teller. I don't do readings on demand, and I don't get to pick and choose what I'm shown."

"Right," I say with exaggerated patience. "Then just make something up. You're a storyteller. It's all the same thing isn't it?"

"No. It most certainly is not." She shakes her head vehemently, then looks at me sadly. "Though I do acknowledge it can look and feel that way at times. Especially to people who are closed-minded."

"I bet," I nod, feigning sympathy. "Sounds tough."

Honestly I'm not sure what else to say. She's talking nonsense. It's like when my sister tells me a certain shade of purple is *too grape*. Or when people think they know what their pets are thinking.

My hand automatically goes to the tiny green medallion on a gold chain at my throat. Murphy was the exception of course. He was the goodest good boy and highly advanced. He was smart enough to communicate with humans.

"Don't patronize me like that," Isla says. I stop spinning on my chair. She glares at me and squares her shoulders. I could swear her hair fluffs up. She runs a hand through the wild mane. Then she rolls her eyes dismissively and stands to pack up her things.

*Shit.*

"Isla?" I say, tentatively.

She glances up disdainfully. Her lips are pursed, and her eyes are still narrowed. I'm speared by her gaze, and there's an aching lump in my throat like I used to get when I was a kid. It happened whenever I would say the wrong thing. Which was often.

Why am I so mesmerized by her? She turns her back on me, but I can't stop staring at the back of her head, my mind grasping for something, anything to say to bring back that easy camaraderie of five minutes ago. Can I pull up a funny video on my phone? Impress her with my ability to make an annoyingly loud horn out of a single sheet of office paper? Gah!

I'm like a nerdy little Sebastian the crab, scuttling around, scrabbling for dinglehoppers to impress Ariel the mermaid with. And, of course, I'm also dying to kiss her.

*WTF actually?*

It's weird. Normally, if I were this attracted to a woman in an empty boardroom like this, I'd be quietly fantasizing in a pretty graphic fashion, speculating about whether the conference table could hold our weight.

But while kissing her has crossed my mind, other thoughts haven't been as intrusive. My mind feels whooshy and my heart races when I'm around Isla. Like I am caught in a riptide. I don't just want a part of her. I'm not sure what I want from her? To be a part of her world?

This is impossible of course. And crazy. This woman is a walking hallucinogen. She needs to be classified and come with a warning.

It's a bad idea to even think about it. *Bad, bad, idea.* Fantastic, but bonkers. I grasp onto logic and common sense in order to swim myself back to the safety of solid ground. Isla Fairfax and I can never be more than friends. It's just the novelty of her that's unsettling me. The accent. Her hair. The bright colors. Her silly belief in magic.

Maybe if we weren't working together there'd be one-night stand potential?

*No Jackson! You need to shut these thoughts down!*

Okay. So maybe I regret my insensitivity. And it's probably unkind of me to be giving her such a hard time. After all, it's going to be bad enough when she comes off like a fool on the show. There's no reason we have to be enemies just because we disagree about magic, right?

The lump in my throat is still there, but I feel less likely to choke on it. I offer up the best apology I can come up with, without sounding insincere.

"Look, Isla, I'd be thrilled if you proved me wrong. But unless you can use your cards to predict the lottery numbers for tonight, I'm not buying it. I'm sorry; it's not personal. I just don't believe in that kind of stuff, so I kind of think you're full of it."

I watch her wrap the tarot cards in a silk cloth and place them into a zippered case. She places the case carefully in her beaded and embroidered tote bag. Her brow is furrowed. With her left hand, she strokes a pink crystal pendant that's hanging around her neck. Rose quartz?

"You think you know a lot about me, don't you?" Isla drops the pendant, and it swings in a circle before landing in her cleavage. I have to cleave my eyes away.

"I mean, not really, but I know your type?" I shrug. "Again it's nothing personal. I'm a data guy."

"You know nothing about me, Jackson Porter," she says, "but I'm pretty sure I know a few things about you."

She glances at the pen in my hand, which I've just noticed I'm slowly clicking again. It's an annoying habit that I haven't been able to break. Suddenly feeling self-conscious, I set the pen down.

"Hey," I say. "I'm sorry I'm being such an ass. My sister and my friends are always telling me I have no manners. Can you at least let me buy you dinner to make it up to you? I'm not flying home till tomorrow morning."

"No," Isla answers. "I've got a deadline and an awful lot to do to get ready for next week. I'm just going to go back to my hotel, do some work, and crash."

"Okay," I say, feeling so much more disappointed by her rejection than I would have expected.

"See you at Peaches," Isla calls over her shoulder before leaving. "And don't worry about *me* looking like an ass there. Worry about your own ass instead. Oh, and Jackson?" she smirks a little, pausing in the doorway, "I see you as much more of a Flounder than a Sebastian."

# isla

. . .



*"My ideal partner would share my love of five-star travel and have enough points and miles to keep up with me."*

*~Jackson Porter, Playing With Matches Confessionals*

THERE'S a dedicated driver waiting for me, holding a sign with my name on it, when I arrive at the tiny island airport. He quickly loads my luggage and escorts me into a brand-new SUV. The backseat is outfitted with cameras, water bottles, and a big box of tissues.

"That's for the confessionals," the driver points to the camera. "It's all set up for you if you want to record something on the way to the resort, Darlin'. Just press the red button."

"Oh, I'm not one of the contestants," I laugh.

"Right," he says, checking his clipboard. "You're the star. You're Isla, the…" he squints at the writing and laughs a little, "Mystic Matchmaker? What's that about?"

"I'm a romance novelist, actually. The mystic matchmaker is the main character in a series that I write," I explain.

"Well, don't let me stop you from recording," he says as we pull away from the airport. "Rob told me it's all good, whatever you wanna say. Also Rob told me if I get his people to fill the drive, he's going to buy me a case of beer. So talk as long as you want, Isla the Mystic Matchmaking romance novelist. Tell us a story!"

"But I look like hell," I protest. "I just got off a long flight."

"Not true, Lady!" the driver laughs, and I see the flash of a gold tooth reflected in the rearview mirror, "You look like a beautiful tropical flower. What's gonna happen when all them boys fall in love with you, Mystic Isla?"

"And you look like a man who really wants a case of beer," I laugh back.

I slap on some lipstick and check my appearance on my phone, thinking about what I want to say. I don't have to think too long or too hard. Rob, or possibly Rory, has made it easy for me, or whoever's in this hot seat. There's a laminated card on the back of the seat with a list of prompts and suggestions for what to talk about.

1. **Introduce yourself**
2. **Tell us why you decided to be a part of *Playing with Matches***
3. **Do you think this experience could be life-changing for you?**
4. **Have you tried any dating apps or matchmaking services in the past? How did that go?**
5. **What are you hoping to get out of this experience?**
6. **Do you believe in soul mates?**
7. **Why do you think dating apps work (or not)?**
8. **Who would you be most likely to swipe right on?**

9.  **What is your ideal first date?**
10.  **What are you looking for in a partner?**

Here we go. I settle back into the soft leather and hit the red button.

*"Hi, my name is Isla Fairfax, and I love to make matches. You might be familiar with some of the couples I've set up in my Mystic Matchmaker Romance Series. But what you might not know about me is that nothing makes me happier than making matches in real life."*

I pause the recording while I think for a moment.

"Keep going; you're doing fine. Tell us about matchmaking!" the driver prompts.

"Fine," I say and hit record again.

*"My theory about matches is not so much that everyone has one perfect mate. But I do think a lot of it has to do with getting the timing right. There's a reason so many love stories start with an awesome meet-cute. It's like a chemical reaction. All the right ingredients have to be there at the right moment, and poof! Alchemy!"*

I pause the recording again, but only for a moment, to catch my breath. I'm on a roll now.

*"Sometimes it's hard for us to see the big picture. We can't zoom out of our own lives and see all the possibilities. But other people can see them for us. I can see that my friend who keeps swiping right on guys from her gym would be more likely to meet the man of her dreams at a bookstore. Sometimes people need to get forced out of their comfort zones to shake things up."*

Here I pause again, but I keep the camera rolling as I briefly look out the windows at the pastel colored buildings and lush green landscape flying by. In between, I keep catching teasing glimpses of the clear blue water in the distance. So very different from Rome, London, and even California. Here the palm trees look rooted. They don't seem fake.

*"When I write meet-cutes in my novels, I think about the people involved and whatever ruts they might be in. My characters rarely like the situations they get tossed into by me. I'm like an emotional hot waxer. It's embarrassing, and it's painful. But ultimately… it's worth it."*

I hit pause and groan.

*Emotional hot waxer?* Did I really just say that? Where did that come from? Good Lord. I'm one hundred percent positive they are going to use that idiotic clip. There's no rewind button. What have I done?

I ought to stick a sock in it now, but of course I foolishly keep going. Now that I've started to opine, I cannot seem to shut up.

*"I guess I just want to do this show because it feels like it's part of my calling? Making great matches on the page is one thing, but doing it in real life feels more meaningful. It makes me feel like I'm doing my part to make the world a happier place. I want to spread a message of hope to people. Hope, love, and magic. Because love IS magic. We're so caught up in petty things - appearances, trends, and technology. We've handed over so much control of our lives to algorithms that I fear a lot of us are losing our ability to trust ourselves, and where does that leave us? Alone. Frightened. We need to be able to trust in what our guts and our intuition are telling us before we can open ourselves up to the universe of possibilities. How can we ever trust ourselves enough to fall in love if we can't trust ourselves to make simple decisions with our hearts? Scary stuff, right?"*

I hit pause. The driver whistles.

"You just gonna leave me hanging like that? You can't stop now, Miss Isla. I know you have more to say!"

I picture Jackson in the boardroom last week, wringing his hands, feeling sorry for me. But he's the one who is worthy of pity. Him with his vision of toilet roll placement compatibility in lieu of a cosmic connection.

"I don't know. Maybe it sounds a little crazy," I sigh.

"No, it doesn't. It sounds like you are some kind of a love prophet to me. Come on… you know you want to say it," the driver cajoles.

"Give me a minute," I swig some of the chilled water from a bottle before going on. Jackson is on my mind as I finish my monologue. I was the one who reminded him that it wasn't a competition. But maybe he was right. Maybe it is. And maybe people need to be reminded that love has never been about ones and zeros. There's never been a simple formula, and there never will be. I hit record and continue.

*"I worry about all these apps that are out there now. They are supposed to make things so much easier, but do they? Or do they make us too lazy to think for ourselves, to use our imagination, and to make an effort. Why swim upstream when it's so much easier to float around the lazy river and stay in your lane while browsing a seemingly infinite menu? That's what apps are best at. Helping us feel like we don't have to lift a finger, unless it's to swipe to winnow away the choices we only review at a glance. Too old, too young, too blond, too short, too fat, too far away, too bald, too bad. Before you know it, you're out of time. You're out of time, out of options, and the funniest thing is, you can't remember the faces of a single one of the people you've rejected. If you ran into them at the store, you wouldn't recognize them."*

The car comes to a stop under a sheltered port cochere, and I press the stop button for the last time.

"Wow. That was really deep." The driver clutches his chest. "You really spoke to me. Even though I met my wife on the Tinder app. I was very lucky. I feel what you are saying."

He hops out and circles the car to open my door.

"You can proceed directly into the concierge lounge for check-in." He launches into a well-rehearsed script now. He holds out a hand to assist me out of the vehicle. "Don't worry about your luggage. I will hand it over to the porter, and he will deliver your things directly to your room. I hope you have a sweet stay, Ms. Fairfax, and that you find whatever it is you're looking for here at Peaches."

"Thanks," I say, reaching for my bag to get a tip.

"No need to tip me, we are a gratuity-free property," the driver says. "But thanks for doing your part in filling up the drive on that camera," he winks.

The lobby of the concierge lounge is furnished with luxurious Italianate furnishings and beautiful handwoven rugs laid over travertine floors. The carved wood furniture, chenille tapestries, and massive crystal chandelier hanging from the vaulted ceiling add to the luxurious ambiance. I feel as though I've been transported to a palazzo, even though the damp chill of the air conditioner on full blast assures me that I am still in the tropics.

"Would you like a drink, Ma'am?" a staff member in full butler attire appears as if out of nowhere. He is wearing white gloves and carrying a polished silver tray full of freshly poured cocktails that sparkle in frosted glasses. "These are bellinis, the signature drink of the Peaches Property."

"Thank you," I say, taking one of the peach-colored cocktails. It's sweet, fizzy, and fabulous - the perfect introduction to paradise. "My compliments to the mixologist, this is splendid," I say, carrying my drink with me to the check-in desk.

"Indeed. There's a little bit of magic in those, and a pinch of good fortune," the concierge winks. "But I see you don't need it. You've already beat the rush and the bad weather. We have a handful of guests who were supposed to check in later this afternoon. I fear they won't make it. There's a small storm predicted."

"Really? That's hard to believe," I say, glancing out at the gorgeous weather. "It looks perfect out there right now."

"You will find that the weather changes very quickly here," the concierge smiles. "Mother Nature likes to keep us on our toes."

"Oh great! Isla!" I hear a familiar voice behind me as I am stepping up to the counter to get my room key. "I was hoping I would catch you in the lobby!"

Rob, dressed in a white linen shirt, khaki cargo shorts, and flip flops, rushes over to kiss both my cheeks.

"Look at you!" he enthuses, appreciating my hot pink Lily Pulitzer dress, oversized straw hat with pom poms, and electric blue sandals. "I just love this whole resort wear look on you. Not everyone can pull off color the way you do. I mean, I'm afraid to wear anything with a pattern. But on you, it's all so good. Part of your whole magical vibe. I hope you packed a lot of it because the camera is going to love you."

I blush at all the flattery. "I mean, I just packed what I would normally wear in the summertime," I say. "I have a thing for vintage tropical clothing."

"Well, you wear it well. We are so beyond lucky to have you," Rob grins. Then he seems to notice the woman who is patiently waiting with my room keys and smiles at her. "I'm sorry to interrupt you, I'm sure you were about to tell Ms. Fairfax about her wonderful accommodations?"

"I was," the woman smiles broadly at me. Her eyes are sparkling, and her bright smile lights up in contrast to her gorgeous, dark skin. "My name is Edwina, and I'm here for you, whatever you need, Ms Fairfax."

In less than an instant I know how much she loves her job here. Even when the customers are a bit needy or grumpy, she loves it. Edwina loves welcoming people at the start of their vacation when the world is their oyster, and she's a little sad when it's time to say goodbye. But she's also glad because she knows if she's done her job right, they will have great memories and they will be back - again and again in many cases. And when they come back, she will remember their names, and they will remember hers. Like family.

I feel her genuine warmth radiating into my bones, an even more welcoming cocktail than the drink in my hand.

"You'll be staying in one of our deluxe suites. There's a king-sized bed in the master bedroom and a daybed and pull-out sofa in the living room. There are bunk beds and a trundle in the second bedroom. And your suite has an oversized patio with a beautiful ocean view. I hope that is acceptable?"

"But it's just me," I protest. "I don't need that much space."

"Nonsense," Rob insists. "The resort puts all their VIPs in deluxe suites with ocean view rooms. Isn't that right, Edwina?" he asks.

"We are very thrilled to have you here, Ms Fairfax," Edwina says. "I must confess, I personally love all your novels." She shyly pulls a dog-eared copy of the first book in *The Mystic Matchmaker* series out of one of the drawers.

"Oh!" I exclaim. "You must let me sign that. How sweet!"

"Oh, that's not necessary," Edwina blushes.

"I insist!" I say, pulling a pen out of my bag. Rob waits patiently while I finish adding a personal note and draw a smiling sun around my inscription to her.

"Mind if I ride along with you and see you to your room so we can talk about the schedule for this evening?" Rob asks, as he points to a golf cart that's pulled up outside the lounge. My luggage has already been loaded.

"Sounds good," I say.

We both step out into the steamy tropical air, and I laugh as a pair of tiny lizards skitters by and into the bushes. Their tails are held aloft, forming jaunty little o-shaped curls.

Rob slides into the rear seat beside me.

"There's a big BBQ dinner tonight for all of us. You'll want to use the next couple of hours to copy any essential contacts into this new phone." He hands me a brand new iPhone in the box. "We had these configured for you, and you should know we may be monitoring messages. We'll store your phone in a lock box for the duration of filming."

The lush scenery rolls by in a green blur of oversized leaves and brilliant blooms.

"Are you kidding me?" I groan. I shouldn't be surprised, there was something about this in the contracts. But I was hoping they would forget about it.

"It's only for the week, and you'll still be able to call and text friends and family. But we do need to keep all the talent, including our experts, off of social media for the duration of the taping," Rob shakes his head. "I'm sure you of all people understand that. We'll be confiscating phones at the BBQ. Laptops, too, if you brought one."

"I'm in the middle of a manuscript!" I protest. "I have a deadline."

"Okay. I'll make an exception for you, Isla," Rob considers this and looks sternly at me. "As long as you promise to delete social and stay off the wifi. Think you can do that for me?"

"Sure. It's only a week. Piece of cake," I breathe a sigh of relief, grateful that I'll still be able to write. "It might actually help me focus," I point out.

"Good for you, Isla! I don't think I'm that strong!"

The golf cart lurches to a halt in the breezeway of a multistory oceanfront block of rooms. The entryway is tiled with a colorful mosaic floor, accentuated with bits of shell and pebbles.

"This way!" The porter jumps out and removes my bags, then leads us to the open-air corridor and the elevators. He hits the up button. "Top floor," the porter says. "The best view."

"Thanks," Rob says appreciatively.

"What about you?" I ask Rob. "Are you giving up your phone?"

"No," Rob looks apologetic. "I know it seems unfair, but Rory and the folks working on the technical side need to be able to keep tabs on the outside world. If it makes you feel any better though, the wifi on the island is pretty spotty. Probably good for people though. Forces them to do things the old-fashioned way. Face to face. We want everyone to have that kind of wholesome experience here."

"Totally - I get it," I say as we step into the elevator. "It's just another source of noise that messes with your mind, right? It's important to set up filters."

Of course, they want the participants to stay off social media. If anyone gets that, it's me. But what about Jackson? I cannot picture the tech mogul taking kindly to this rule. I bite my lip, picturing how he's going to react to this news when Rob breaks it to him.

*But Jackson's not my problem, is he?*

He's just another distraction I'll need to filter out this week. During our conversation at Goodfellow Productions, he seemed so determined to get a rise out of me. I've met his type before. Closed-minded, smug, logic-thinkers who feel like they need to break me down, just so they can continue to cling to their narrow-minded beliefs.

His face when I'd read his mind! I only sensed a snippet of him relating to that funny singing crab from *The Little Mermaid*, but it was enough. It was clearly a direct hit. I'd seen the crab, and I'd felt his disgusting sense of superiority. He had the nerve to feel sorry for me? Pretty ridiculous when he's the one being set up to fail here.

I was almost feeling sorry for him, up until the moment I unintentionally read his arrogant mind.

Sometimes my gift really is a blessing. For a moment there I'd considered it. I'd thought about my mum's proclamation. Maybe she was right. Maybe I do need to get laid. I'm a grown woman. Would it really be such a terrible thing to have a little fling while I was in the tropics? Don't I deserve to have a little fun, too? I finish my bellini in the elevator on the way up.

There was something achingly familiar and magnetic about Jackson Porter. Even though I'd wanted to wring his neck all day. I've wanted to wring his neck ever since the Lupercalia episode of his podcast. But I've also wanted other things. And I know he's thought some of those things, too. *What else had he been thinking?* I guess it's not all ones and zeros in that hard head of his.

I have to quell my curiosity before it drives me crazy. The things I do know instantly rule him out. *I'm not sleeping with someone who feels sorry for me and who thinks I'm a crackpot.*

"Look, Isla, you've been such a great sport, and I know I've said it several times but it bears saying again. So many of the cast members look up to you. Idolize you even. And I think they'll be taking their cues from you with regard to this digital detox. I'm so glad that you'll be here to help them with it. It's always one of the hardest things for the cast members to get over, those first few hours of being unplugged. But by day three, everyone always feels better," Rob says as the elevator doors open.

The porter leads us to my room and uses his card to open the door to a large, airy sunlit suite. It's practically a whole apartment! I am quite literally blown away by the cool, ocean-scented breeze that rushes out to greet us. From the entry door, I can see a wall of glass with sliding doors that lead to a large patio. And beyond that, the shocking turquoise water of the Caribbean. Brighter than the saturated color of my favorite lucky dress. So intense it almost looks computer-generated.

"Wow!" I exclaim.

A crack of thunder rumbles behind us, and rain begins pouring down in sheets beyond the covered corridor outside the hotel room door.

"Looks like you got here just in time," the porter smiles, leaning on the doorframe. "Lucky."

"That's just so crazy," I say, nudging Rob and pointing to the wall of glass in the room as I stride closer to get a better look. "Look out there on this side of the building, it's still so bright and sunny. It's like a whole other world from back there." I point back towards the open door, where the sky is an ominous shade of dark gray and the rain continues to come in sheets.

"Welcome to the tropics," the porter says. "Where the sun and the storms can kiss and make up and make baby rainbows."

"I love that! And I am thrilled to be here," I answer. I turn in a circle, taking in all the thoughtful touches everywhere. The suite is lavishly furnished with a deep sofa and separate dining area. The door leading into the master bedroom is open, and I can see that it contains an enormous four-poster bed, romantically tented with semi-sheer curtains. The master bedroom shares the same ocean view and has its own separate entrance to the patio.

"Wow! Could this suite be any sexier?" I exclaim. "I'm going to love staying here and writing on that patio." So long writer's block! I can feel my creativity firing up just from staring at the view. It's almost too much though. I'm embarrassed to be this spoiled. I turn to Rob. "I can't believe all of this is just for me."

"We want you to be comfortable here. It's the least we could do," Rob insists. "This show wouldn't be possible without you, Isla."

"We've stocked your bar with alcohol and soft drinks." The porter opens a cabinet to show me the selection. "And please enjoy the fruit platter and the champagne with our compliments." He gestures to a colorful spread of artistically-carved fruit set up on the dining table.

"That's not all," Rob says, leading me to the bedroom. He parts the curtains to the bed, revealing a mountain of totes and gift bags. "I made sure that you were included in all the swag bag drops. I mean, if anyone on this show is a household name and bonafide celeb, it's gotta be you!"

"That's all for *me*?" I ask, incredulous. The entire king-sized bed is covered with bags from clothing designers and makeup brands. I spy red-soled shoes and three couture purses. There's even a camera. It's almost obscene.

"It's hardly enough, but consider it a small perk? We know that the gig doesn't pay much, and the brands actually pay us for the privilege of giving their stuff to you guys so it's a win-win, right?"

He checks an incoming message on his phone. "Oh no, Isla, I'm so sorry. I have to run and check on something. Seems like the storm might have delayed some late arrivals." He turns urgently to the porter, "Do you think I can get a lift back to reception?"

"Of course," the porter nods.

Rob squeezes my hands reassuringly before he goes. "I'll see you later at the BBQ, Isla. I can't wait for you to meet everyone. You're the catalyst. We're going to make some magic here. I just know it."

I can't help myself. His enthusiasm is contagious. I find myself actually believing him.

# jackson

*"Who would I swipe right on? I just said I don't swipe. I guess the main thing is someone who is kind. Patient. Good natured. Humble. But honestly, guys, you know this is not about me. I'm here to help other people meet their soulmates!"*

*~Isla Fairfax, Playing With Matches Confessionals*

"LADIES AND GENTLEMEN, this is your captain speaking." The message coming through the loudspeaker is so garbled that at least three people look around anxiously and ask their neighbors, *"What did he say? Is the plane okay?"*

I am crammed into a middle seat in the back of the plane. There's a white-knuckler to the left of me chanting Hail Marys and a puker on the right.

The plane lurches and plummets, slipping sideways like a hockey puck that's been dropped on the ice.

"I have good news and bad news," the captain continues with his garbled announcement. "Looks like we are not going to be rerouted today. But it's going to be a bumpy ride, and I need you all buckled in nice and tight for the remainder of the flight. Flight crew, please take your seats."

Three more drops and a shudder. Outside the windows, it's disturbingly dark, with the occasional lightning flash. When we finally break through the clouds and I see the shock of blue water, it seems much closer than it should. We're almost about to touch down. The wings wobble from side to side like an unbalanced gymnast that might fall off the beam as the ground speeds towards us. Someone cries out. I close my eyes.

This is not how I die. I am not dying on a plane. *In coach.*

After the violent turbulence we've just experienced, we almost don't feel as the plane touches down gently. When the wheels finally kiss the runway, everyone, myself included, bursts into applause. People who don't know each other start high-fiving, and at least a few couples who I don't think were coupled before this flight embrace.

"Sorry about that," the captain says, "And I'm sorry as well that you're all going to get a bit wet on your walk to the terminal. We don't control the weather. Hopefully, you packed an umbrella. On the plus side, you've all made it here today. You're a lucky bunch. The airport just closed for the remainder of the day. The forecast calls for clear skies later this evening. Have a great vacation!"

Naturally, since I'm one of the last ones to get out of the plane and stuck behind slow walkers on the single file staircase, I'm completely soaked by the time I get inside the terminal.

*Who packs an umbrella for a tropical resort?*

Dripping and disgruntled, I pass through passport control, then join the crowd gathered around the single luggage carousel inside the tiny terminal. My plan is to change in the airport bathroom as soon as I get my stuff. I hadn't wanted to check a bag, but the gate agent in Miami had forced me to due to the overhead compartments already being full by the time they loaded the back of the plane. She hadn't even given me time to transfer anything to my backpack.

*Coach problems.*

One by one, the bags tumble onto the carousel. Everyone seems in a hurry to grab their bag and get out of there before the storm gets even worse. Pretty soon the rate of new bags dropping down the chute starts to slow down. The luggage carousel grinds to a halt. The only item left on it is a plastic crate sealed with duct tape.

It appears that my bag never made it onto the flight.

*Perfect.*

After I file all the necessary paperwork, the lost luggage lady advises me to keep my phone handy.

"They'll call to arrange delivery of your bag."

"Any idea when that will be?"

"This airport is about to shut down till further notice. Buy some new clothes at your resort," she looks at my wet khakis and polo with a complete lack of empathy or concern. "I don't know when you'll have your stuff."

"Fine," I grit my teeth. I'll just have to get my current clothes cleaned. The sooner the better. They must have laundry service at the resort, no? The show is supposed to start taping tomorrow.

I've been flying for almost sixteen hours now. They couldn't even get a direct flight from Seattle to Florida. I had a three-hour layover in Texas and another three hour hours in Florida in a terminal that was under construction and standing room only. All I want to do is take a nice hot shower. And a nap.

"We are closing the airport, Sir. Do you need to arrange for a ride?" The lost-luggage lady seems impatient to get rid of me now.

This is when I notice that I am one of only a handful of people left in the terminal and almost everyone else works here. All the tourists and hugging high-fivers have vanished into waiting vans or disappeared with their sign-holding chauffeurs.

There's apparently nobody here to meet me. No driver. No car from the resort. Nothing.

I check my phone. No signal.

"Hey, can I use your phone to call the resort?" I ask.

"I'm sorry, Sir, I can't let you use the phone."

"Can you call the Peaches resort for me then? Someone was supposed to meet me here." I say, exasperated.

She eyes me dispassionately, and considers my request, tapping one long, cheetah-painted talon on her ancient, corded phone. Then she finally relents and picks up the receiver. She consults a printed directory on a sticker in her drawer and dials a number slowly, holding the receiver aloft between us like a speaker. The line rings and rings, and finally after ten rings the call is automatically answered and funneled directly into muzak. She hangs up.

"Nobody there," she says.

"It's a five-star resort," I argue. "*Somebody* has got to be there."

"Big storm," she shrugs. "They must be busy."

This is getting ridiculous.

"Could you at least call me a cab?" I ask, slinging my tech backpack over one shoulder.

"No cabs. It's raining, so there might be flash floods," she says.

*Ok then.*

"Right, so apparently, I live here in the airport now? You want to show me to my room?" I snark. The overhead lights go off, and I hear the rattle of the steel grate as the one shop in the airport is being locked up. "Oh great, next you're going to tell me no electricity. What the hell do you expect me to do exactly? Where am I supposed to go?"

I look at my phone, and there is still no signal. The battery is getting low, too. Did the production team really forget to send someone to get me?

"I don't know what to tell you. You can't stay here." The luggage lady turns off her computer and reaches under her desk for an umbrella.

"This is flipping ridiculous!" I shout. "First you lose my luggage on your shitty flight, then you refuse to help me to get where I'm going? What is it you want me to do? Conjure up a magical boat to ferry me to my destination?"

I hate feeling so helpless. I'm remembering all the times I was stranded as a kid, due to my mom not showing up because she had to deal with my dad. He was a bit of a tropical storm himself.

"Sir, I am going to have to ask you to calm down or I'll have to call the authorities," the luggage lady threatens, and I have to wonder if that might not be a good thing. Maybe they could drive me to the resort. Then again, the idea of spending the night in a mosquito - or worse, *lizard* - infested cell on a cold, hard bench is not appealing.

"Fine," I say. I open my wallet and pull out a hundred-dollar bill waving it around at whoever's still here that wants to make some fast cash.

"All right, Folks. I'm looking for a ride," I say loudly. "It's only around five miles to the resort where I'm staying, and I have no suitcases. I'm ready to go right now. Surely someone wants to take me?"

"I'll take you," a voice booms out from the far corner of the airport near the bathrooms. A grizzled-looking old man is still zipping up his fly. He's wearing a sea captain's hat pulled down over his eyes, and he's sporting at least three months' worth of facial hair.

"Call me Cappy," the man says. "You want to give me a hand with this bin, Son?" He gestures towards the battered plastic crate that's still sitting on the motionless carousel.

I help him haul it onto a luggage cart. It weighs a ton.

*What the hell has he got in there?*

"Were you on the flight out of Miami?" I ask, thinking I don't recall seeing him on the plane.

"No, I just came down here to do a favor for a friend. Had to pick up his package." Cappy shoves the cart towards the exit. "I've got my boat moored not far from the resort. I'll be wanting to check in on her on the way there," he says.

"You can't drop me off first?" I ask.

"You want a ride, or would you prefer walking?" he asks.

"Fine," I shove the bill back in my wallet and follow Cappy out into the storm. The wind is blowing now, sending sheets of rain across the parking lot.

"You got any rain gear?" Cappy asks, pulling a rain poncho out from a compartment in the back of a Jeep. An open-air Jeep. He's got to be kidding me.

"I didn't pack for the monsoon season. I thought I was planning a trip to a five-star resort," I grouse.

"No need to be churlish, Son," he scolds, pulling out a plastic tarp from another compartment. "This'll have to do you, then."

"Thanks," I say, visions of complimentary cocktails and scented hand-towels popping and vanishing like soap bubbles. This is not the VIP arrival I was anticipating.

*And where exactly is Isla? I'd expected to see Isla Fairfax at the airport.*

"Shake a leg! I promised my buddy I'd get his jeep back before 4 pm." After we get the plastic tub loaded in the back, Cappy leaps nimbly into the driver's seat. It occurs to me that he probably isn't that old after all. I follow suit, buckling in and stashing my backpack underneath my seat, where I hope it will stay reasonably dry.

Lucky for me, Cappy seems to be a competent driver. We pull away from the airport and make decent progress down the empty, water-logged streets. I'm glad that I'm in a rugged four-wheel drive vehicle even if I'm wrapped in enough plastic to conceal a corpse.

"So what brings you to the island?" I make an attempt at small talk.

"This and that." Cappy cinches the cord on his hood. "I'm normally based in the Bahamas, but I came down here for a few weeks for a gig. Staying with an old buddy of mine. Lucky I got to the airport when I did. You seemed like you needed some rescuing." He glances sideways at me, squinting into the wind. His thick, gray brows are drawn together.

Suddenly, and without indicating, Cappy takes a sharp left turn onto a sandy, muddy road. I grab the roll bar to steady myself. Up ahead, I spot a small, weatherbeaten sign advertising a marina. The Jeep bounces over roots and ruts and jerks to a halt in a dirt lot on the hillside above the marina. Cappy parks under a scruffy tree that offers little shelter from the downpour.

"Wait here," he advises. "I'll be right back."

"Got it," I say. I check my phone again under the makeshift tent of my tarp. Barely two bars. Not even enough to gather email. I sigh, hunched over my phone, scrolling through and re-reading all the messages I cannot respond to.

"Well that's a relief," Cappy seems more relaxed, when he gets back. "My boat's just fine. I left her in the best berth, and she's all covered up, snug as a bug. I think I'll drop off the new parasail tomorrow when it's a bit drier." He gestures to the heavy crate we loaded in the back of the Jeep and sighs contentedly. Then he cracks his knuckles, not in any hurry to get going. It's almost like I'm not sitting here dripping wet, freezing and shivering my ass off.

"That's great, Cappy. Think we can get going then?" I ask.

"Course, course," Cappy mumbles agreeably, starting the engine. He throws the Jeep into reverse. The wheels spin. He throws it into forward. They spin in the other direction. He tries something else. Still spinning.

"Well crap," he says. "Looks like we're stuck. You're going to have to get out and give her a push."

"What?!" I ask, in disbelief. "Isn't this a Jeep? Do Jeeps get stuck?"

"Have you seen the ground out there? Just look at my Wellies!" Cappy gestures down at his muddy boots. "Those loafers of yours are gonna take a real beating in that muck," he laughs. "Sorry Son, nothing's to be done."

"You want me to push the Jeep?" I repeat. I'm pretty sure at this point that this is either a fever dream or I'm being punked. "Are you messing with me?"

"Well," Cappy says, "if you want to get out of here any time today, I'd sure appreciate a good shove."

"Fine," I bite back my irritation as I step down into the soupy muck that is the parking lot. My left shoe immediately gets stuck. I have to retrieve it with my hand and end up tossing it into the back of the Jeep. I sigh and toss my other one with it for good measure.

"Okay, I'm gonna gun it, just give 'er a good hard shove," Cappy says. "Ready, steady, go!"

I lean into the back of the Jeep, pushing as hard as I can, my bare feet slipping and sliding through the muck as I struggle to stay upright. Cappy guns the engine, and the Jeep lurches forward. I trip, almost falling, and in slow motion I see my phone fall from my pocket into the mud, just below the wheel of the Jeep as it rolls back towards me.

"Nooooooo!" I shout, shoving the car for all I'm worth, but I know it's too late. I hear the crunch.

"Atta boy!" yells Cappy, gunning the engine again. This time when the Jeep jerks forward and free, I do fall. Face down in the mud, right next to my completely smashed cell phone.

We drive the last mile in total silence.

"Sorry about the mud," Cappy says when he drops me off at the gate to the resort. The guard takes one look at the two of us in the Jeep and apologizes to Cappy that he can't let him drive onto the property without some kind of a pass.

"Well then, I guess this is far as I can take you," Cappy shrugs

"Here you go," I hand him the hundred-dollar bill.

"What, no tip?" he looks insulted.

"I had to push your Jeep!" I say.

"Yes, but I saved you from the storm," he tuts. He shoves the bill back at me. "I can't take your cash. It was the decent thing to do. Sorry about the phone. Good luck with your trip, Son. See you around."

IT'S SURPRISINGLY FAR from the gatehouse to the resort proper. The only nice part about the walk is that the rain has settled into less of a lashing gale and more of a gentle shower. It washes some of the mud off of me on the way. When I finally get to the Mediterranean Village and see the coffee station outside the ornate double doors to the concierge lounge, I could cry. *Civilization!* I use some of the napkins and hot water to clean off my hands, and face. I'm Jackson Porter, millionaire tech mogul, I remind myself, reaching into my pocket to get out my passport and pull up my reservation on the phone.

*Shake it off.*

A fresh wave of horror washes over me as I look down at the smashed screen. RIP phone.

At least I have my laptop in my backpack. I pat my shoulder where my bag should be slung. There is no bag.

*I left my backpack in Cappy's borrowed Jeep.* This is not my day. At least the laptop inside of the backpack is backed up and insured. I'm pretty sure I'll never see it again.

If I were in a movie, or even one of Isla's novels, this would be the meet-cute moment. Except it's usually the girl who gets pulled into a mud puddle by the adorable mutt she's volunteered to dog walk or some other dumb shenanigan. I glance around, half expecting to see Isla Fairfax in a fluorescent pink raincoat. If this were a movie, she'd be walking by and walk smack into me right about now. I know how this shit goes. I do the podcast.

"Can I help you, Sir?" an employee wearing a name tag that says Edwina peeks through the door of the lounge, looking concerned. "Are you a guest here? Have you been in an accident?"

"Something like that," I sigh, glancing down at my shoes. My pants are rolled up, and my legs look like they used to look when I was a kid and my friend Hudson and I would play in the adventure park, slinging mud patties at each other.

Edwina follows my gaze to my wrecked shoes and quickly looks back up to my face, wide-eyed. She's curious but too polite to come out and ask what happened.

"I'm checking in. Got caught in the storm. I probably should just wait outside here while you get my room keys. I don't want to mess up the lobby," I explain. "Jackson Porter, I'm with the *Playing with Matches* production."

"Oh!" her face lights up. "I checked in some of the other people from the show earlier. We are so excited to have Isla Fairfax here. Have you met her? I am such a fan!"

So Isla *is* here already. She managed to check in before the storm. Of course, she did. And she probably packed her dinglehoppers and an umbrella, too.

"I'll just be a minute," Edwina says. "Can I get you anything in the meantime? Unfortunately, we're out of our welcome bellinis. I'm so sorry. We weren't expecting any more guests to arrive today," she apologizes.

"I'm fine," I say. "I just need a shower."

"Right away, Sir," she says, turning to go back into the lobby and leaving me dripping next to a wooden bench. I sit down, leaving an embarrassing brown puddle. *Whatever.* They can hose it off later.

"Jackson! You made it! Thank goodness you're here. I have been calling all over the Island trying to locate you. We were so worried!" Rob rolls up on a golf cart, leaping out before it comes to a complete halt and rushing to my side. "What the heck happened to you?!"

*So they hadn't forgotten me entirely.*

"Long story," I grumble. No point in bitching about it now. "Nothing a hot shower and a quick shopping session can't fix. There's a store here, right?"

"Yes, but I think it's closed for the rest of today. Something to do with the storm," Rob looks almost apologetic. "But really, what happened–"

"I'm so sorry. Mr. Porter, was it?" Edwina pokes her head out the door again.

"Yes," I look up expectantly. I can almost feel the hot shower water cascading over my tired body.

"There seems to be a problem with your reservation."

"Oh no! What do you mean?" Rob looks surprised.

"I mean there's no record of his reservation, Sir," Edwina says apologetically.

"Surely you have a record of the reservation, no?" Rob says. "Can you pull it up on your phone, Jackson?"

"My phone is out of commission," I pull the smashed phone out of my pocket. "But whatever you've got, at this point I don't even care how much it costs," I extract my black card from my wallet and shove it at her.

"I'm so sorry, Mr. Porter," Edwina says, handing the card back. "I don't think you understand. The resort is *at* capacity."

"Oh come on, Edwina," Rob dials up the charm. "Do you know who this is? Jackson Porter is a very important member of our cast, quite possibly the MOST important member of our cast. Surely you have an empty room here somewhere?"

"Let me check again, Mr. Goodfellow," Edwina makes eye contact with Rob. "There was one garden view economy room that is being retiled."

"Thanks much, Edwina! You're a true peach!" Rob winks at her.

As soon as she goes back inside, Rob lets out a deep breath. "I think I know what happened."

"Dude," I say, "It's not that big of a deal. As long as there's a bed and a shower, I can stay in the economy room." I have reached the numb stage of weary.

"No," Rob says. "I feel like it's all my fault. I should have said something earlier when it happened."

"When what happened?" I ask.

"When they gave Isla Fairfax your room. I am mortified, Jackson. This is unacceptable."

Edwina comes out again, and I can tell immediately she doesn't have good news for me. "I am so sorry, Sir. Unfortunately there is no running water in the room that is being renovated, and I don't think there is any other availability in this resort. We are going to have to call another hotel."

"That won't work," Rob shakes his head. "I need my whole cast here on the Peaches property! If we wanted to film at the Four Seasons, we would have booked the Four Seasons."

"Actually, the Four Seasons is also sold out," Edwina shakes her head sadly. "I already checked. I've located one bed in a shared room at the hostel next to the airport."

"There's a hostel near the airport?" I ask, incredulous.

"Right across the street," Edwina agrees with a friendly smile.

*Might have been nice if the luggage lady had mentioned that.*

"No way. There is no way we are sending our MVP to a hostel," Rob protests. "I'd sooner stay there myself!"

"I don't know what else to say. Perhaps someone from your cast might be willing to share?" Edwina raises her eyebrows hopefully.

"Hmmmmm…. There's only one bed in my room. Sharing won't work. Unless–" Rob rubs his hands together as he thinks. Suddenly he claps and then shakes one finger victoriously. "That's it!"

"What's it?" Edwina and I both look at him.

"Well, you just gave me an excellent idea, Edwina. Isla Fairfax is in a two-bedroom deluxe suite, right?"

"She is," Edwina smiles and nods at Rob encouragingly.

"I know this is a huge ask, Jackson, but would you mind sharing with her?"

*And here we have it. The would-be rom-com moment. Forced proximity it is.*

But beggars can't afford to be choosers, and a multi-bedroom deluxe suite sounds a lot better than the hostel.

"Sure," I say. "At this point, all I care about is a hot shower and a bed." The mud is starting to drop off me in chunks as it dries. I'm leaving a trail.

"Great, let me just make a call to make sure it's okay with her. If she's cool with this, I'll let her know we're on our way," Rob says. He pulls out his phone and walks down the path. I can see him smiling and laughing as he chats with her. A moment later he returns, giving me two thumbs up.

"All's well, that ends well!" he says. "It'll probably make things simpler in the end anyways, since you two will pretty much have the same filming schedule. I know she seems a little kooky, but she's ok.

"Interesting," I murmur distractedly.

On the way to Isla's suite, I apologize profusely to the golf cart driver for the mess I'm making. Rob reaches into his bag and hands me a cell phone. "Here you go. I assume you saw the clause in the NDA about cell phone use?"

"I know you don't want us posting spoilers - we have to stay off social while filming and till the show airs," I say with no hesitation, acknowledging the clause.

"Right, but it's more than that. We don't want any of the cast members posting anything on social or viewing any social media during the taping of the show. Just to be safe, we've got everyone a phone without a data plan. We'll keep your phone and your laptop in a lockbox for the duration."

"Are you kidding me?" I ask. There's no way. No can do. "But I'll need access to my database and my server. And to communicate with my team."

"We cleared it with your team already, actually. They've already run the data on all the participants prior, but they've agreed to work directly with me, get us whatever additional data we need," Rob pauses. "And of course you can still call or text with them."

"You're telling me that everyone here is unplugging?" I ask, looking dubiously at the proffered phone. "What about you and Rory?"

"We're the exception. We need to stay in touch with the team here and back home, monitor social for sentiment, and turn the episodes rapidly. We are only two weeks ahead of the schedule to air this show. So exciting. I've never worked on a show with such a truncated production schedule!"

"Sounds stressful," I say.

"Not with you here," Rob grins. "You are our ace in the hole, Jackson. Secret weapon. You and your incredible app are what I'm banking on to make magic happen." He slaps me on my shoulder for emphasis.

"I think you mean logic," I say.

"Right, LOGIC," Rob taps his head.

"Isla Fairfax is okay with this?" I ask. She has a pretty robust presence on her author social accounts. Not that I stalk her. But she'd posted about heading to the tropics last night and hadn't said anything about going dark for the week.

"Oh yeah," Rob nods. "She was saying how thrilled she was to be off the grid and do a tech detox. Crazy, but hopefully she'll help convince the others."

We reach the oceanfront block of rooms where Isla is staying. The sun is peeking out from between the clouds, and the rain has finally stopped.

"Here we are," Rob says. "Room 777. Isla is expecting you. Sorry to drop you and dash, but I'll see you both in about half an hour. We've got a big BBQ for the cast and crew on the beach by the Jerk Hut."

"Dude. Sorry. I can't go to dinner like this." I kick off one of my destroyed loafers. The sole is detached, flapping like a loose jaw. "I'd change but my luggage was lost. And I don't think I'll be getting the call when they find it." I wave my smashed phone.

"Shit!" Rob smacks his forehead. "That's a bummer about the luggage. Here's what I can do. I will let my PA know to contact the airlines and look into getting you some new clothes when the resort shops open again. Just make a list. You can take my shoes," Rob shoves his flip flops at me. "But in the meantime just rinse off. Stuff dries fast here, and anyways it's casual. Most of the cast will probably be in their swimsuits."

"Okay…" I take the flip flops. A little small but better than my decimated loafers. Hesitantly, I step out of the golf cart.

"Room 777. I gotta run, Jackson! Can't wait to introduce you to the rest of the cast and team. You're our biggest rockstar!" he taps the driver on the shoulder to go. "Thank you for being here! Say hi to Isla!"

**"OH MY GOODNESS!"** Isla exclaims when she sees me. Her blue eyes are wide with surprise and amusement as she takes me in, standing outside her room, clutching a borrowed pair of flip-flops. "Look what the tide washed in."

Her hair is damp and she appears to be freshly showered. She smells like lily of the valley. Clean. So achingly clean. She's wearing a simple chic caftan with a graphic blue and white geometric print, and she's barefoot. Her toes are painted seashell pink.

"Very funny," I quip. "Next you're gonna tell me that you knew this was going to happen, right?"

"Not at all," she shakes her head. "Like I told you, my intuition doesn't work that way. I get random snippets. Little bits and puzzle pieces." She studies the wall behind me and breaks out in a grin. "Aw! look at that little guy! Isn't he cute?"

Slowly I turn around to see who, or rather what, the "little guy" is.

*Please let it have fur. Or even feathers.*

It's worse than I feared. He's clinging to the wall and doing push-ups like he's showing off. How long has it been there? I must have missed it when I walked up because it's blending into the background. I freeze and crouch, assuming an action stance.

"Back away slowly," I whisper. "It'll be okay. They're not dangerous."

I feel the feverish sweat gathering on my neck.

"Of course they're not!" Isla laughs and claps her hands loudly. The lizard scurries down the wall and onto the floor. Why did she have to do that?

*It's coming right at me.*

I yelp and leap straight up in the air as if I can fly away from this monstrosity.

At the last minute, the lizard veers left and over the railing. It leaps onto a plant and disappears into the foliage. I shudder.

*That was a close call.*

"Jackson?" I only recall I am not alone when Isla cautiously says my name.

"Yeeeeeeees?" I slowly look back up at her.

"Do you want to maybe come inside the room?" Isla asks. She is biting her lip.

"It's not funny," I say. "There are a lot of toxic species of reptiles."

"But none of them live on this island," she says, calmly waving me inside.

"Good to know," I say, trailing behind her into the massive, immaculate suite.

"I would shake your hand but, I'm a bit dirty," I prattle on, trying not to think about the lizard. Reptiles are my kryptonite. I've had herpetophobia since I was a child. It's not debilitating. I'm able to cope with breathing exercises and simple coping strategies. But that one caught me off guard. "Thanks for taking me in on such short notice. I'm so sorry to impose like this. If you could direct me to the shower, I'll head straight there."

Isla stops suddenly in front of me and we nearly collide.

She turns and blinks slowly at me. "Wait. Did you want to use my shower? Rob didn't mention anything about that."

I stand stock still, staring back at her. "What?"

And then I see her mouth tick up at the corners.

"My goodness, your face, Jackson! I'm kidding! I don't mind at all. I love to rescue strays. And besides, this place is huge. Ridiculous that they gave it to me. It sleeps seven people. I feel like I'm putting some poor family out. You can just leave your things in here," she says, taking my filthy hand and pulling me into the second bedroom. It's a children's room with a bunk bed and a trundle. There's a pile of stuffed animals, including one of a gecko, that Isla quickly tucks under her arm.

"You don't have to hide the stuffie," I say. "It's only the real thing that gives me the heebie-jeebies."

"Okay," she says solemnly. "I will chase away the lizards if you promise to take care of the spiders. They are *my* kryptonite."

"That's a solid deal," I agree thankfully. "Arachnids are not an issue for me. I got you."

"Hey, where's your stuff?" Isla glances around behind me, as if my bags might be trailing me like puppies.

"My luggage was lost, and I misplaced my backpack on the way from the airport to the resort," I explain. "Some guy named Cappy just scored himself a brand new MacBook."

"Oh, I'm sure he'll return it when he realizes," Isla says cheerily. So hopeful. So naive. It's cute.

"Right," I laugh a little bitterly. "That's not happening. Good thing I have everything backed up in the cloud."

"So not to rush you or anything," Isla says, leaning against the wooden bunk beds. "But we have to be out of here in fifteen minutes to make it to the BBQ on time. You might want to change."

"I'll have to rinse my shirt before I put it back on. Got any laundry detergent?" I toss the flip flops on the floor and peel off my filthy shirt. Mud is caked on my chest. It's even in my belly button.

"Oh come on. You can't wear that shirt again. Possibly ever." Isla looks horrified at the prospect of my rinsing and re-wearing the shirt. She holds out a hand. "Give it here. I'll set it to soak, but we'll have to find you something else to wear tonight. Jump in the shower real quick, and I'll see what I can pull together for you."

"Really? Do you have another cool dress like that one that I can borrow?" I lean against the bathroom door frame, admiring her.

Maybe it's the adrenaline from my close encounter with the cold-blooded monster. But I don't think so. I think the electric buzz that has me suddenly feeling so reanimated is one hundred percent Isla.

"Sadly, I don't think my dresses would fit you, but I did bring a few oversized tees to sleep in. And there were some sweat pants in the swag bags," she says.

"You got gift bags?" My jaw drops. I feel a rogue pang of jeal-ousy. I bet a driver met her at the airport, too.

"I'm sure you will get some goodies, too," Isla says. "And if not, I'm happy to share mine. There's plenty to go around. Just please get in the shower quickly? I hate being late!" Her vaguely schoolmarmy voice makes me smile. I'm surprised that punctuality is one of her quirks. I never would have guessed that. If anything, I would have expected her to be the type that's chronically late. Too dreamy to stick to a grown-up schedule.

"Okay, okay." I kick off my muddy pants and throw them directly in the trash can. I can feel her eyes sweeping unapologetically over my abs, pecs, and other places. "You don't have to ask me twice to get out of these clothes." I hook my thumbs in my boxers watching her face for a reaction. Of course, I have no intention of actually getting naked in front of her. But I like the way her eyes feel on me. It's an almost physical sensation. Warm and cool at once. I can't resist meeting her gaze.

Much to my delight, Isla doesn't look away. She meets my eyes, challenging me. Calling my bluff.

"Oh, you can keep going," she says. "Take it all off. I'm not easily shocked. My parents are nudists."

Now it's my turn to blush.

Isla smiles triumphantly and spins on her heel. "There's soap and shampoo and stuff in the bathroom," she calls over her shoulder. "Just shout if you need anything."

Although lightning fast, the shower is the best thing that's happened to me in over twenty-four hours. Hot, with great pressure. I lather my hair twice with the coconut-scented shampoo and use a washcloth to scrub off all of the mud. No time to shave, and no razor to do it with, but afterwards I am a new man.

Isla is sitting cross-legged on the bottom bunk waiting for me when I emerge in a towel.

"I have this shirt," she says, holding out a brilliantly tie-dyed tee, "and I made you these shorts." She holds up a pair of light pink sweatpants that have been cut off mid-thigh.

"You didn't have to destroy your clothes for me," I object.

"I didn't. They were in the gift bag and they were a size xl and bedazzled. She holds up the rhinestone-studded cuffs that she's cut off. "Not my size or my style. I'm sorry I don't have any underwear for you. You'll have to go commando." She tosses the shorts at me.

"This is the outfit you want me to wear to meet the cast?" I raise an eyebrow.

"I don't see what other options you have right now," she says. "Unless you want to go in that towel."

"Rob did say it was casual," I smile.

"I'm sure everyone will understand that your luggage was lost. Anyways, I thought tech guys weren't supposed to be so particular about their clothing," Isla teases. She checks the time on her phone.

"And I thought artsy, magical types weren't concerned about getting to company picnics on time," I say, holding out a hand for the clothes.

She's annoyingly spot on about me. I am not actually that fussed about the clothes. It's not what I'd normally choose to wear, but it's better than the stuff I just threw in the trash.

"Give me two minutes," I say, "and I'll be good to go."

"Great," she bounces out of the room. I can still smell her though. She's all over the clothes I'm pulling onto my body. The colorful tee is steeped in her floral scent.

"Hey, Jackson, come out here quick! You gotta see this," Isla calls me out onto the balcony before we leave. There's a brilliant double rainbow spanning the horizon over the water. The colors are practically vibrating against the sky; they are so obnoxiously bright. Kind of like my borrowed shirt.

"Let's take a quick selfie? It's a wonderful omen," she says. "Don't you think?"

"If you say so," I allow myself to get pulled into her orbit and appreciate how well we fit together. She passes the phone to me to do the honors because my arm is longer.

I take my time, and not just because I want to get the shot right.

# isla

. . .

*"Chemistry is overrated. Think about what ends up getting released in a toxic dumpster fire. Chemicals."*

*~Jackson Porter, Playing With Matches Confessionals.*

JACKSON PORTER IS such a study in contrasts. A hipster and a nerd. Grumpy and silly. Overconfident and scared of tiny lizards. What else? Every time I'm with him, I feel like I'm doing one of those seek and find puzzles where you have to find all the pictures hidden in plain sight.

Also, somehow this incongruous and infuriating man has managed to pull off my oversized sleep tee and an improvised pair of sweat shorts like they're haute couture.

On him, my tee is on the small side, and the shorts are a little tight, but he's got one of those lean yet sculpted surfer bodies, where there's nothing that you need to hide. The close fit seems intentional. Every time he gets ahead of me on the path

- which is often due to his ridiculously long legs and brisk stride - I can't help but admire his bum. So round. Looks firm. It's surprising given the fact that most tech dudes spend so much time sitting.

What on earth is the matter with me? Are they putting something in the water here? It's not like me to ogle. And yet I cannot seem to stop looking. Is it because he practically dared me to?

*He wants me to look at him.*

Knowing this makes it harder to stop.

I've never seen anyone look quite as bedraggled as Jackson when he showed up on my doorstep. There was mud in his light brown hair and in his ear. His shirt was torn and his knuckles scraped. His shoes were entirely done for. And he had no bags. Nothing. Just a pair of borrowed flip flops. He'd looked so vulnerable. And when he saw that lizard? Oh my.

He hadn't been humbled for long though. Five minutes later the swagger was back, volume up.

"So when did you get in?" Jackson asks, slowing his stride to match mine.

"Around noon."

"So you missed the storm."

"I did. I actually slept through most of it. I had such a lovely nap," I admit.

Jackson rolls his eyes. "I am going to sleep like a log tonight. I've been up for forty-eight hours. I call top bunk."

"Very funny," I shake my head at him.

"Have you turned in your phone yet?" He asks.

"No," I open my purse to show my phone to him.

"Good," he says. "Let me see it a second."

I raise my eyebrows.

"I'm not going to read your messages, I promise," he says. "Just give it here."

I hand him my phone and he turns it over in his hands. "Can I borrow one of your earrings?"

"Seriously?" I ask, but I still remove one.

Jackson looks around and then pulls me close, holding the phone between us. He smells like coconut shampoo and sandalwood soap. It's even better than whatever scent he was wearing last week at the production company. He smells like himself.

Quickly he pops my earring wire into the hole to eject my sim card and removes it. He hands me the phone back. Then he reaches into his pocket, pulls out a smashed phone, and ejects the card on that one, too. He hands both sim cards to me.

"Just in case. Can you hold onto mine for me too? I get why they want to hold onto our phones, but I still feel a lot better keeping my own SIM card on me."

"Would it even work with the phones they're giving us?" I ask.

"There are ways," Jackson nods solemnly and slips his phone back into his pocket. He hands me back my earring and waits while I put it back on. We walk along the boardwalk beside the white sandy beach towards the area at the far end of the resort where the reception is being held.

"My mom would love it here," he muses, looking out at the water as it changes colors along with the sky.

"What's your mom like?" I ask.

"Actually?" Jackson laughs wryly. "She's a little like you. Into crystals and chakras and all that crazy woo shit," he says. "She would love you."

"Crazy woo shit?" I ask, raising an eyebrow. That's awfully cocky of him. "Why are you even doing this show with me if that's the way you feel about my matchmaking methods?"

"Someone's gotta keep things from going off the rails. I mean, with all due respect, Isla, your romantic notions are fine for novels, but this is real life. There can be serious consequences," Jackson frowns.

"You think I don't know that?" I ask, thinking of my parents' loveless match. A match made with the same sort of methodology Jackson uses. My parents look great on paper. Same background. Same taste. I don't think I've ever heard them argue about toilet rolls. I don't think I've ever even heard them argue. Not even when confronted with each other's affairs.

"Chasing rainbows is too risky," Jackson presses his lips together and shrugs in a #sorrynotsorry fashion.

I get that Jackson's got some kind of a chip on his shoulder, but why should that entitle him to be so rude?

"Do you think you're the only person on the planet with a backstory?" I ask. I think coming from a broken home is the norm these days. "You're not the only one who's ever had to deal with the fallout from a less than ideal match. Don't you see that?"

"Here's what I see, Isla," Jackson pauses by a copse of spiky beach grass. "I see that *you* clearly come from a wealthy, privileged family, but you like to wear thrifted clothes and live in tiny little garrets and write your fantastical fiction and pretend like you're not part of the one percent. People like you don't get really screwed when relationships go wrong. They get a first-class ticket to somewhere else and a free pass to try again."

*The nerve of him!*

"So only poor people are entitled to have feelings?" I ask.

Jackson shrugs.

"You do know my parents separated for a while when I was quite young," I say. "They were very unhappily married. Still are, in fact. But they soldier on."

"Let me guess," Jackson smirks. "They sent you to a posh private boarding school which is where you developed a penchant for Ouija boards and regency romance novels?"

He really can be such an ass. What happened to the vulnerable guy who appeared on my doorstep with mud in his ear?

"Let *me* guess," I fire back at him. "You made your first million just to prove your bitchy second-grade teacher wrong about your ADHD quirks. Then once you got rich, you used your success to try and convince yourself you were smarter and better than everyone else, but you were still miserable, so you decided to take it one step further and build a ridiculous app that would ensure that everyone else would have to remain as miserable as you for the rest of time!"

One of the curly tailed lizards suddenly dashes across our path, and I reflexively throw out a protective arm like my mum used to do to try to "save" me when she'd had to slam on the brakes with me in the passenger seat.

"Look out! There's a lizard!" I say. Jackson stops in his tracks.

"Thanks," he says, eying me suspiciously. "How did you know about my second-grade teacher? Did my sister say something?"

I pick up the pace again. I can smell the food, I'm getting hungry, and I really don't want to be late. "No," I smile sweetly. "I asked my Ouija board about you."

"WELCOME!" Rob says. He's standing on a makeshift stage, holding a mic. "I am so excited to have you all assembled here at last! So much energy! Can you feel the energy on this beach?"

The six contestants, along with the various cast and crew members who have assembled, clap and cheer.

Across the table from me, Jackson swats at a bug and curses.

"I wanted to introduce everyone to each other tonight, but I know everyone is probably starved and some of you are still jet-lagged. So I had the team put together this montage of your confessional videos while you were arriving and since you've been here. Some of you got here more conventionally than others. He looks our way and waves at Jackson.

"Why is he waving at you?" I ask

"I have a bad feeling about this," Jackson says.

"I thought you didn't believe in premonitions," I tease. A server sets a platter of crabs on the table. "Oh look, your friends are here."

Rob steps off the stage, and the video begins with security footage from the gate house. There's a jeep parked at the gate-house, and a security guard with an umbrella is speaking to a grizzled old man in the driver's seat. Sitting next to him is Jackson, wrapped in a blue tarp and covered with mud.

"Not the most auspicious arrival for tech guru Jackson Porter, but things can only go uphill from here, right?" Rob narrates the film montage, which suddenly cuts to me in the back of the car.

"I guess you could say I'm like an emotional hot waxer."

*I knew I'd regret that.*

"Ouch!" Rob says.

Cut to a sexy-looking blonde in a low-cut tank. Chloe. "I've tried every app, but all the guys just want one thing from me. And it doesn't involve putting a ring on it."

Ryker, the "digital nomad" contestant from Australia, wolf whistles in his seat. Most of the singles from the show are sitting together at a long, banquet-style picnic table. Chloe is surrounded by all three of the men, laughing and joking as if they've all known each other for ages. Lacey and Paula are sitting together a few feet away. Lacey is distracted. She keeps stealing jealous glances at the cluster. If looks could kill, Chloe would be in serious trouble.

"Do you have a pen on you?" Jackson nudges me. "I need a pen. Cappy's friend's license plate was in that video. I want to write it down. Maybe I can find a way to contact him."

"Oh right! That's the guy that has your laptop?" I hand him the pen and he jots something on a napkin while I go back to watching the video.

"I'm looking for *the one*," a tall, dark, burly man is speaking into the camera. "As a former firefighter, I've come face to face with the consequences of dangerous combinations. This show is called *Playing with Matches,* but I'm not playing here. I'm ready to embrace the next chapter of my life, and I'm ready to embrace the woman I plan to spend the rest of my days with." A buzz of appreciative cheers and clapping follows.

"That's kind of morbid, don't you think?" Jackson asks.

"I think it's kind of sweet," I say, closing my eyes, trying to shut out the noise so I can picture Owen and Paula together with their grandkids.

I get nothing. But I try not to let it worry me. They seemed like they'd be so great together when I looked at their files. I glance at Paula again. She's crocheting something, without looking at it, which makes sense, given that she is almost completely blind.

Lacey's up next. "I'm still learning about who I am, but this is definitely the year of ME! I know I'm a lot, but I'm not willing to settle. Come and get me if you think you can handle me. I'm Lacey, and you'd better be ready to treat me like your queen," Lacey pouts, flutters her furry lashes, and blows a kiss.

"I'm Ryker, and I'm a full time nomad. I'm looking for the right woman who shares my sense of adventure. If it works out, we can talk about going the distance." Ryker slings his backpack over his shoulder and winks at the camera.

"Duuude! This place is the bomb!" a brawny man does a cannonball into the pool. I recognize Darwin.

"There's more to me than meets the eye." Paula is walking towards a lounge chair at the pool. The tiny woman is wearing dark sunglasses and a pale pink bikini that shows off her natural curves. At the last moment, the camera pans around to show her sparkly cane, and it becomes clear she is blind. "I guess you could say I'm 'looking' for the perfect match, but it might not be love at first sight for me."

The power cuts out, and the screen suddenly goes black.

"Sorry! Sorry!" Rob jumps back up on the stage and speaks loudly, so everyone can hear. "There's still some power issues from the storm earlier. Take some time to introduce yourselves to each other. Don't stay up too late. We'll be starting filming tomorrow afternoon, and you'll want to be at your best for our first matchmaking ceremony. We have loads of fun planned. In case you haven't noticed, this place is amazing. Take advantage of all the amenities and activities as you mix, mingle, and get to know each other. That's what we're here for!"

"I feel like I'm on a singles cruise," Jackson mutters in my ear. "Does this feel like a singles cruise to you?"

"It reminds me more of a summer camp," I whisper back. "Have you ever been on a singles cruise?"

"No. Have you ever been to camp?" He slaps his arm. "A cruise might be preferable. Fewer bugs."

"Try and keep an open mind," I say. "Great things could be happening here. You saw that rainbow earlier; why not wait and see?"

"Because I'm seeing the people that they gave us to cast. They're not looking for love, Isla. They're looking for a SAG card." Jackson shakes his head.

"Can't they want both?" I ask.

Rob whistles loudly to get our attention.

"A couple of housekeeping items," Rob says. "I was hoping to introduce you all to our host Marco tonight, but he and a few other last minute additions to the team got caught in the storm and won't be arriving till early tomorrow morning.

"Please be sure to check in your phones and any other wifi-enabled devices before you head back to your rooms. And hey, no hooking up yet!" Rob points at Ryker, who has an arm draped around Chloe. "Save it for the show! Otherwise, get a good night's sleep. And cast members - don't forget to stop by the production tents before bed to do your first impression confessionals."

"WHAT DO YOU KNOW ABOUT MARCO?" Jackson asks on the way back to the room.

"Well... He's a lot." I can't help but let out a little laugh recalling him stripping off his shirt and leaping on the table at my Rome book signing. Jackson doesn't miss it.

"Uh oh. You gonna share the joke?"

"I don't actually know him very well," I admit. "But he's a type. Very handsome and hunky. Charismatic in a goofy way. Huge social following, and he's a bonafide celeb in Italy. Anyone who reads romance novels will recognize him immediately. I'm sure he appeals to the show's demographic or they wouldn't have chosen him," I say.

"Isn't his demographic the same as yours?" Jackson asks pointedly. "You're a romance novelist, no?" The sky overhead is clear now, and the moon is shining bright.

"He's a 'chest cover' model," I explain. "He's mostly popular with the smutty billionaire romance readers. Actually, *you're* more their demographic, aren't you?"

Jackson smirks, "Right. I'm familiar with the trope stereotype."

"Rich? Check! Nerdy? Check! Grumpy? Double check!" I can't help ribbing him. He's the real-life version of the nerdy tech billionaire types that show up so often in the trades.

"Very funny," Jackson rolls his eyes.

"I mean, if the shoe fits?" I bite my cheeks and look down at the ground, trying not to smile and failing miserably.

"I'm not really that grumpy. And these shoes definitely don't fit." Jackson kicks off the flip-flops and sticks them in his pocket. The path is sandy, and he doesn't really need them anyways.

We are passing an outdoor bar kiosk and he stops. "Drink?"

"I'll take a gin and tonic," I agree gratefully.

"So British," Jackson observes. "Plain soda water for me." He waves a hand in front of his face and then smacks it against his own chin. "Shit. I'm getting eaten alive."

"Must be because you're so sweet," I say, taking my drink from the bartender.

"Yeah, sure," Jackson shakes his head. "Or my blood type or something. This always happens. I packed extra bug repellant, but of course it was in my bag. I think I gotta take cover. Mind if we take these back to the room?" He holds up his drink.

"No problem," I say.

BY THE TIME we get back to the room, Jackson's lower lip has started to significantly swell. He's holding his drink against it, but it's not doing much.

"Has this happened to you before?" I ask, rifling through my medication bag for allergy meds. I hand him an antihistamine, and he finishes the rest of his drink as he takes it.

"It's not a big deal. I usually pop a Benadryl, take a nice nap, and I'm good to go." He sets the glass down and leans to look at himself in the mirror.

"Let me see it?" I step closer to check. He still smells great. Even with a little sweat in the mix. Especially with the sweat.

"Are you a medicine woman now, too?" Jackson's eyebrow shoots up, but he doesn't step away.

"I have some training," I say.

"Are you going to make me a poultice or give me an amulet to ward off the bloodsuckers?"

"Actually, I've got some extra garlic and oregano tabs if you want to try them. They repel the little guys pretty effectively. That and some lemon eucalyptus." I stand on my tiptoes trying to get a better look. "Come on, I'm properly trained. I did a first aid course in London as research for one of my books."

"Fine," he sighs and leans back against the desk, lowering himself and resting his bum on the surface. "It's just a mosquito bite though. No big deal. I just need to sleep it off."

"Open your mouth?" Stepping between his legs, I take his chin in my hands to see it more clearly. His eyes are closed. I run my thumb over his lip, checking for the boundaries of the swelling. I was right about his jawline. There's nothing to hide. I like him better clean-shaven.

"You're sure it was a mosquito?" I ask. "You're not having any trouble breathing?" The swelling seems to be purely superficial, but I'm still a bit concerned by how quickly it flared.

He swallows.

"The *mosquito bite* is not affecting my breathing," Jackson's eyes flutter open, and he takes a long deep breath. There are circles under his eyes, and his pupils are wide in the dim room. He seems to be considering saying something, but he changes his mind. He gently pushes me away, then stands and glances at himself in the mirror again.

"I just need to sleep it off. I think the meds are already starting to work," he says. "I'm super tired."

"Okay," I say, "But do me a favor. Lie down in my bed for a bit? I'm going to go and get some ice."

"You want me in your bed?" He smirks. "That didn't take long."

"I want to make sure the swelling is going down, or I'm not going to be able to sleep," I say.

*And if my sheet ends up smelling like him? It won't be the worst thing in the world...*

Jackson raises an eyebrow at me. "You're really setting me up so well here, Isla. It's taking *all* my self restraint not to run with the obvious jokes."

"Good," I say. "You could do with a bit of practice on the self-restraint front, I've heard the way you tease your co-hosts on that podcast of yours." I shove the swag bags aside to clear off a spot on the bed and fluff a pillow. "Now be a good patient, and lie down here. I'll be right back with the ice."

Jackson eyes the bed with the weary desperation of someone who's crossed too many time zones without a proper place to lay their head. Two long strides and he's down.

"Wake me up and send me back to my room if I fall asleep," he says."You got it," I say. "Just a minute." I duck into the hall with the ice bucket.

Even though I'm back in under sixty seconds, Jackson appears to be fading fast. He has pulled off his shirt and rolled onto his side.

"Got the ice," I say.

"Mmmmm, just wanna sleep," he protests.

I pull an ice cube from the bucket. "Let's just ice it for a couple of minutes? Humor me?" I hold the cube to his lip, sliding it over the affected area. He's right; his lip seems to have stopped swelling. It's enlarged but not grotesque. Come to think of it, his lower lip was already pretty plump to begin with. He has extremely sensual lips. My fingers are tingling and damp with the ice that is quickly melting against the heat of his mouth.

Jackson's hand closes around my wrist and he opens his mouth to bite the half-melted ice cube.

"This is one way to keep me up," he says quietly. "But I assure you, it isn't cooling me off. Why are you doing this, Isla?"

"I'm just trying to help, Jackson," I answer, barely above a whisper.

He turns my hand over, kissing my palm and spitting the ice cube back out into it.

"Thank you for trying to make it better. But I think you skipped the important part."

"Which is?" I say stupidly, feigning confusion.

*Kiss it and make it better.*

The ice cube is almost fully dissolved. There's a tiny pool left, cupped in my palm. I can still feel his hot breath, and I realize I am panting. Jackson releases my wrist, and I pull my hand away, careful not to drip on the duvet. He sits up.

"Just go to sleep, Isla. I'll be fine. Take your bed back." Jackson pulls back the covers and stands up. He doesn't even bother to make any attempt to hide his arousal as he heads back towards the other bedroom.

# jackson

. . .



*"I'm so excited for all the couples! This show is such a special opportunity, and I'm truly honored to be a part of it. I can't wait to reveal the matches. I have the feeling that this is going to be magical!"*

*~Isla Fairfax, Playing With Matches Confessionals*

BETWEEN THE BENADRYL, my less than ideal arrival, and the blackout shades in my bedroom, I sleep until 11 am the following morning. I wasn't in a rush to wake. My normally black-and-white dreams were coming at me in vivid colors. I can't remember much. Only that Isla was in them, and I wasn't in any rush to wake. I could have binged a whole season. I haven't slept in this late since I was in college.

I peek out my door to see if she's around. There's a bag of clothes from the gift shop sitting on the floor in the hall outside my door. I peel off the sticky note on the bag.

*Good morning, Jackson! Rob had these clothes sent over for you, and I've tossed in some bug repellant wipes, too. Didn't want to wake you. I'm headed down to breakfast and to check out the pool. - Isla*

The suite is silent. I step out into the hallway. That's when I see the typed letter that's been slid under the front door of the suite. The envelope has my name on it.

*Greetings Mr. Porter,*

*I checked with the airport, and your luggage was located in Miami. It was put on a flight this morning and should be here by later this afternoon. We are also tracking down your laptop bag, and should have news shortly.*

*Edwina*

Things are finally looking up.

The Mediterranean Village is a chaotic flurry of activity when I head down. The cast and crew have taken over this entire section of the resort. Cameras are set up all around the iconic swimming pool at the center of the village. The pool occupies most of the courtyard with the far end of the courtyard open to the beach.

It's a clear day with no sign of yesterday's storm. Parasailers are riding high in the sky beneath rainbow-colored parachutes. There's a pink and aqua one out there that's emblazoned with the *Playing with Matches* logo.

As I walk the perimeter of the pool, I smell suntan oil and hear reggae music pouring from the speakers. Lacey, Ryker, and Darwin are sprawled out on the lounge chairs, lazily sipping fruity cocktails.

I glance around, trying to locate Isla, which shouldn't be difficult, given the color of her hair and her penchant for bright colors.

"Oh good, you got the clothes," Rory pauses as she dashes by, taking in my new Peaches-branded tee and peach print board shorts. Given that the resort's emblem is the peach emoji, I kind of feel like a giant walking ass. But I'm trying to convince myself that it's cool, in an ironic way.

"Only you could pull this off," Rory waves a hand at me.

"It doesn't make me look like I'm a creeper with a bum fetish?" I ask.

"No, dude, you look awesome. It's so 'I don't give a fuck what anyone thinks' that it's cool," Rory insists.

She's swapped her business suit for some cutoff overalls with a million pockets, all of which seem to be full of random items. "Have you seen the robot yet?"

"Robot?" I ask.

"OMG, just wait," she looks over my shoulder, smiling and waving flirtatiously at one of the camera men before dashing off. He looks to be around her age. Good. Now that I see her again, I realize she's definitely not my type and definitely too young for me. Even for a fling.

I feel like I dodged a bullet.

I continue my search for Isla. There are multiple hair and make-up stations set up under two pop-up tents off to one side of the lawn. In one of the tents, having his make-up done and chatting animatedly with Rob, is a shirtless, tanned, oiled, and ridiculously buff-looking man with long, dark hair that can only be Marco. Whatever Rob's saying to him, it's making him smile. He's nodding enthusiastically, and he and Rob share a fist bump and shoot a selfie together. Something tells me Marco's one true love is definitely here on the island. And it's himself.

*I've gotta hand it to Rob. He's really good at handling the annoying personality types.*

Two jacuzzis flank the swim up bar at the oceanfront end of the pool, and I spy a couple more contestants there. Owen the firefighter is in the hot tub with Chloe the blonde nurse, and they seem to be getting along great. Maybe they're getting along too well?

We haven't even kicked off the show officially. We have yet to reveal the contestants' match-mates, and I'm already second guessing our choices. Were we too hasty? I'm tempted to run back to my room to review their compatibility with the partners we picked for them versus this new pairing. Could I have missed the best possible match?

If I can't get at least one solid match out of this show, I think my app will actually be done.

I just don't get it. I don't get why the app is still having issues getting people to use it. We've redesigned the user interface several times and even tried to gamify the process. But people are addicted to swiping. It's a dopamine thing.

The latest iteration of my app gives users the ability to sort their matches by swiping. It's doing much better than the previous version. Swipers gotta swipe.

Still scanning for Isla, I see a flash of someone's red hair on the beach-facing side of the swim-up bar. It's just the top of her head, but I'd know that shade of red anywhere. I skip down the three steps headed towards the path to the beach and circle around behind her. Isla's chatting with a bartender whose back is to us both, making drinks.

I pause, feeling uncharacteristically nervous. I'm still considering whether placing my hands over Isla's eyes would seem spontaneous and fun or childish and weird when she greets me without even turning around. I can hear the smile in her voice. She sounds smug. Like she caught me.

"Hi, Jackson."

*How the hell did she see me?*

"Good morning, Isla!" I say, rounding the corner of the bar and into her line of sight. She's perched on a stool, sipping some kind of yellow fruit smoothie.

"It's nearly noon." She laughs, checking me out. "Your lip looks better."

I run a hand over the bite. It still feels itchy and in need of her attentions. I close my eyes. It's probably not a great idea to think about her rubbing my lip with an ice cube right now.

Isla is wearing another short, colorful frock today. It's a loose vintage-style dress with an oversized tropical leaf pattern that's just short enough not to be frumpy. And she has no reason to hide those legs. A patterned purple scarf is twisted into a headband to hold back her hair, and gold and enamel tropical leaf earrings dangle from her earlobes.

I have to give her credit for going the extra mile and matching. There's something so fun and playful about her wardrobe choices. It makes me wonder what she'll wear next.

"Nice tee," Isla stifles a smile as she sips her drink and gestures to the giant peach emoji on my chest.

"Suns out, buns out," I read the legend. "It's a Peaches Resort exclusive."

"What can I get you, Jackson?" The bartender suddenly turns around, and I do a double take as I recognize the curvacious, curly-haired woman behind the bar.

"Alexis! What the hell are you doing here?" I blurt.

"Surprise!" Alexis flicks some water at me. "Turns out you're not the only one from the *Lit Lovers* podcast who got scouted to be on the show. The producers contacted me to see if I had any interest in being on the show, and when I told them I worked my way through college tending bar, they asked if I wanted to bartend on the show, too!"

"Oh crap! Did I miss the surprise?" Rob trots down the stairs smiling expectantly.

"I'd say you're here just in time; he hasn't picked his jaw off the floor yet," Alexis laughs.

"But? What? Why? How? When did this happen?" I stutter.

"We brought Alexis in right after we got you. Rory and I were listening to the podcast again, and we'd been thinking we need someone to stir the pot."

"Reporting for CPS duty, Sir!" Alexis salutes Rob.

"CPS duty?" I ask.

"Chief Pot Stirrer," Alexis explains.

"Ah. That's a better title than CLITO," I manage to say with a straight face.

"Did you just say 'Clito', as in *Clitoris?*" Now Alexis's mouth is hanging open.

"I can't even recall what it stood for now," I admit.

"Chief Love Information Technology Officer," Rob supplies, slapping me on the back. "Jackson will always be my CLITO. I don't care what anyone says."

"Well the CLITO certainly is important," Alexis agrees, eyes twinkling at Rob. "The CLITO should never be ignored."

*Ha ha ha.*

"Are you sure this is a good idea?" I ask Rob. "What if her meddling messes things up?"

"Nah," Rob dismisses my concerns. "Sometimes you gotta shake the tree to get the ripe fruit to fall off, right, Isla? Don't you always say it's all about timing?"

"Yes, but we don't want to shake the tree before the fruit is ripe, do we? If you don't give people enough of a chance to get to know each other–"

"Isla! Bella! Is that you?" I am interrupted by the shirtless god from the tent. He approaches with arms outstretched and steps between me and Isla to envelop her in a big bare-chested hug that goes on entirely too long for my liking.

His heavy cologne coats my nasal passages like an inescapable sticky substance, making me wish I had something to blow my nose with. Like his shirt. If he were decent enough to be wearing one.

"Mi Isla Bonita!" he effuses as he kisses both cheeks before releasing her. I'm surprised he doesn't leave streaks on her dress when he pulls away from her. His abs look like they've recently been enhanced with airbrushing.

Isla is flushed, clearly overwhelmed by the sudden attention. Alexis, meanwhile, is staring with such comically wide eyes that it can almost hear the old-timey cartoon sound effects. *Ah-oooo-gah! Thump, thump. Thump, thump!*

Marco doesn't disappoint - the ladies, at least.

"When Marco hears that his dear friend Isla is doing this show, Marco says, this is the show for me!" Marco announces, in his heavy Italian accent.

*Referring to himself in the third person. Charming.*

"I mean, this is all so very flattering, but we only met the one time in Rome," Isla stammers.

"Si, si. But it was a very special way for us to finally meet, no? Very *cute*, if you know what Marco means? Even though Marco has never graced the cover of one of your books, Marco is your biggest fan, mi amore." He places his rude, meaty hands on her shoulders, swiveling her on her barstool to face the same direction as him. The nerve of him. Touching her like that. Manhandling her. I feel my own hands forming fists.

"Rob, take a photo of us together," Marco demands. "Marco doesn't want to forget a single special moment!"

"I got it!" A staff photographer suddenly appears out of nowhere, snapping photos like a madman. Isla, who is blushing a shade of red that only natural redheads can achieve, doesn't even have a chance to protest.

"That's enough," I snap at the photographer after he's taken enough shots to do a documentary. "Go take pictures of something else now."

"Perfetto, Bella!" Marco kisses Isla's cheek again and releases her. He's still standing directly in front of me, between her and me. I step sideways and shove my way past his beefy bicep, to perch on the barstool beside her.

Alexis's whole face is animated as she looks from Marco to Isla to me. It's like she's doing a whole play-by-play report with her eyeballs, eyebrows, nostrils, and lip twists. I can practically hear her thoughts..

*"Marco is fawning over the beautiful British romance novelist. She seems a bit surprised by his attentions. But who can object to shooting selfies with this hottie? Could Isla Fairfax and Marco be the hottest match to come out of Peaches this summer? But wait, why is Jackson Porter scowling and shoving Marco out of the way?"*

Alexis winks at me and grins. I know she's enjoying every second of this celebrity-studded scene. Rob could not have cast a better pot-stirrer.

"What can I get you, Marco?" Alexis speaks in her sexiest, most provocative podcast-host voice and bats her lashes at the buffoon.

"How about some sex on the beach?" He smolders at her.

Rob, who is standing behind Marco and Isla, swiftly catches my eye and rolls his own.

It's comforting to know I have at least one ally, and it happens to be the most powerful guy on the production team.

"Don't forget you were getting me something, too," I say. "I'll have a Perrier with a splash of grapefruit juice."

Alexis wrinkles her nose at my request.

"Perdone. But, who are you?" Marco turns and waves a hand at me, as if I am one of the infernal mosquitos. His hairless chest is jutting into my face, nipples pert, pores perfected. I can't help but notice he doesn't have a single bite mark on his perfect flesh. Probably because he is not, in fact, human.

"Marco, this is *Jackson*," Rob says, mouthing a silent apology to me over the beefcake's shoulder. "Remember I told you about him?"

"Right, right," Marco waves a hand and turns his back to me again. "The, how do you say it, *geek squad*?"

Alexis stifles a giggle and places Marco's drink in front of him. "One second," she holds up a finger as she slowly unfolds a paper umbrella, garnishes the rim with an orange slice, and drops in a whole cherry. "Now it's ready."

"Guys, I wanted to go over some pre-shoot notes," Rob says, pointing at Marco and Isla. "Jackson, do you mind if I grab Isla for a minute?"

"Sure," I offer, trying to ignore the overwhelming prickle of jealousy I'm feeling. Over what? Being left out?

"Here you go," Alexis says, pushing my drink at me. "I made you a virgin mojito."

Marco freezes and turns back to me. "Jackson is a virgin?" He announces loudly. "Not to worry; we can fix this. Marco is an excellent wingman!"

"I'm not a virgin; it just means there's no alcohol in my drink!" I sputter.

I can see Isla and Alexis trying not to laugh. They're not trying hard enough.

"Yes, yes, of course, my friend. Not to worry. Marco is here," he taps the side of his nose and holds out a hand to Isla who politely allows him to pull her off her stool.

And then the three of them are gone. Alexis rushes to the other side of the bar to make some drinks for the cast members on the pool side, leaving me alone to steep in the muddled mint of my virgin mojito.

# isla

. . .



*"Nothing's going to work if you don't have the right attitude and put in the effort. You gotta stay focused. Committed. Eyes on the prize. You snooze, you lose."*

*~ Jackson Porter, Playing With Matches Confessionals*

ROB PULLS us into the resort's coffee shop and insists on fetching us both drinks before revealing what he wants to chat about. I get a latte. Marco orders hot cocoa. With marsh-mallows. His bare chest is dimpled with goosebumps from the chill of the air conditioning.

"Here's the thing. I'm not saying you two actually have to get involved," Rob stirs a little sugar into his tea. "I'm just saying, it couldn't hurt the ratings if you two flirt a little, you know, for the camera. It'll add a certain level of dramatic tension. This is reality TV, but there's still an element of theater. I'm sure you of all people get it, Isla. You are a *master* story crafter."

"So you're saying we should fake a relationship?" I ask Rob.

"Not as such. I'm just recommending you two play up the obvious chemistry on camera. Imagine what a thrill this will be to your devoted fans. They want to believe in romance, and what could be more magical than the possibility that their favorite author is hooking up with their favorite cover model?"

The curveballs keep coming today. First Alexis shows up, and now this request. But it all makes a weird kind of sense. I trust that Rob knows what he's doing.

"Marco does not need to pretend," Marco says. "Marco is a huge fan of Ms Fairfax. *The Mystic Matchmaker* is my mama's favorite series. And you know what my mama says? She says, 'Marco, why can't you bring home a nice girl like this beautiful English rose?'"

He's looking at me with such pure puppy dog devotion that I'm not sure if I should laugh or cry.

"I'm sorry, Marco. You're a very handsome man, but I'm not really looking for a relationship right now," I explain to him. Then I turn to Rob. "Are all your reality shows fake like this?"

"What do you mean, *fake*?" Marco protests. "This is reality for Marco! Just give me the chance, mi amore. Marco will prove it to you! Marco will put a tattoo on this body, right here. It will say your name. There will be no other author on Marco's chest." He pounds his naked chest and pouts. The gesture is totally ruined by the chocolate milk mustache above his upper lip.

I take a deep breath, trying not to laugh at how preposterous this all seems. I can't believe this hunky model suddenly thinks he's in love with me.

"What have you done to him, Rob? Did you drip a love potion in his eyes?"

"This has nothing to do with me, I assure you, Isla. The idea wouldn't have even occurred to me if this poor bloke hadn't confessed to me what a massive crush he has on you. We work with what we have in reality TV, you know. We 'sculpt' it." Robs shrugs. "I'm open to your ideas if you have any better ones. I just want the show to do well for all of us."

I picture my agent's face. I need this show to cement my place in the U.S. market. I don't want to blow it. At least Rob is being totally upfront with me. And Marco? My gut is telling me he is genuinely infatuated with me, which is both flattering and ridiculous. This man could probably have any girl he wanted. A million women would kill to be in my shoes. They'd literally claw each other's eyes out for a date with the supermodel. I watched it happen every week on the *Pazzi per Amore* show.

But of course, like all overindulged men, Marco only wants the thing he thinks he cannot have - the author that ducked out the back door of her own book signing, without even getting a single shot with the supermodel, let alone his sharpie signature on her left breast.

Marco continues to stare at me with blind adoration. I have to resist the urge to pat him on the head like a prize spaniel. Rob hands him a napkin and points to his lip.

"Fine, I do see your point, Rob. I don't have a problem with a little lighthearted flirting, but let's be clear," I make eye contact with both men, "it is just for the camera, okay?"

"Okay, it's a deal. And thank Venus," Rob says. "To be honest, I'm not feeling one hundred percent confident about the combinations Jackson's software suggested. I'm not seeing the chemistry. We need to give people a reason to tune in and see what happens next on the show, you know? The two of you are such avatars in the world of romance, and having you both on screen at the same time is powerful. But having you both onscreen at the same time with the hint of a possibility that there might be a little something more going on?" He opens his fists by his head in the "mind blown" gesture. "This is going to be great, Guys. Great for the show and for both your careers."

JACKSON and I are sitting crammed together in a sweaty, crowded pop-up tent, along with three crew members. We're all waiting for the filming to begin. The tent, which is loaded with equipment and monitors, has been set up as a control room a little ways away from the shaded, beachfront gazebo that's been styled as an outdoor living room.

At first I was relieved to hear Jackson and I wouldn't need to be on camera today but now I feel a little jealous that we're in here and not on the set. The gazebo looks dreamy on the monitors. The backdrop of the brilliant blue Caribbean is perfect. The three women are lounging on colorful pillows on the daybed to the right of the camera, and the men are all seated on the oversized sofa to the left. Gauze curtains float in the breeze. They've placed three massive fans just off-camera to keep the gazebo cool and bug-free.

There's an atmosphere of hushed anticipation in the tent, and it's hot. Super hot and stuffy. I'm grateful for the personal mister fans I found in the swag bags. Alexis packed mine with ice from the bar earlier. Thank goodness for that. I mist my face and decolletage with icy water and switch on the fan.

"Mmmmmphhh," I can't help but breathe out with relief at the instant cooling effect.

Jackson turns away from the monitors to stare at me, eyes traveling jealously from the fan to my damp cleavage. I realize that I offered to share the swag with him, and here I am hogging it all up for myself.

"You want me to do you?" I hold up the fan. Jackson tips his head down and raises his eyebrows.

"I was wondering how long it would be till you propositioned me again," he smirks.

Just for that I spray him in the face without warning.

Rob chooses that moment to poke his head into the tent and address us. "Thanks for hanging in there, you two. I see you're both mic'd up. That's great. I appreciate your standing by in case we need you for anything. We're just about ready to get started."

Rob gives a thumbs up to the crew members, and they all jump to attention, rushing to don headsets and check their assorted equipment.

"Okay. Buckle up. This is where the games begin," Jackson says. I turn sideways to study him. He looks so serious, staring at the monitors.

"Is that how you think of it?" I ask. "Love is a big game?"

"Hmmm," Jackson considers this. "Sometimes. Other times it's more like a battlefield."

"With winners and losers?" I ask. I'm still trying to understand his theories about relationships.

"I mean, yes, and no." Jackson's brow furrows as he considers my question. "We're all trying to be winners in life and that includes love, but it's not necessarily about *beating* someone else, so much as doing the best you can do for yourself, given the hand you've been dealt."

"Okaaaaaaaay," I somewhat reluctantly agree. I have to concede that this makes sense. It's not even all that different from my own philosophy about relationships. "So what's your personal game strategy?"

"For myself? I haven't ever really felt the urge to merge my life with someone else's. I'm not the market my app is targeted at. If I want to get *laid*, I reach for the same apps as everyone else. You know how it goes, swipe right, have a nice night." He mimics waving goodbye to his booty call. I spray him in the face again.

"I'd be mad at you for that if it didn't feel so damn good," Jackson smiles, wiping the water from his eyes. He pulls down the collar of his shirt, exposing his chest, and I notice the small green medallion on the chain around his neck again. It looks like a pet tag. "Hit me again?" he says tilting his head back.

I spray the water at his face, aiming up his nose, but he doesn't seem to mind. He just uses the hem of his shirt to mop it up.

"So what makes your app different from all those others?" I ask, a little pointedly.

"I'm so glad you asked, Isla," Jackson smiles charmingly, and I see the college professor side of him rise to the surface as he launches into his pitch. "My app isn't just about facilitating hook-ups. My app makes compatible life matches based on proven data points, rather than fleeting attraction. We've done over a decade of computer learning enhanced research. In short, my app makes it easier for people to find *their most ideal partners.*"

Somehow, while he's distracted me with his talking, he's also managed to sneak the mister fan off the table. He sprays me in the face now, catching me completely off guard. I gasp at the icy blast. Unexpected, but not unpleasant. It reminds me of the shock of running through sprinklers as a child, chasing rainbows.

"All's fair!" Jackson gloats.

"Do it again," I say, closing my eyes this time and sighing with pleasure when he switches on the fan and holds it in front of me.

"Can you two please turn that thing off? We can't risk getting the equipment wet." One of the tech guys pointedly reprimands us and mops his brow with a microfiber rag. He's a large man, and he's sweating profusely, a situation which isn't being helped by the beanie and flannel shirt he's got on.

"Sorry," I apologize, reflexively.

"We haven't aimed the fan anywhere near the electronics," Jackson argues. "It's a pretty targeted spray. Here. Just chill." He offers the fan to the techie who stubbornly waves it away and returns to his console.

"Or not," Jackson shrugs. "Now *that* is a real-life grumpy nerd," he whispers in my ear.

We both turn our attention to the monitors now, as a four foot tall robot rolls into the center of the filming area. It is decorated with a colorful "Playing with Matches" themed vinyl wrap and has a flashing LCD screen for its face. Right now the screensaver is cycling through a deck of playing cards featuring each of the contestant's faces and animated hearts. There's a little shelf on top of the robot's "head" where a stack of envelopes is arranged.

Peeking outside the tent, I can see the robot is being controlled by Rory. She's standing next to Rob's folding director's chair, and she is clearly holding the controller. She says something to him and he nods, then she presses a button and fidgets with a dial. The robot starts to loudly play the theme song for the show, the 80s classic "Playing with Matches." The robot spins around at the center of the clearing in the middle of the stage, doing a little dance of sorts. Alexis watches from the sidelines, and she shoots me a thumbs up.

Everyone stops and claps. "Three minutes everyone!" Rory calls out.

The robot suddenly spins around, revealing Jackon's company logo in the middle of the back side. Right where the robot's "butt" would be. If a four foot high rolling robot could have a butt.

I snort.

"What?" Jackson smiles and raises his eyebrows at me. "You want to let me in on that joke?"

"You called your app AI Swiper?" I say, blinking back tears of laughter.

"Yeah, that's because the research showed that people are totally addicted to swiping. It's all about the dopamine." Jackson sighs, "Powerful stuff."

"No, that's not what I mean," I fan my face with my hand. "Didn't you run the name past anyone?"

"Of course!" Jackson rolls his eyes. "We did the market research, hired a firm, ran focus groups...."

"And you're sure that none of them were trying to sabotage you?" I ask.

"Of course!" Jackson is looking at me like I am crazy.

"Then how could they ever have let you name your app 'Asswiper', Jackson?"

He looks at me quizzically, then follows my gaze back to the robot that is still doing a little dance center stage, shaking its branded booty. His eyes suddenly go wide, and he blanches.

"Oh my God," he says, seeing it for what I can only assume is the first time. "Oh my fucking God."

"Places everyone! Quiet on the set! We are ready to roll!" Rob calls out.

MARCO STRIDES out into the center of the gazebo to greet the cast. Jackson is still scowling, and his fingers are twitching, likely with the unmet urge to text someone.

"Welcome, Everyone. I want to tell you how excited Marco is to be here. It is Marco's first big American show. Some of you may know Marco as the cover model for the international best selling romance novels. But what you don't know about me, is that Marco is not just a model. Marco is a man. A man who, like all men, is also looking for love."

He shoots the camera an imploring look, laying it on thick with the sad dog eyes. I look down. Beside me, Jackson's hands are now clenched into fists.

"So who is ready to get started?" Marco asks. The cast claps and cheers.

The robot does its dance again, and the cameras zoom in on it. It starts to make chirping and buzzing noises like R2-D2 from Star Wars.

"What is that, my little friend? You say you have a match?" Marco hams it up, speaking to the robot. The robot in turn flashes a photo of Marco and then the small screen reverts to animated heart eyes. The robot shakes exuberantly.

"Well this is odd," Marco announces. "It looks like Marco is up first! My little buddy Cupidbot is telling me he has a match for *me*." Marco pats the robot and mugs at the camera. "I wonder who the Asswiper program is going to tell me is my soulmate, Cupidbot? Will it be the same woman who I cannot stop thinking about?"

The robot produces chirping noises and Jackson clenches his fists even tighter at Marco's pronunciation of his app. He jumps to his feet.

"Cut!" Jackson yells, bursting from the tent.

Everyone turns to stare at us, but they continue filming. I follow behind

"Jackson," I tap his shoulder, trying not to speak too loudly. "I don't think you're authorized to yell that?"

He ignores me, rushing forward onto the set, where he marches up to Marco.

"It's A-I Swiper. *Ay eye.*" He pokes Marco in the chest as he over enunciates the letters, making his point. "AY. EYE. Not Ass. I didn't give you exclusive use of my proprietary technology in order to be insulted!"

Marco rolls his eyes dramatically, shoves Jackson back, and Rob stands to yell, "Cut!"

"Why is this *man* being such an ass?" Marco argues petulantly, affecting a ridiculous American accent when he says the word ass. "Here is what Marco say, I say 'Aaayyssswiper.'"

Even when he tries to say it right, it still comes out sounding like *Aaya-swiper.* I can feel the tension rippling off Jackson in waves. He is seething.

"Okay, okay, you know what, this is nothing we can't fix in post," Rob says. "Let's take it from 'the woman I cannot stop thinking about?' Jackson, Isla, can you two please make your way back to the tent?"

"We didn't even do a profile on that douchebag, so how could he have a match?" Jackson mutters under his breath as we head back into the sweaty tent.

"We're rolling again!" someone shouts, and on screen, Marco snaps back into character.

"So this is how the matchmaking ceremony works on the show," Marco says. "Cupidbot here, who is powered by Asswiper, already knows who should go on a date. But we are not leaving the entire fate up to the robots." He smiles at the camera and winks. "We humans have a vote, too."

"Hmmm," I say to Jackson. "I thought they were going to reveal the matches right off the bat, weren't they?"

He nods, eyes narrowed.

"So how is this supposed to work exactly?" I ask. The techie hushes me as Marco goes on to explain.

"Everyone has a deck of cards with all the other contestants on it. And if they play their cards right today - that is, if we have a match, tomorrow they will get to go on a very special date, organized by the resort and the *beautiful* mystic matchmaker, Isla Fairfax, herself. But what Marco is wondering right now, is who the computer has matched Marco up with. Could it be the person I hoped for?"

The robot makes a series of beeping noises and plays some animated hearts and fireworks on the screen. Jackson huffs beside me. Finally the screen displays a spinning card and the robot starts playing jackpot sounds. When the card stops spinning, I see it is a photo of *me*, taken from my author site.

"Perfetto!" Marco claps. "Oh my God, Marco knew it was meant to be!"

The robot makes more noises, interrupting him.

"What's that, Cupidbot? What do you say? I still have to open the envelope?" Marco feigns nervousness. "If she didn't select me, too, we don't get to go out on the date?"

The robot beeps and spins, and a series of lights shooting upwards direct our attention to the envelopes on the tray top. Marco picks up the biggest envelope and turns it over carefully. He shakes it next to his ear, as if he could discern the contents by listening.

A crew member holds up a sign encouraging the cast to clap and laugh, and everyone out there whoops it up.

In the tent, Jackson is still glowering at the screen. "What the fuck is happening? I thought we were just going to announce the matches during the first episode."

"Change of plans," the techie says. He must have snagged my fan while we stepped out, as he mists himself and basks in the coolness. "Rob thought it would be more dramatic if we mix it up a bit."

Back on the set, Marco is still hamming it up, chatting with the robot. "Oh I am so nervous, Cupidbot. I don't know what to do. Tell me what I should do?"

"Open it, Dude!" Darwin yells.

"I'll go on a date with you, Marco!" Lacey offers. He turns to blow her a kiss.

"Okay, here goes nothing," Marco tears into the envelope and a stream of confetti and waterfall of cards fall out. "Oh my!" he mocks shock. "I think that is the whole deck! Marco is so flattered by *everyone* wanting to date him. But there is only one card I am looking for… could it be?" He bends to pick up a gold foil-embossed card with my face on it. "It looks like it is!"

"Get out there, Isla." The techie holds the tent flap open and gestures towards the set. "Rob wants you on camera. It's your moment to shine." He mists himself again.

*For God's sake.*

I said I'd put up with a little light flirting, but this is ridiculous. Rob could have been a little more explicit. But it's too late to do anything about it now. I wish I hadn't misted off most of my makeup.

"You don't have to do this," Jackson growls at me.

"In for a penny, in for a pound," I sigh.

Pasting a smile on my face and thinking about book sales, I walk out onto the set to greet Marco. I tolerantly allow him to kiss my hand, closing my eyes to hide the eye roll at this act. When I open them, Rob shoots me a thumbs up and indicates I can get out of there. He pantomimes walking fingers, waves, and blows a kiss.

Obediently, I blow Marco a kiss and then I skedaddle, back to the relative safety of the tent.

"Put on your dancing shoes, mi amore. It looks like we have a hot date tonight. Now let's see who else chooses each other!"

Beside me Jackson is tapping out a message on the temporary phone to show to me. It's simple and to the point.

> WTF is happening here? This is total bullshit. Did you know?

# jackson

· · ·

*"I just want the best for all of the contestants. I want them to be happy. Whoever they end up with."*

*~Isla Fairfax, Playing With Matches Confessionals*

**"WE'RE NOT GOING** to tell you who you've matched with, till the next episode," Marco trills.

This isn't what was supposed to happen today. Today was supposed to be about revealing the matches *we'd* made. We were supposed to be taking turns with the reveal. One for me, one for Isla, and one we'd both agreed upon.

No wonder why Rob had relegated us to the tent. And the robot? My software personified as a dumb droidy sidekick named Cupidbot? Total bullshit. Insulting.

*But not as stupid as the product name that I single handedly came up with.*

Had nobody thought to point it out before now? Surely someone else had seen it? My skin feels too tight.

I'm not comfortable speaking in front of the crew member, so instead I type out a message for Isla on the loaner phone. I'm pissed. At no point did Rob mention that the show was going to be a free-for-all, with contestants choosing their own dates. This isn't what I signed on for.

> WTF is happening here? This is total bullshit. Did you know?

I show the message to Isla, watching and trying to gauge her reaction. She shrugs and shakes her head a little, then she reaches for my phone and taps in a response.

> Talk later

If any of the contestants couple up and get too cozy before we reveal the matches, the whole thing is likely to get blown. We're in a tropical paradise here, with open bars and dreamy sunsets. It's sexy, it's romantic, and it's going to *ruin everything*.

How can we expect any of these people to do the right thing when the wrong thing is right there in their face, sharing their space and giving them a hard-on?

I click my pen in my pocket till the tech guy gives me a warning look.

By the time Isla and I came on board with the production, the casting director had narrowed our choices down to a few dozen men and a dozen women. All of them completed AI Swiper matchmaking profiles prior to that. At first, I was a little worried that we wouldn't have any strong matches working with such a small pool. But I'd been wrong. I was surprised to see how many strong possibilities there were.

I was dubious about some of the contestant's intentions, but the AI Swiper app is really more about predicting long term compatibility than it is about sussing out motives. I always like to say, you can lead a horse to water, but you can't make an ass drink.

*Ass. AI Swiper. Asswiper.*

I feel heat radiating from my face again, and I don't think it's because it's six hundred and sixty-six fucking degrees out here. In the shade. At least the bugs aren't sinking their tiny tubular fangs into me anymore. Isla's herbal products seem to be working even better than the DEET spray that I packed in my lost bag.

*Asswiper.*

Something has to be done about the app name and about Marco. We'll have to look into a last minute re-brand. In the meantime, I may pay a visit to the wardrobe tent. I'd like to rebrand the butt seam of Marco's pants with a thread ripper.

I watch as Owen, the firefighter, steps up to the robot to play his choice card: Chloe.

But then Chloe picks Ryker.

Next Lacey picks Owen.

Darwin and Ryker both pick Lacey.

And in the end, nobody picks poor Paula, who has chosen Ryker strictly because "his accent sounds cute."

How is it even possible that there are no matches amongst the choice cards and that only one person has chosen the same person that we wanted them to match with?

I do some quick math in my head. While it's not statistically impossible that everyone could miss the mark so perfectly, it is rather unlikely. It just goes to show that nobody has a clue what's best for them. Even when it's standing right in front of their faces.

"I cannot believe it!" Marco says when the last member of the group sits down unmatched. "Can it be that Marco and Isla are the only fated mates on the island?"

I steal a sidelong glance at Isla who is sitting tensely beside me. She doesn't crack a smile at his idiotic banter.

*Good.*

The robot is now making sad sounding beeps. Womp, womp, womp, beepity, beeps.

"Not to worry!" Marco throws the last envelope over his shoulder and pats the robot.

"It's okay, Cupidbot. We will try again soon. In the meantime, why don't you go plug yourself in and take a nice nap while we figure out what we do next. Maybe we have to send someone home?" He adopts a pensive, serious look and stares into the camera.

The robot rolls away and the camera pans over the anxious contestants. Chloe's knee is bouncing. Lacey is twisting a lock of hair. Darwin is actually biting his nails.

Finally Marco speaks.

"Not to worry! We won't be sending anyone home tonight. We will be sending *everyone* on a group date instead! And tomorrow night, after a cocktail party we will have the first Shell Ceremony and find out who everyone's ideal mate is. Will it be the person they have chosen or somebody else? Until then, 'Suns Out and Buns Out,' my friends. Every day you spend at the Peaches Resort is a sweet escape."

"And that's a wrap!" Rob stands up, clapping enthusiastically. He shoves some papers in his tote, and the crew rapidly surrounds him. Everyone is asking questions at once.

Isla and I step out of the tent. The air almost feels cool by comparison. We both wait while the participants give each other high-fives and hug. After a few awkward moments of standing around unsure what to do, Alexis makes an announcement.

"Come on back to the pool bar, Guys! Drinks are on me!"

*Very funny at an all-inclusive resort.*

She doesn't have to ask the contestants twice. They all follow Owen in her direction, and she proceeds to herd them back towards the bar like sheep. Rob taps a cameraman to follow.

Spying us, Marco rushes over to Isla's side. He tries to do the thing again, where he stands between us and gives me his back. But this time I kick out a foot, stealthily tripping him. I catch him before he falls and give him a good shove to one side, placing myself between him and Isla. He seems dazed by the maneuver. Dazed but undeterred.

"So, Bella, we will have dinner tonight, no?" He practically stands on his tiptoes, speaking over my shoulder.

"Isla's eating with me," I say. I don't even know why I say it, but she nods and confirms this when I do.

"I'm sorry, Marco. Maybe another time," she says. "We'll be here for the whole week."

Marco sighs sadly. "Okay. Until then, Marco dines alone," he lifts her hand and kisses the back of it gallantly before sauntering off towards his room.

"Thank you," Isla says. "I really didn't want to have dinner with Marco tonight." She hikes her tote bag up her shoulder and glances in Rob's direction, clearly anxious to have a word with him. He's holding court with the crew, while Rory packs the robot into an oversized case. "I need to speak with Rob about a few things," she says.

"Me too," I mutter with annoyance. "This wasn't how I pictured things going down today."

"Me either," she confesses. "And what's worse, I have no experience with matchmaking via group dates. I have no problems creating the intimate one-on-one opportunities that bring folks together, but a group date just seems like a random free-for-all. I can't *see* it." She sounds as frustrated as I feel and keeps stealing glances in Rob's direction. The line of people waiting to speak to him only seems to be getting longer.

"You really didn't see these changes coming?" I ask. "What exactly happened when you left to have that little chat with Rob and Marco before we started taping? And what's with Marco's whole lovesick act? I mean, there's no way he's actually *that* into you, that quickly, is there? Don't you find that a little bit odd?"

"What makes you so sure it's an act?" She bristles. "You don't think I'm worthy of that kind of attention from a hot cover model?"

"With all due respect–" I start to say, but she steps away, silencing me with the palm of her hand. She lowers her sunglasses to obscure her eyes.

"If you manage to get an audience with Rob, please tell him we need to speak ASAP to sort out the details for tomorrow's group date. And In the meanwhile, I've got some writing to do, so if you come back to the suite, I'd appreciate it if you don't disturb me."

The infamous Jackson Porter foot-in-mouth disease. I can see I've said the wrong thing again as she dashes off. Sometimes I need a muzzle.

I should have immediately made it clear that the issue wasn't a fame disparity or related to her looks. The issue is that she is *so much better* than him. So much smarter, cooler, quirkier. In the best ways.

My eyes trail her as she crosses the lawn. I follow her flaming red hair and colorful green dress until she ducks behind a copse of trees and disappears between two buildings.

"Grab a drink?" Rory hooks an arm through mine and tugs me back along the beachfront in the direction of the bar. I glance around and notice that Rob is already gone.

"Sure," I say, allowing myself to be led.

**ALEXIS**, who is truly in her element behind the bar, tries to cheer me up with creative mocktails.

"I can't even believe you guys got this one here to do the show," she says to Rory. "He's usually such a stick in the mud."

Most of the cast have already gone back to the pool or their rooms to tape confessionals. Rory, myself, and Owen have the bar to ourselves.

"Rob can be pretty persuasive," Rory flashes a grin. "And I'm not always on board with his choices, but in this case, I was all in." She leans closer to sniff my guava, pineapple, and ginger-spiked soda. "Is this any good?"

"Try it," I shrug.

She leans forward and wraps her lips around my straw, glancing up seductively at me as she sips. But all I can see are her freckles and sunburnt nose. In her overall shorts and pigtails, she looks like a child that spent the day at the beach after their mom forgot to reapply sunscreen

"Hmmm. Needs vodka," she proclaims.

"You should wear more sunscreen, Kiddo. Skin cancer is no joke." I tap her nose, and she leans back, scrutinizing me.

"Okay, Pops," she says. She turns to Alexis, "Maybe you need to make this guy a real drink. Is he always this way?"

Owen glances at Alexis, raising his brows and waiting to see if she'll throw me under the bus. He's just been sitting there quietly, drinking his beer.

Of all the participants, Owen is the oldest - an old man at thirty-five. Sort of like me. I have the feeling that we'd get along if we met in other circumstances. I also think he's genuinely on the lookout for a life partner, unlike some of the other cast members. He doesn't seem particularly motivated by fame. He didn't even have an instagram account before signing up to do the show.

"If you think Jackson's rude now, you should see him with a few drinks in him," Alexis comments. "Zero filter. None."

"See, I'm doing you all a favor keeping it G-rated." I toast Rory with my very non-alcoholic soda.

Alexis is right. I kind of am an asshole when I have a few drinks. I say shit I always regret later. And it makes me nervous. Does it mean I'm like my dad? He was a really mean drunk.

To date, I've never had a problem with alcohol. But I'm still wary of it, and I probably always will be. I know alcoholism can be hereditary, and I don't want to tempt fate. I'm saving my indulgences for celebrations and toasting occasions - wedding toasts and holiday parties. I'm happy to always volunteer to be the designated driver. When I do drink, I almost always cap it at two drinks. The truth is, I'm a bit of a lightweight. It doesn't take much, which is all the more reason to be cautious.

"On the other hand," Alexis says absolutely stone-faced, "You all should hear Jackson sing karaoke after he's had a drink or two."

"Shut up, Alexis," I growl.

"Do tell!" Owen slides closer and leans towards Alexis, all ears. She's got that mischievous look in her eye. I know it well. It's the same look she gets when she's about to say something scandalous on the podcast.

"Yes," Rory raises an eyebrow. "I want to hear this, too."

I shoot her a warning look, wishing that I hadn't agreed to singing at Emily's engagement party. But it isn't every day your good friend and podcast co-host gets engaged, and I'd been truly happy for her and Blaze.

Emily and Blaze. Hudson and Georgia. Dean and Chelsea. My forest of friends is starting to look more like a clearing full of felled trees.

"All I can say is that Jackson's got some pipes," Alexis comments not-so-innocently, "which makes sense given that his dad was a bonafide rockstar."

"Really? Who?" Rory asks.

"Nobody," I say. "Nobody, a kid like you would know."

"Of course she would know. Your dad recorded the theme song for this show!" Alexis blurts excitedly.

"No way!" Owen looks impressed. "That's wild. I've always loved that song," he says.

"Wait. That's your dad? Does Rob know about this?" Rory asks, taking out her phone.

"He mentioned it once," I say. "It's not a big deal. Anyways, my dad and I haven't talked in years. It's just a funny coincidence."

"I'll say," Rory murmurs distractedly as she checks an incoming text. She scrolls down quickly. "Ooops - that's my boss now. Looks like party time's over," she says.

"Hey, do you think you could tell Rob that I need to talk to him?" I ask her.

"Sure, what about?" she asks.

"The shooting schedule." I shoot a glance over at Owen, not wanting to say too much in front of him. But he's not even listening to us. He has his head together with Alexis sharing a laugh over something.

"I was just hoping he'd have a minute to talk. Or maybe you can." I glance at Rory's phone, "I'd love to conference in my team and go over the plan for shooting. I'm concerned about the potential matches being compromised by the delay."

"Hmmmm…" Rory slips the phone into the bib of her overall shorts. "That's more of a Rob thing. I'll let him know when I see him."

Rory loudly slurps the dregs of her drink through the paper straw and stands to go. Her hands fly over her pockets, checking for pens and doing some kind of silent inventory before she takes off. At the last minute, she stuffs some napkins and a couple of sugar packets in a back pocket. She's rarely still, I note. It's funny how some people are always flapping like birds prepping for liftoff. And other people manage to cover miles and miles on steady outstretched wings. Isla is like that. She seems relatively still, and yet she's always going places, soaring.

After Rory's gone, Owen turns to me and says, "You seem like a numbers guy, Jackson. What do you think the odds are of Isla and Marco actually getting together? He seems really into her, and it seems like they're a perfect match doesn't it?"

"No way," I say. "He's full of shit. I am not buying it for a minute."

"I dunno," Alexis cocks her head at me, "I think he seems genuinely into her. He was just asking me for advice on how to woo her."

"Oh my God, he's not snowing you, too, is he? Come on, Alexis, you know better. Marco's a puffed up cheeseball in hammy, spammy, processed man-meat form."

Alexis gives me a scathing look and glances sideways at Owen. I clap a hand over my mouth. I've done it again. Even without alcohol. No filter. But to be fair, I'm so used to dishing with Alexis. It just popped out.

Owen chuckles. "Tell us how you really feel, Man."

"My bad," I apologize. "I'm very sorry, Owen. I should not have said that about our host. It was unprofessional of me."

"Maybe," he laughs. "But I'm not gonna disagree with you." He looks at Alexis. "I guess this is why he can't drink, huh?" He laughs again.

"Yeah," she says, still looking at me funny. "But I'm not so sure that's all there is to it. If I didn't know better, I'd say my old pal Jackson here has a little crush."

# isla

. . .



*"I just wish more people would listen to me. You can lead a horse to water, but you can't make a jackass drink."*

~Jackson Porter, *Playing With Matches Confessionals*

WHEN I GET BACK to the suite, I see Jackson's left my tee on the bed, neatly folded. It smells like him. In fact, the whole room smells subtly like Jackson. I like it a little too much. It's distracting.

I carry my laptop out to the patio where the only sounds are wind and waves, distant laughter, and the occasional rev of an offshore boat engine. It's warm, but the breeze is delicious, smelling of seaspray and tropical flowers.

There's something about working on a book without the distractions of wifi and social media. When I eventually look up, two hours have passed, and I've managed to bang out three chapters. These are the most words I've clocked in weeks.

Jackson gets back just as the sun is setting and I'm packing up my laptop. He cautiously slides open the patio door.

"I'm not interrupting you, am I?" he asks.

"No, I was just finishing up," I say. "Did you see that your luggage arrived?" I'd practically tripped over it when I came in earlier.

"Yes!" he says. "Thank goodness. Although I will always treasure my Peaches ensemble," he smooths his hands down his chest over the branded outfit from the gift shop.

"Did you get to talk to Rob?" I ask, folding down the screen of my writing device. I've texted him and Rory multiple times about the group date tomorrow, and as yet - no response.

"Not yet," he frowns. "I chatted with Rory, but she didn't have anything useful to say. I actually think I might have seen Rob parasailing. How about you - heard anything?"

"Nothing," I say, checking my temporary phone again and placing it back on the table where I can see if I get an incoming message. "I don't know if they want me to weigh in on the group date or whether they expect me to be ready to go on camera tomorrow. It's a little rude."

"Agreed!" Jackson lays his borrowed phone on the surface, face down next to mine, and takes a seat next to me. "I dropped everything to be here, and I thought I understood what was going to happen. Feels like we're being messed with a bit, doesn't it?"

Suddenly, the table vibrates. My screen lights up, and both of our devices ding loudly at the same time. Jackpot. We both grab our phones and read the message.

"It's a group text," Jackson says, successfully opening his phone first.

"I see," I say, "I'm reading it...."

The message is for me, Jackson, and Marco, and the sender is R. Goodfellow.

> Hi, Guys. Sorry for the confusion. Still working out the schedule for tomorrow, but it looks like we'll be taking the group out snorkeling and parasailing at a local nature preserve. Gotta keep the resort happy - they want to highlight their day trip options. I'm giving you three the day off. We'll resume group filming the day after tom*orrow. Plan is to reveal your matches then. Stay tuned.*

I didn't realize how tense I was till I feel it lifting. I don't have to figure out the group date. I'm off the hook. I have a whole day to write. This is great news!

Jackson, on the other hand, does not look pleased. He slips his phone into his pocket.

"See, this is what I'm talking about. They dragged me down here to cool my heels? They're not even using the matches we made, and God knows what kind of alliances or hook ups or whatever are going to happen on that boat. Parasailing and snorkeling? It's not only irresponsible, it's dangerous! It's not in their best interests. We're talking adrenaline, dopamine, booze, and bikinis!" he shakes his head worriedly.

"Don't forget the cortisol," I roll my eyes.

"Huh?" Jackson looks at me confused.

"All that cortisol from worrying can't be good for *you*," I clarify. "Look, we've just been given a day off in paradise. Is that really the worst thing?"

"Yes. I could be getting some work done," Jackson grumbles grumpily. "I have things I need to take care of."

"Like what?" I ask.

"Like a rebrand," he scowls.

"Maybe you could sketch out some ideas poolside? I have a deadline, too, but my editor doesn't care whether I get the work done while laying at the beach. It's all about balance," I suggest.

I feel Jackson's eyes on me as I stand and stretch, rolling the tension out of my neck and shoulders. His gaze feels wrapped around me like a weighted blanket as I walk to the metal and glass railing of the balcony. Heavy, but not unpleasant. Late afternoon rays of sun float across the balcony in orange slices, coloring everything golden.

Jackson squints at me and shades his eyes protectively. "Damn, Isla, why does looking at you always make me feel like I'm looking directly into the sun?"

He lowers his sunglasses.

"Oh. Did you come out here to insult me again, then?" I ask, swiveling my back to the setting sun and meeting his gaze. He flinches.

"No. *Shit.* I am so bad at this." He drops his head into his hands for a moment before looking back up. "I didn't mean it as an insult. You actually look *gorgeous*. Breathtaking. Your hair–" he gestures with his hands, "backlit like that, it's like a ring of fire."

"Oh," I say, completely taken off guard by his compliment. "Thank you?"

This seems to encourage him to keep talking.

"Earlier today, I didn't mean to disparage you when I was questioning Marco's intentions. It was just that everything seemed so off about the way filming went down, and I guess I'm not sure who I can trust anymore. I want to trust you, Isla. Can I trust you?"

He removes his glasses, and the sunlight pools in his gray-green eyes, illuminating flecks of brown and deeper greens that shimmer like bits of beach glass on a rocky shore. His lashes are thick and bronzed in the sunlight, a shade lighter than his hair. And his lower lip is still so deliciously full. I guess the mosquito bite wasn't entirely to blame.

I feel a pulse of desire coursing through my body, gathering between my legs. But it's more than just wanting. It's almost like a premonition. Tangled sheets and whisper-soft kisses. The feeling of stubble against my neck and chest, the taste of something sweet, and the slip of salty, sweat-soaked skin. Every hair on my body stands on end as the phantom sensations wash over me. Like a memory of something that hasn't happened. *Yet.*

I spin back around to face the ocean and slowly count to three.

"Yes, you can trust me," I finally say, without turning around. "But can I trust you?" I know I'm asking the wrong person that question.

*I'm not sure I can trust myself around this man.*

Jackson stands and steps to the rail beside me, staring at the same vista silently. He doesn't answer immediately, and with each passing second, I feel the crackle of electricity between us amplifying and building, like we're both over-loaded conductors passing the energy back and forth. The sparks should be a warning, but it feels more like the prelude to a show.

"There's no possible scenario in which I would benefit from sabotaging you," Jackson says, turning towards me. "Or vice versa. We may have totally different philosophies, but this truly isn't a contest. Especially since Rob seems to have changed the format. The only way either one of us 'wins' is if we do it together." He places a warm hand on my arm.

Another wave of desire crashes down. Hotter. Harder. Does he feel it, too? I search his eyes as his face moves infinitesimally closer. The breeze is ruffling his hair. I note the freckle on his right cheekbone and the curve of his ear. He's already got a light tan, despite copious use of my sunscreen this morning. His skin is glowing with a new golden tone. Our lips are just inches apart, and then - an alarm goes off on his phone.

"Shit!" Jackson snatches his hand away and shakes it, like he's just touched a hot stove. He fumbles to retrieve the phone from his pocket and stop the alarm. He glances back at my folded laptop.

"Well, I know you were working. I really didn't mean to disturb you," he says. "I set the alarm as a reminder for dinner. I was actually hoping we could talk then."

"It's okay, I was ready to take a break," I swallow my disappointment. "And appreciate this glorious sunset."

*Which would have been more glorious, if he had actually kissed me.*

"It really is spectacular," he agrees, darting a hand out to tentatively move a strand of my hair. He brushes it back quickly, like someone passing a finger through a flame. Then he shoves his hands into his pockets. "Do you think you'll be ready to go to dinner in an hour?"

"You don't actually have to eat dinner with me, Jackson," I say. "I did appreciate you running interference with Marco, but I'm fine with grabbing a plate at one of the buffets and bringing it back to the room."

"I made a reservation at The Rooftop for us for eight o'clock," he says, mentioning the resort's fanciest table-service restaurant. "Maybe we could chat a little more about our thoughts on the show and the matches we chose? So we can present a united front?"

"Okay, sure," I say, studying him for a moment.

He's not making eye contact anymore. His eyes seem hooded. Avoidant. The wind blows past him, toward me, mingling his scent with the sea breeze. I brace for the next overwhelming wave of attraction to crash on the shores of my overactive imagination.

"I'm just going to go shower. Can I get my SIM card back from you?"

The moment has passed, and Jackson slides the door to the suite open.

# jackson

*"The tricky thing is learning to trust your gut. It's so easy to decide you're just imagining things. The harder you are working to convince yourself that it's just your imagination, the less likely it is that it's just your imagination."*

*~Isla Fairfax, Playing With Matches Confessionals*

THE MAITRE D' shows us to a table on the outer ring of the candlelit rooftop terrace. The night air smells like gardenias and mimosas, sand, salt, coconut, and ocean. I close my eyes, inhale, and try to capture it, making a memory.

"I'd love a vodka soda," Isla tells the waitress when she shows up to take our drink orders.

"For you, Sir?" she asks. I hesitate, considering whether I should ease up and have a drink tonight. I want to, but I'm worried about what might happen if I do. I'm worried I'll lose what inhibitions I have left around Isla. It's already taking all my self control not to drag her back to our shared suite and lock the door. The nonstop, near pornographic images in my mind are lapping away at my reserves, wearing me down like a weathered stone. The sun washing over her on the balcony? She looked almost unreal backlit like that. Her flimsy, semi-sheer dress was no match for the sun. It called out her silhouette in relief, crowned by a mane of fire. She's like a video game goddess from my mushy, frontal-lobed, teenaged dreams.

"Jackson?" Isla says. "Did you want to order something?"

"Whiskey soda," I say. Just one drink. I'm a full-grown man, with a fully-formed frontal lobe. I am in control of my faculties. I'm not going to lose it. I have a professional relationship with this woman. Nothing more.

*It can't be anything more.*

"So I spoke to Emily today," Isla says, while perusing the menu.

"You called her?" I raise an eyebrow. "On the loaner phone?"

"Yes," she smooths the napkin on her lap. "They didn't say we couldn't *call* people. Just that we can't go on social media."

I am fascinated by the symmetry of her collarbones and the way her squared shoulders appear to be double the width of her waist. Her body is a perfect combination of triangles and circles, hard and soft, sharp corners and voluptuous round–

Isla catches me staring at her breasts. Breasts sheathed in an elaborately and colorfully beaded, embroidered top. Tiny round mirrors circle each mound, reflecting the candlelight. She meets my eye and smiles knowingly. I feel my face heat. There's no use pretending I wasn't looking.

"That's um – a really cool top," I shake out my napkin and stare down at my lap as I place it there.

*Smooth, Jackson.*

"Thank you," Isla smiles, looking genuinely flattered. "I got it in Morocco." She meets my eye. "But I get the feeling you didn't ask me to dinner tonight to talk about fashion, right?"

"Right," I sigh, accepting my drink from the waitress. "To making matches," I say, and we clink glasses, ice tinkling.

I take a sip, enjoying the warming burn of the alcohol as it goes down, cooled by the fuzz of the soda. Like an itch being scratched. So good.

"I have to be careful with this stuff, " I find myself saying. "My dad was an alcoholic. I don't drink often. I like to save it for toasts and stuff." *Why did I just tell her that?*

"My mum drinks a bit too much, too," Isla sets her drink down. "But I don't know that she has a problem with drinking so much as that her drinking tends to occasionally create problems."

"Is there a difference?" I ask.

"I'm not sure. I think that she's not addicted to drinking so much as she is to creating drama. The two go hand in hand for her. I don't think she'd mind giving up the alcohol, but she'd definitely mind giving up the drama. Anyways, she's never done anything truly terrible. She's just a pain in the ass when she's had a few."

"Ah well, that's where my dad's situation was different. He was a mean drunk, and he did do terrible things." I feel for the small medallion on my neck. I don't even know why I still wear it. It's been over fifteen years. I'm just used to it being there.

I sigh and sip my drink, enjoying it less. This was not at all what I wanted to chat about tonight.

"You say his situation *was* different?" Isla takes a tentative sip of her drink. "Has he passed?"

"He's no longer in my life," I say. "Haven't seen him since I was eighteen. No idea if he's dead or alive." I pick up the menu, desperate to change the subject. "So what do you think you'll get? The short ribs sound good."

"I was thinking scallops," she says, following my lead. *Thank God.* That was close. I don't know why I went there. I never talk about my dad with strangers. I barely talk about him with my own sister.

"So what did you and Emily talk about?" I ask casually, still looking at the menu. Of all the members of my podcast crew, Emily is the one I've known for the least amount of time. She's a childhood friend of Alexis's.

"How did you and Emily meet again? Alexis introduced you?" Isla asks, as if she's reading my mind. It's uncanny.

"Yes. I know Alexis from the college where I teach part time," I say. "She and Emily grew up together."

"She's a good egg," Isla smiles, reminding me of the good egg/bad egg scene in *Charlie and the Chocolate Factory.* I am instantly reminded of my fantasy from the diner. I can still imagine Isla saying Veruca Salt's lines. "I want it *now*! I want *you* NOW!" Not helpful. I shake my head, take a slug of my drink and squeeze my eyes shut for a moment, trying to picture anything else.

"What? Was it something I said?" Isla asks.

"I'm sorry," I admit, eyes fluttering open. "I keep imagining you as Veruca Salt. I think it's the accent? Maybe also the hair?"

"You really don't have a filter do you?" she snorts.

"Nope." I hold up the glass as if to toast and drain it.

The conversation pauses while we place our dinner orders. I decline the refill on my cocktail, even though I know I'd like another. I need to pace myself. I've probably said enough already.

"You go ahead," I say when she glances at me before ordering a second. "I'm fine."

"Are you?" she cocks her head.

"Stellar," I say. "I've just got a lot on my mind."

"Okay then, why don't you tell me about it?" Isla lowers her chin. Her blue eyes are wide and dark in the candlelight. All pupils.

I want to bite her neck and slam her up against the wall. I want to claim her with a hickey with twice the landmass of the one on Kenna, the barista back at that diner. I cannot say any of that out loud. It's bad enough that I thought it. I wash the dirty thoughts down with some clean, cold soda water and a squeeze of lime.

*Data. Think about numbers, Jackson.*

"So I'm pretty sure that Rob – the show, whoever – is not actually interested in using the data from AI Swiper," I say. "And that presents a problem for both of us."

"What do you mean?" she furrows her brow.

"They were supposed to start with the matches, not let things devolve into some sort of free-for-all," I explain. "It's going to be twice as hard to get people together if they are distracted by budding relationships with the wrong people."

"Maybe there are no wrong people," Isla shrugs. "Maybe this is the way it needs to play out."

"Are you kidding me?" I rattle the cubes in my glass. "This is more like a recipe for disaster. And I'm starting to get the feeling that Rob knows it."

"Why would he do that?" Isla asks.

"Why?" I roll my eyes. "Who the hell knows? I don't understand any of it. I don't know why people make these stupid dating shows or why anyone even watches them."

"Um? Maybe it is because love makes the world go round?" Isla shakes some salt on her hand and licks it off before doing the tequila shot that a server just dropped on the table. She sucks seductively on a slice of lime. I am mesmerized by her tongue. If I kissed her right now, would she taste like tequila?

*Stop it, Jackson!*

"I don't know," I shrug, sipping my sober soda. "I've never been in love. I'm not in the love business. I'm in the matchmaking business. My matches lead to long term partnerships."

"What?" Isla sputters. "What does that even mean? What's the point of matchmaking if love isn't a part of it? Why not use one of those marriage brokers like in the dark ages?"

"I mean, that's not a terrible idea," I say. "But most brokers look at social and financial assets and liabilities. They don't look at a couple's core compatibility. And that's what my algorithm is great at. I can predict which couples are most likely to remain long-term friends. That's a better predictor of marital longevity than love."

Of course the stats are still a little fuzzy on this, but my team is compiling enough data to make a compelling case for compatibility.

"That's bollocks and you know it," Isla rolls her eyes and me, calling me out. "And what about sex?" She leans forward, providing me with an enticing view of her cleavage. I swallow and force myself to look away, examining my cuticles instead.

"What about it?" I say. The wick on the candle separates, sending up a spark that becomes an ember floating between us. We lock eyes.

"I don't want to have sex with my friends," Isla says, still holding my gaze. Our knees are barely touching, brushing up against each other under the table. I want to scoot in and capture her legs between mine.

"Friends with benefits isn't a terrible thing," I posit.

"No thanks," Isla leans back so the server can place her plate in front of her. The server looks confused, and she apologizes to her. "Sorry, that looks lovely. I wasn't saying 'no thanks' to you!"

The server lays my dish in front of me next. "Bon appetit," she says.

We both look at our plates. "That looks good," I point at her perfectly seared scallops. Round and succulent.

"Your short ribs look delicious, too," she eyes the succulent meat on my plate. "Now I have restaurant remorse. I should have ordered that."

"Want to trade?" I ask.

"Oh no, I couldn't," she says.

"I'm not offering for your benefit, Isla. Your plate looks irresistible to me," I say. I watch her lick her lips, thinking a bit before capitulating.

"Fine then, give it here," she says, passing her plate to me while I pass mine to her.

The waitress pours us both glasses of wine. I swirl mine, enjoying it as an accessory even though I'm not really planning on drinking much of it.

"So tell me, if you're such a cynic about love, why are you even here, Jackson?" Isla asks.

"It's simple," I say, "The app isn't doing great. My investors thought it would help if I was on the show."

"But so what? You don't need the money." She bites into a chunk of meat and closes her eyes. "This is so good."

"Listen, Veruca, I may not be in it for the money, but this app is important to me. If I can save one couple from the strife my sister and I went through, it's all worth it."

"You parents didn't love each other then?"

"Oh they loved each other. But in a toxic, dumpster fire kind of way. Their love blew up everything around them, spewing black ash for miles. It didn't make any sense."

"Was that due to your father's alcoholism?" Isla asks.

"Absolutely," I say. "His drinking decimated our family."

"So if he'd suffered from dementia or been stricken with another kind of illness or brain injury, maybe cancer, would you have been so down on love?"

I freeze with my fork halfway to my mouth. "What do you mean?"

"I just mean that maybe you're working on the wrong equation."

"That's ridiculous," I say.

*Preposterous.*

I take a cautious sip of my wine.

"Look at you. You're anxious about having two drinks in one night. You've clearly read up on alcoholism and the hereditary predisposition. So good for you for being cautious. But I have to wonder about your rationale for the app. At least your parents loved each other before their lives got messy. Mine never did. They merely tolerated each other because they had so much in common. You might even say they were *compatible*. That's not something I'd wish on anyone."

"You think love is a cakewalk?" I ask.

"I wouldn't know. Seems like it though." Isla shrugs and spears a bit of potato.

"So you've never been in love either?" I ask, surprised to hear this. *The irony.* "How exactly can you be a best-selling romance author if you've never been in love?" I slide a succulent, tender morsel of scallop in my mouth and savor it.

"I don't have to be the one in love to recognize the emotion. True love is all around us, even if it's not for me. I don't know. I think I might have a disability when it comes to falling in love." She shrugs.

"Okay, now I see it," I say, rocking back in my chair. "You've got some kind of martyr complex. You're like the Mother Theresa of romance." I adopt a mocking tone "Don't mind about me," I say, with a fake British accent in falsetto. "I will wash your wounds and make you whole again. I need only subsist on the occasional dry crust of human kindness."

Her eyes flash angrily at me. "That is not it at all, you arrogant ass."

"Looks like from where I'm sitting. You're like some sort of emotional holy virgin statue."

There's no such thing as a love disability. And even if there were, nobody who writes love stories like the ones she writes has one. I have read her books. I can't even let myself dwell on the passion I've uncovered between her pages.

"Okay, you know what, Jackson? From where I'm sitting, you look like a scared little boy who's looking for a scapegoat to blame for his father's *health* problems. You're so afraid of repeating history that you're afraid to live your own love life. How's always playing it 'safe' with casual hookups really working out for you? " Isla's eyes are blazes of blue as she fires back at me with both barrels.

"Dessert?" the server approaches warily, holding a plate of delicious looking confections.

"She'll have the chocolate cake," I say, without breaking eye contact.

"And he'll have the fruit tart," Isla says.

A few more seconds pass before either of us looks away.

"So what do you think we should do?" I ask. She raises her brows and tips her head sideways, chin out, defiant. "About the *show*," I clarify.

"I don't know," Isla says. "But Emily seemed to think I was overthinking things. She reminded me that things have a way of working themselves out, and I think I'm going to go with that for now. There's not much we can do at this point anyways. So I say we let it ride. "

"Let it ride?" I repeat, swirling the last of my wine.

The waiter sets our desserts down, and we immediately trade plates without comment.

I can't think of anything more terrifying than leaving things to chance. It's been my experience to date that nothing good can come of that. But Isla is staring at me with so much determination in her eyes that I'm not sure I have the will to fight. More than that, I have the feeling that I've been bested.

"Do you think you can handle that?" she challenges, digging into her fruit tart.

"I think I can handle anything," I say, stealing a bit of straw-berry from her plate before digging into the luscious slice of chocolate cake, "as long as we're in it together."

# isla

. . .

*"Will they make good choices? Will their libidos get the best of them? I hope they'll hold their horses and wait to hear who they matched with before getting too attached and entangled. But I have no idea how the group date is going to go. It might be a disaster."*

~Jackson Porter, Playing with Matches Confessionals

IT'S ONLY 8 am when the sound of someone talking on the balcony wakes me.

I peer out the sliding glass door.

"That's what I thought," Jackson is clutching his loaner phone to his ear and pacing. He's wearing a pair of running shorts and a sweaty tank top. His hair is damp.

"Right. I honestly don't care what we call it, but it can't be *'Asswiper.'* How is it that nobody caught this?"

When he sees me, he waves.

"Okay, I gotta go. Nope. No spoilers. You'll have to watch the show when it airs next week like everyone else." He hangs up the call and grabs onto the railing, dropping into a lunge and a stretch. There's music playing on his phone.

"You're up early," I slide the door to my bedroom all the way open.

I squint at the morning brightness. The sun is reflecting off the water in a million glittering sparkles. I can see a small crowd has gathered on the pier, and when I look closer, I realize it's the cast and crew loading onto the catamaran.

"Looks like the cast got an early start," I say. "Hope they have fun."

"But not too much fun," Jackson says. "Have you eaten yet?"

"I just woke up," I laugh. "I'm still in my pajamas." I gesture down at my sleep tee.

"Well throw something on," Jackson says. "I passed by the breakfast buffet, and they were just putting out the bacon."

"I was just planning to bring something back to the room and get to work," I say.

"What happened to the 'let it ride' Isla?"

"What happened to the 'I have work to get done' Jackson?"

"I did it already. That was the call I was on. Now you're seeing vacation Jackson. It might surprise you to learn this, Isla, but I can be a lot of fun. Let's call a truce for today. Have breakfast with me?"

I glance back at my bed a little longingly. The laptop is still sitting open on the bed, right beside my pillow where I left it last night. I'd been in the middle of a scene but too tired to finish at 1 am. I duck back in the room to shut it down.

Jackson frowns and looks at me imploringly. "Please don't make me eat alone? It's a little triggering for me. I don't know if you can tell but I was picked on as a kid. I was kind of a nerd, and nobody wanted to sit with me."

"Bullshit," I throw a balled up tee at him. It's the same one he wore the other day. It lands on the table muffling the music. Jackson fishes out his phone and tosses the tee back. That's when I see his screen. He's listening to music on a streaming service. The lyrics to the song are flashing across the screen.

"Wait a minute. Are you streaming that music right now?" I ask. "How?"

"Nevermind," Jackson shrugs and shuts the phone off, shoving it into a pocket. "Hurry up, and put one of your colorful suits on. I don't want the bacon to get cold."

"You hacked your phone, didn't you?" I gasp. I step back out onto the patio to confirm my suspicions.

"Mayyyyybe," Jackson smiles coyly. "What's it to you if I did?"

"But we're not supposed to be on the wifi!" I say primly.

"No, we're really not," his mischievous grin blooms, and his eyes twinkle. "Breaking the rules would be *bad*, right?"

"Right," I nod.

"Then I guess you don't want me to do yours?"

It would make it a lot easier to back up my chapters, I think longingly, but I can't do it. I'm too much of a rule follower.

"No thanks," I shake my head. "I promised to stay off social media. The whole point of us turning in our phones was to save us from being tempted."

"If only it was that easy to avoid temptation." His slightly feral gaze makes my heart stutter. "I'm starving. Meet me out front in five minutes?"

"Okay," I capitulate. "I could eat." My stomach is starting to growl, as well.

"Beautiful." Jackson runs a warm hand down my arm as he passes me on his way back in. I'm not sure if he's referring to breakfast or me.

Back in my room I choose a hot pink and yellow sundress with a pineapple print. I throw it on over a yellow swimsuit. Naturally I pair this with a straw hat, pineapple slice earrings, and a stack of fruit-scented jelly bracelets. Then I quickly pack up a pool bag with my sunscreen, a couple of magazines, a book on vampire lore, a water bottle, and my laptop.

Jackson's right. I might have to work today, but there's no rule that I have to do it in my room.

Now that we've gotten to know each other a little better, I finally think I understand what Jackson's software is really about. It doesn't have anything to do with data or numbers or love. His app is an attempt to fix his own broken family.

There's something so sadly sweet about it. If love is the disease, then logic must be the cure. I can picture a younger version of Jackson feeling powerless to protect his mom and his sister from the man who was supposed to be his role model. More than that, I can *feel* him.

No wonder he's leaned in so hard into numbers and logic. Numbers are predictable. Logic makes sense to him. It's safe. Emotions aren't.

# jackson

· · ·

*"What do I think of Marco? I think he's not what most people would think. Sure he's super campy and a little over the top. And no question, he's a hottie. But what most people don't realize is that he's also got a heart of gold. That's what makes him the perfect host for this show. He genuinely believes in love.*

*~ Isla Fairfax, Playing With Matches Confessionals*

"SO, can you explain the appeal of meet-cutes to me again?" I quiz Isla over breakfast. "What is it, in your *professional* opinion, that makes them so important to people?"

"I think it's about the story. We all see ourselves as central characters, and when something important happens in our lives, it had better have a great story. Nobody wants to tell their grandkids about a boring meet-cute." Isla explains.

"I get that," I say. "That's why people embellish so much, even if they meet in a totally mundane way."

"I think there's nothing mundane about meeting someone you're destined to fall in love with. Even the mundane becomes epic, simply because it's such a momentous thing."

"Do you think the ancient Romans were all, 'Hey Dad, how did you and Mom meet?'" I adopt a kiddish voice then switch it to dad-mode. "'Well, Son, we hooked up at Lupercalia. Your mom was really into my leather thongs and thank the gods I drew her name from the jar. It was so magical.'"

"Maybe," Isla shrugs and helps herself to a blueberry from my plate. "I don't think human nature has changed all that much over the centuries. People are still people."

"But what if he'd drawn someone else's name," I ask, realizing the flaw in the story. "I mean it all seems so random. How do you know when someone is *the one*?" I pop a blueberry in my mouth. "Please do not say 'you just know.' That's such bullshit. I still hold that compatibility quotients are a much safer way to figure things out."

"You have a major flaw in your logic," Isla argues. "You assume people are finite, and unchanging."

"Aren't they?" I refill our coffee cups from the carafe on the table.

"Nothing could be further from the truth," Isla rolls her eyes at me. "There's a whole world of possibilities in each of us."

"Oh goody. Is this a multiverse theory of matchmaking?" I set down my cup and rub my hands together. "Because I am a huge fan of the multiverse."

"That's surprising given how static you seem to think people are." Isla stirs cream into her coffee.

"Well, they are. In this universe. Doesn't mean there's not other versions of people in other universes."

*I've spent way too much time thinking about the universe where my dad was more like Dean's.*

"I don't see it that way. I think we all contain a universe of possibilities within us at any given moment. And when our universes collide, it changes us. Everything about us. Our tastes change, our habits change, our hopes and fears change. We're not the same people anymore. It's like we're all constantly changing each other's DNA." I catch Isla staring dreamily into space. "I totally believe the right meeting can turn the wrongest people into a perfect couple."

"So if that's true, can the wrong meeting destroy a perfect couple's chances of ever getting it together?" I ask.

"Totally," Isla shakes her head sadly, "Everyone knows that sad couples who were just perfect for one another but they met two years too early and one of them wasn't in the *right place.*"

"But that's about timing, not the meet-cute," I argue.

"The meet-cute is timing! Pure, cosmic timing!"

"So tell me about how *we* met?" I lean back in my seat. "Where does the story start? With Lupercalia or the diner?"

"I don't know, if I was writing it, I might have to start it when you showed up homeless and bedraggled outside my hotel room," Isla's grin makes her eyes crinkle a bit at the corners.

"Okay then, that's the story for our grandkids," I say.

I'm aware that I am acting like a posturing idiot. Is it because of her campy pineapple dress and that adorable tropical fruit-trimmed sun hat? Isla even smells like a fruit cocktail. Like she's candy. Delicious candy.

*Why am I feeling so desperate to charm her?*

When I first got back online this morning, for a hot second I'd thought about buying a few thousand copies of her books using separate dark web accounts. It could get her back on the bestseller lists. But considering that she wouldn't even let me hack her phone, I don't think she would have taken kindly to the gesture. It might even have upset her.

I just want to make her happy. I love how unwaveringly optimistic she is about matchmaking. Like it's merely a matter of getting any two people together under the right circumstances. I could almost write a mathematical formula for it. And then spend the rest of my life trying to solve for the variables.

Was that my parents' problem? One of their variables was off?

"Bella! You look so sweet!" Marco suddenly rushes over to kiss Isla on both cheeks. His plate is loaded with a selection of high-protein, low-carb items. No fruit. All the bacon. No wonder the serving platter was empty when I got there. Marco was hogging it all for himself. "You mind if Marco joins you?" He sits without waiting for an answer. "Marco hates to eat alone. So what are we doing today, Bella?" He takes Isla's hand and slavers all over it.

Oh wait. That's just my imagination. He is not actually drooling, but he looks like he might if I rubbed a little bacon on her.

Isla pulls her hand away.

"I actually thought I'd get some writing done today," she says. "I'm running behind on my current deadline."

"Oh! Marco would love to watch you work. What a special privilege. Should we reserve a cabana by the pool?"

"We were thinking about checking out the lazy river," I say to Marco, shooting a quick wink at Isla.

"Oh! Marco loves the lazy river! Marco already ran six laps around the river this morning. Running against the tide is very good exercise." He looks sideways at me, sizing me up and apparently finding my bulk lacking. "Maybe you should try it."

"I went for a run on the beach," I say officiously. "The sand also provides a fair amount of resistance."

*Damn it, Marco. I wish I'd come up with the idea of running in the lazy river.*

"Hmmph," Marco sniffs at me and turns back to Isla.

"You won't even know I am there, Bella. Marco will be as quiet as a mouse. Marco will fetch you drinks –"

"Oh for goodness sake, Marco," Isla laughs. "You are welcome to join us at the lazy river. You just may be floating in circles with Jackson and not me. I'm going to be parked in my lounge chair, writing."

"We will stay busy, eh, Jackson?" Marco punches me in the arm and winks. "You still need Marco to be your wingman, no?"

"Is that Edwina?" I notice the concierge coming through the door, smiling and waving. Perhaps she's found another room for me? My heart judders unexpectedly. I'm not so sure I want another room now. She threads her way to our table.

"Good news, Mr. Porter! We've contacted the man who drove you here and apparently he has retrieved your backpack. He's off island today, but he'll be around tomorrow and he said he can bring the bag by then."

"See!" Isla snaps. "I told you! Have a little faith in your fellow man!"

"Don't count your chickens before they hatch," I say. "I'll believe it when I have my laptop back in my own hands."

"You are using a laptop to warm the eggs?" Marco's face is screwed up as he tries to untangle the colloquialism. "I am confused, Jackson. You know we are not supposed to have the social media here."

"I know," I grit my teeth.

Marco leans in and winks conspiratorially at Isla. "But I tell you a secret, Bella. Marco has an iPad. You want some insta-gram, some TikTok, some Netflix and chill? No problem. You come see Marco."

**MARCO SQUEEZES** a snot-like snake of his jellified skin lotion onto the back of his shoulder and leans over to Isla on the shaded chaise lounge between us, where she is sitting, happily typing away. He flexes his biceps as he asks a favor.

"I am so sorry to bother you, Bella, but I need a little help with the rubbing," he angles his beefy shoulder towards her.

Isla looks up, then glances down at her keyboard. "Sorry, Marco. I don't want to get any sunscreen on the keyboard. I'm sure Jackson can help you." She smiles and looks between us, and we both freeze.

Neither one of us wants to be the awkward asshole who says, "Ew no, I'm not touching another *dude*."

So naturally, I go to the other extreme. "I got you, Bro!" I announce, getting to work rubbing the lotion into Marco's shoulder like a pro.

"Wow! You have such good hands, considering they are so tiny," Marco effuses. I deliberately miss a large area and then slap him with a sunscreen covered hand in it. That'll leave a mark.

"You're done, Dude," I say.

"Do you want Marco to do you, Bella?" Marco holds out the sunscreen to Isla.

"Oh, no thanks. I put mine on back in the room. As a ginger, I can't be too careful," she points to the umbrella and her hat. "But maybe you should get Jackson's back?" I see her licking her lips and smiling a tart little smile at me. And then, the moment Marco glances away, she winks.

"Of course, of course," Marco says. He makes minimal effort to rub the sunscreen into my back, performing flappy little pats, instead.

"Interesting technique," I say.

A burst of reggae music comes on over the speakers as an invisible emcee makes an announcement.

"Ladies and gentleman, we are about to open the flow rider in the waterpark. Who's up for a surfing safari?"

I hear a loud rushing noise as the jets for the surf simulator come on. A bunch of little boys come running over to the area where we're seated, lining up to take a turn on it.

"Have you ever gone surfing?" Marco asks.

"Not since I was a kid," I admit. Surfing and sailing were things I'd done with my dad when I was very young. Before the drinking got bad. I'd kept up with the sailing when I joined Boy Scouts, but I probably haven't been on a board since I was ten.

Still, how hard can it be? I watch as a kid who can't be older than nine or ten bounces up and slices back and forth on the artificial wave.

"Marco loves to surf! I learned in Portugal when I dated a surfer girl," he brags, then dials it back a smidge. "Not to worry, Bella Isla. She was not so pretty as you. She has thighs like… Jackson." He looks at my legs and shudders.

That's it. I'm calling his bluff.

"Let's do it," I point at the flow rider. "Loser picks up the drinks."

"But everything is free," Marco says, baffled by this.

"It's just a joke, Marco," I explain, exasperated.

"Oh, yes. You mean that the loser must go to the bar to pick up the drinks."

"Sure." I stand to get in line behind a tweenager. "Isla, will you time us when we're up?"

She sighs. "Okay, you guys, but honestly, I need to work. After this, I'm putting in my earbuds."

"Got it," I say, looking doubtfully at Marco. "Don't worry, this shouldn't take too long."

When it's my turn to surf, the attendant hands me a helmet. "You been on one of these before?" he asks.

"No, but I've done the real thing," I say confidently, failing to mention that the last time I was in an ocean anywhere near a board was at least twenty years ago. I wave at Isla, who's watching now, and tap an invisible wristwatch, reminding her to time me.

"Ah, righteous. You got this!" The attendant slaps me on the back and gives the board a shove, propelling it to the center of the nonstop, rushing wave. The nonstop, rushing crushing wave that picks me up and slams me back down so hard that I forget I can't breathe under water. I skin a knee and come up choking and sputtering.

Still in line, Marco is laughing. Several of the little boys standing beside him are also laughing and pointing. I glance at Isla. She has her hand over her mouth and a look of horror.

"Oh my God, Jackson. Are you okay?!" she calls out.

"I'm fine! Fine!" I shout and pop back up. "I forgot I like to surf goofy."

"No," Marco says, "you did not forget. You *are* Goofy." He snickers with the small children.

"It's okay, Man. Do over. Go again," the bored attendant flags a lifeguard, and he hops into the simulator with us. This time when I get up on the board the two of them walk it to the center of the wave, holding it steady so I don't wipe out again. "You good?" the attendant asks. I give the thumbs up sign and slowly they let go and back away.

Fifteen seconds later, I'm back in the gutter. Who knew this damn thing was so hard? It must be rigged for kids.

"Still fine!" I smile and wave at Isla and the other resort guests who have started to gather. One of them has recognized Marco and is shooting a selfie with him. It's triggered a chain reaction as several other guests flock over to do the same.

I console myself with the certain knowledge that I am about to see Marco landing flat on his ass, as well, and climb out of the small pool, unstrapping my helmet.

"Here you go," I say, passing the helmet to Marco.

Marco scoffs and tosses his signature chestnut locks. "Oh no, Marco doesn't need the helmet."

*Because Marco is already brain damaged?*

"Suit yourself," I say, taking my place on a nearby bench.

The attendant counts down and gives Marco a shove. I hold my breath, waiting to hear the splat. All around me, guests are filming. This could end up being a viral TikTok, I think, with a small amount of malicious glee.

And then Marco does a trick. He jumps up on the board and switches directions. Then he switches back. He shakes his butt and holds up two fingers in the international signal for "hang loose." I hold up a single finger in my armpit for the international signal for–

"He's really quite amazing at this, isn't he?" Isla comes to sit beside me, phone aloft and filming as she gazes at Marco with budding admiration.

His run lasts a full five minutes, during which time he does multiple kickflips, a full 360, and stands on one leg. An even larger crowd amasses to cheer him on. When he finally steps down - not because he falls, but because "Marco wants to give the kids a turn," everybody claps.

AT LUNCH TIME, the three of us head to the beachfront cafe near the pool in the Mediterranean Village. We settle into a picnic table.

There are assorted board games set out on the tables. Backgammon, chess, and on our table an oversized version of Jenga. I stack the wooden pieces into a tower, trying to ignore the non-stop buzzing of my phone in my pocket.

I made the mistake of looking earlier, and apparently my wipeout is making the rounds on social. Marco made sure the kids tagged me when they posted it, using that famous 60s era song as the sound.

Now I kind of wish I hadn't hacked my phone. I can't unsee the videos and I can't respond.

"Anyone want to play?" I ask, raising an eyebrow at Isla and Marco.

"I just want to get this thought down before it flies away," Isla takes out her laptop again and starts typing quickly. She pauses to twist a piece of hair and bites her lip, then she smiles and resumes typing at an even more furious pace. I could watch her all day. I love trying to figure out what she's writing about, imagining scenes based on the expression on her face. Earlier when she blushed, I tried to sneak a peek, but she wouldn't let me see.

On the other side of the table, Marco is shooting ridiculous selfies with a filter.

"Don't you ever get sick of that?" I ask Marco as he tries yet another filter. This one puts fruit on his head and lipstick kiss marks all over his cheeks and chest.

"What? No!" Marco preens. "I am proud of my body, Jackson. I want to share it with the world. But mostly, I want to share it with one special woman," he looks piteously at Isla who's so lost in thought she doesn't even notice.

"How old are you, Marco?" I ask, pulling blocks carefully from the tower.

"Marco is thirty-two," he says. "A good age to settle down." He gazes at Isla again. She keeps typing. He pulls his long hair into a man bun.

*Marco is actually thirty-seven.*

"Huh," I say. "I could have sworn you were older."

Marco reaches out and pulls a piece from the bottom of the carefully balanced stack on the table, causing the entire thing to come crashing down. "Oops," he says. "My bad."

Isla sighs contentedly and slams the laptop shut. "Got it!" she says. "Sometimes my muses are like slippery fish. I think I've got a big one but then the line snaps or they flop right off the deck of the boat. I can't even record the idea before it's gone again. But I got this one."

"Tell us more," Marco says. "Did you write about me?"

"Maybe," Isla smiles enigmatically. "You'll have to wait and see. I did include a handsome surfer in one scene."

"Show me?" Marco begs. "I must read it!"

"Oh no," Isla shakes her head. "This is a very rough draft." She looks down at my knee. "Oh no, Jackson, your knee is still bleeding. Let me get you a bandage. I know I have some here somewhere," she mumbles as she reaches into her bag and pulls out a pink floral band aid and some fruit-scented hand sanitizer. "This might sting," she warns, squirting the pink gel at my skinless knee.

*Mother of God. Just cleanse my wound with a blowtorch next time, Woman.*

I flinch at the pain, but mercifully it passes quickly, and she sticks the floral bandage on my knee, kissing two fingers and passing them over the flowery dressing. "All better," she says.

"I could use a drink, how about you two?" I say, thinking I should have had the drink before she tended to me.

Isla glances over at the bar, thirstily. "I don't see anyone there. I'll go see if I can find someone."

"Marco will come with you," he jumps to his feet. "You stay here, Jackson. Order Buffalo wings if the waiter comes." He jumps up and takes Isla's elbow, and the sight of this makes me feel like I have an electric eel writhing in my belly.

"You're just going to leave me here alone?" I complain.

"Only for a moment," Isla promises, sympathetically patting my arm. She glances down at the menu. "You should order the lobster mac and cheese for yourself," she winks. "And order whatever you fancy for me."

*I fancy so many things. But none of them are on the menu.*

Isla heads towards the empty outdoor bar kiosk with Marco. He says something to her, and she laughs merrily. The green eel of jealousy writhes in my gut some more.

I'm not alone for very long. A moment later, Alexis drops down into the seat across from me.

"'Sup, Jackson?" She grins. She is wearing a red tube top and floral sarong with a matching red hibiscus flower in her hair. Her naturally-curly, brown hair is even curlier than usual, and her skin is two shades darker.

"How did you manage to get a tan like that in only two days?" I marvel. She looks good. Great in fact. I hardly ever see Alexis in anything but yoga pants and baggy sweats or boring business suits. The tropics suit her.

"It's the Puerto Rican genes," she smiles. "I still can't believe we're here, can you?"

"The twenty-seven mosquito bites I got that first day go a long way toward convincing me." I scratch at a bite on my arm.

"Try to loosen up a little and enjoy it, Jackson," Alexis looks at me with pity. "A lot of people would kill to be able to visit a resort paradise like this."

"Yeah," I say, absentmindedly, watching as Isla and Marco appear to be debating something. Marco nods and then launches himself up and over the bar, landing like a cat. Isla claps. Marco locates a cocktail shaker and bottle of rum, placing them on the bar.

"Holy shit," I say to Alexis. "Did you see that? Is he allowed to do that? I mean, that can't be okay?"

"Eh," Alexis shrugs. "The crew asked me to fill in for the regular guy, but I'm on a break. If Marco wants to make drinks, I'm not going to stop him." She leans back, smiling. "I would not have placed great odds on those two, but they actually seem to be getting along," Alexis raises her brows and pauses, considering. "Crazy, huh?"

"Oh, come on," I roll my eyes. "Isla is not into that buffoon."

Marco turns the music up at the bar and begins to dance to the beat. It's that song from *Beetlejuice* by Harry Belafonte - "Jump in the Line." Not only is he shaking the cocktail shaker to the beat, he's also twerking his pecs in time with the rhythm. He still has the rum bottle balanced on his head. Once again he's gathering a crowd, and everyone is filming and clapping. Including Isla.

"Aren't you and Isla sharing a room?" Alexis asks. "You have a crush on her, don't you?" She pats me on the shoulder sympathetically.

"It's not like that. I just think she can do so much better than that idiot," I retort. "She deserves better than him."

Alexis shakes her head at me, curls bouncing, and rolls her eyes. "I dunno, Jackson. It's like you enjoy being grumpy, horny, and alone all the time."

With a flick of his wrist, Marco tosses the cocktail shaker into the air and catches it behind his back. The crowd gasps and cheers and the clapping reaches a crescendo as he pours the drink. For a final flourish, he grabs a lighter and sets the cocktail on fire before sliding it across the bar to Isla. Everyone falls silent, ready to snap when she blows it out.

"I am perfectly capable of getting laid any time I want to get laid. There are plenty of other apps I like to use for that!" I shout back at Alexis, timing my words almost perfectly with the expectant hush.

Suddenly, it feels like all eyes are on me.

# isla

. . .



*"According to my mom and my sister the reason I am still single is because I have no filter and I am always sticking my foot in my mouth. But really, I'm okay with my single status. I'm not stuck or anything. I'm just not actively looking for a mate at this time."*

*~Jackson Porter, Playing with Matches Confessionals.*

I'VE ALWAYS admired writers with the ability to cut to the chase. Literally to cut directly to the chase, getting straight to the action and ignoring all the other boring details in their characters' lives. But so far, there's no chase in the final novel of *The Mystic Matchmaker* series. I've just been following my main character around in my mind, waiting for something to happen, for her to undergo some kind of metamorphosis. It's about as exciting as staring at a cocoon.

I've been stalled. I know where my character is, and I know where I want her to go. But today I've finally broken through the slump. Who knew that all I needed to do to summon my muse was set up camp at a ritzy, all-inclusive resort in the Caribbean?

Even with frequent interruptions and distractions, and a few fun diversions, I've been able to draft the scenes that I've been stuck on. I feel like it's a genuine breakthrough.

It's impossible not to smile watching Marco making cocktails. The man is such a ham, of course, but he's also *fun*. He's drawing a crowd, and it's easy to see why. He's a natural entertainer. The Life of the Party. The embodiment of the Fool card in the tarot deck. The way he just leapt over the bar and how fully he embraces new experiences is impressive.

My initial assessment of him was incorrect. He's not egotistical. He's a little insecure. Afraid that nobody will love him if he doesn't keep up the cover model front. Which is a pity. His most endearing quality is his openness and lack of inhibitions. It's almost inspiring how Marco's not afraid of diving right into new experiences. Or of making an ass of himself.

*Asswiper.* Poor Jackson. He has no filter, but all the inhibitions. He's sensitive. I glance back at our table, happy to see that Alexis has joined him.

I take out my phone to film Marco swirling the cocktail shaker with flair, a bottle of rum balanced on his head. I find myself wishing the metal canister contained a magical elixir. Some kind of spell to release me from my family's curse. The notion comes to me in a flash as Marco sets my drink on fire. If only it were as simple for me as it is for my main character.

To end her curse, the mystic matchmaker must complete the task at hand and pass the torch to someone else. Possibly the handsome surfer that I added into the last scene? She's made her hundredth match, and it's time for her to embrace a new, curse-free life. It's time for her happy ever after.

For the first time, I can see the shape of that. I can feel the outlines of her next chapter taking form, even if it will have to happen off in the sunset, beyond the horizon of my reader's view. It's bittersweet, this send off. The end of an era. I'm not quite sure who *I'll* be without her to write about.

I take a deep breath and hold it before blowing out the drink. It's not my birthday and this isn't a cake, but it still feels like a wishing occasion. Inspired by Marco's willingness to make a fool of himself, I make a frivolous impetuous wish of my own.

*I wish I could have my own happy ever after.*

I open my eyes and blow.

# jackson

. . .

*"I guess I do relate to my main character. She's so great at putting people together, but she can't find love of her own. I feel that way too sometimes. Like I'm out there writing happily ever afters, but so far, no great love of my own. But who knows? It's wise to keep an open mind, right?"*

*~Isla Fairfax, Playing With Matches Confessionals*

AFTER OUR AWKWARD LUNCH, I elect to do some solo windsurfing, enjoying the solitary time on the water. It's been ages since I've done any water sports, and I hadn't realized how much I miss it. Surfing, sailing, and waterskiing. These activities were such a big part of the better part of my childhood. My dad, having grown up on the coast in a fishing family, was always dragging us to the water. Somehow, in my attempts to purge the bad memories, I might have blocked a few good ones, too. I remember one particular day of unsuccessful sailing when my dad fished me out of the "soup" so many times, I was ready to quit.

"Just keep at it," he'd said. "One of these times, you'll get the wind and the angle of the sail just right, and then like magic, you'll be off. You'll be flying!"

Cutting through the waves right now does feel a bit like flying. I've managed to get up on the board, and the wind is in my favor. Unlike the murky Pacific where I first learned to sail, the water here is clear. No worries of unseen monsters lurking below. I feel completely in control, having both the perspective and skill to navigate these waters.

*You've got this, Jackson.*

I find myself wishing my dad could see me now as I skip across the waves, catching air. I feel redeemed from my earlier wipeout on the flow rider. Like a child, I almost want to shout, "Yippee! Look at me!"

I balance on one foot, dragging the other in the water, flipping the sail around. Then I throw the sail into the wind, experiencing a thrill as it magically boomerangs back into my waiting hands. Glancing back at the shore, I can't deny that I'm hoping that Isla might be watching. But she doesn't seem to be. She's back to work, seated in a shaded cabana typing away. A few feet away from her, Marco appears to be napping, a hat on his face.

*There's nobody to witness my triumph. Nobody but me.*

Oh well. It still feels fucking fantastic.

After a bit more play and practicing some long-forgotten tricks, I start to feel tired. My body has a worked-over and pleasantly weak feeling that you just can't get in the gym. It's time to head in before I run out of energy. I turn back towards the pier to return the equipment.

As I'm bringing it in, I notice a plume of smoke streaking the horizon. I wonder who - or what - it might be. Whatever it is, I hope it's not too serious.

I'VE JUST FINISHED re-applying sunscreen and getting situated on a chaise in the cabana. Isla is working, and Marco is still asleep. He's snoring and drooling like a warthog, I note with silent glee. No point in waking him up.

I spy Alexis running towards us. "Guys!" she calls out.

"*Guys!*" she repeats with more emphasis. "Did you hear? There's been an accident on the catamaran that the cast and crew were on! They're just pulling into the pier!"

When we get there, the scene at the end of the pier is pure chaos. The resort's security staff won't let us pass, so we're forced to wait on the beach with the rest of the onlookers as the paramedics back up an ambulance. I can see Rory standing with Rob, who is talking to what appears to be some kind of coast guard official. When Rory sees me, she pushes past the line of security and rushes toward us.

"Jesus fucking Christ," she curses. "I need a hug. This has been one of the scariest days of my life! And I did a season as a PA on *Real Housewives*!"

"What happened? Who got hurt?" Alexis asks Rory. She's on her tiptoes scanning for the other passengers.

I see Lacey, who is being carried piggyback style by Ryker. Darwin is walking alongside, stroking her back. And then I see Paula, the blind girl. She's wearing dark sunglasses and using a cane as she makes her way to the end of the pier, flanked by the blonde nurse Chloe and the dive instructor who was passing out the snorkels this morning.

They guide Paula onto a waiting golf cart. I can't help noticing that Chloe suddenly seems pretty cozy with the dive guy. He gives Chloe a ten-second long hug, complete with a tender, soothing mini back rub afterwards. His hand is resting gently and protectively at the small of Chloe's back as she climbs into the golf cart beside Paula.

Shit. I hadn't factored in resort staff as a potential additional spoiler for our matches. This doesn't bode well.

"Is Paula okay?" I ask Rory

"Paula? She's fine. She was sitting far from the fire, and she didn't even go in the water."

"But, what's wrong with her eyes?" Marco pipes up, staring after the departing golf cart with what seems to be genuine concern.

"She's blind?" Rory says, looking at Marco like he's a complete idiot for not catching on to this already. "I mean, not *blind* blind, she can see shapes and colors and stuff, but considering the day we've just had, I don't think anyone wanted to take any chances of her taking a tumble off the pier." Rory turns back to me and sighs. "Can I get that hug now?"

"Sure," I oblige, pulling her in and wrapping my arms around her bony, bikini-clad frame. She lays a hot, sticky cheek on my bare chest. I pat her back tentatively, in a "there, there" way like you would with a little kid, hoping to hasten the end of the embrace. Her spiky hair is itching the crap out of me, and the buckle of her life jacket is scraping against my ribcage.

"It's okay, Bella. Everything will be fine," Marco croons reassuringly. He's massaging Isla's shoulders, which isn't doing anything to soothe me. Isla catches me glaring and raises an eyebrow at me. I cease to pat Rory's back and hold my hands out in a "there, we're done here" fashion, but she doesn't budge.

"Excuse me? Rory? Has anyone seen Owen?" Alexis taps Rory's shoulder insistently, "He didn't get hurt, did he?"

*Thank you, Alexis.*

"Mmmm, what? No. Owen is fine." Rory says, reluctantly backing away. "He's just gathering everyone's stuff. See - there he is." She points at the figure walking off the pier holding six backpacks. He looks like a proper pack mule.

Alexis takes off running, shoving past security to rush to his side to help him.

"Oh good. I was hoping I might run into you here - save me a trip." says a familiar voice behind me. I turn around, surprised to see the shaggy weather-beaten face of none other than Cappy. He's wearing the same faded sea captain's hat as he was in the airport, along with a striped tee and jeans that might have been white, once upon a time. More importantly, he's holding my backpack.

"Cappy!" I exclaim, taking my bag. "I am so glad to see you! I didn't think I'd ever see this thing again."

"Pleasure's all mine, Son," he says. "Sorry, I couldn't bring this back sooner. The crew kept me so busy, testing out the new parasail and such. Just lucky I was there today when the mishap happened. Followed the cat back in to make sure everyone got back safe."

"I can't thank you enough," I say, rifling through the contents of my bag. Everything is still tucked neatly in its place.

"Maybe I can buy you a drink or something?"

"No, no, sorry! That will have to wait till tomorrow, unfortunately." Rob strides over, interrupting. "I apologize, Cappy, I do appreciate you bringing Jackson's bag by. Maybe you can come back tomorrow night after dinner? I hear there's going to be a karaoke contest. Maybe you can sing a sea shanty or something?" Rob winks at the sea captain before turning back to Rory, "Listen, Rory, I need you to go check in with the crew. I want the gazebo set up and ready to shoot STAT. Let's get it going while we still have some light."

"We don't have time to buy Cappy *one* drink?" I ask skeptically.

"No," Rob says. "We're moving up the schedule. We're going to shoot the Shell Ceremony in one hour. I'm sending everyone back to their rooms for a quick shower and to freshen up. I want to shoot while the near-death experience memories are still fresh."

"Oh. So soon! Marco will need to wash his hair and apply moisturizer!" Marco exclaims, looking around anxiously.

"Chop chop!" Rob hurries us along with a karate chop gesture. "We'll send someone from hair and make-up straight to your room, Marco. There's no shooting this episode without our handsome host!"

"Isn't anyone going to tell us what happened out there?" Isla asks Rob as Marco dives into another waiting golf cart.

"I would," Rob says, "but I'd rather save it for the camera. The story's always better when it's fresh. See you both back at the gazebo in an hour." He jumps in the golf cart beside Marco and taps the driver to get going.

"Well, that was rude," I say to Isla. "They didn't even offer us a lift."

# isla

. . .



*"I gotta say, I was afraid of this. This is what happens when you defy logic. Total chaos."*

~Jackson Porter, *Playing With Matches Confessionals*

THE GAZEBO HAS BEEN SET up like a living room again, this time with four colorfully upholstered, outdoor loveseats flanking a tall, tiled throne embedded with shells and topped off with tridents for finials. The furniture has been arranged in a horseshoe shape around a large fire pit. The firelight makes the blue, cut-glass filler in the center of the bowl sparkle like diamonds. Three large conch shells rest on the ledge of the firepit, each one personalized with one of the female contestants' names.

Once again, Jackson and I are watching on the monitors from the production tent, but this time the flap is propped open, so we also have a wider view of everything that's happening in the gazebo. We're anxious to finally hear Chloe tell the story of what happened on the boat earlier.

"It all started when Lacey got stung by the sea urchin," she explains to Marco, who is seated on the throne, presiding over the group. Chloe looks gorgeous in a simple, sparkly, black gown. No injuries. She seems more annoyed than stressed. She brushes her long blonde locks away from her face. "I took a look at it. I could see it wasn't a serious injury, but it was the reason for the pissing match."

"Pissing match? What is this?" Marco asks. He too, is freshly showered, shaved, and coiffed. I don't know how he managed to get so pretty so fast. It takes me at least an hour just to blow dry my hair.

Ryker, who is seated with Darwin on one of the loveseats to Marco's left, snorts. Darwin looks away, appearing slightly shamed-faced.

"Maybe Lacey should tell you this part?" Chloe wrinkles her nose at the woman seated next to her. "I'm not sure I can even explain what happened next." Behind the cameraman, Rob is shaking his head at Marco, and pointing both index fingers at Darwin.

"No, Marco will ask Darwin," Marco smoothly takes the hint. "Come on, Darwin, tell Marco."

"This is so good," I whisper in Jackson's ear. "I feel like I'm watching a real TV show."

"That's because you *are*," he whispers back. "I just hope this isn't going where I think it is."

"So, Darwin, now you will tell us what happened?" Marco cajoles. "We want to hear what it was like for you."

"Well, Marco, I was genuinely concerned about Lacey, and I know when someone gets stung by an urchin, you're supposed to pee on them," Darwin speaks bluntly.

"No. That's a myth," Chloe calls out, still irritated. "Peeing does nothing for urchin stings. You're thinking of jellyfish, and even then, it's not the best way to treat a jellyfish sting. I tried to tell them, but they wouldn't listen."

Darwin might be blushing, but it's hard to tell given the fact that he's so sunburned. His face is pink and shiny, just a shade or two off from his cerise polo shirt.

"I tried to tell them, too," Owen comments from the far corner where he is sitting alone.

Lacey, who is wearing a short red dress and matching lip gloss, raises her hand and waves it like a student vying to be called on in class. She's got a large white bandage on her hand, but it doesn't seem to be affecting her ability to seek attention. If anything, it makes her stand out more.

"Yes, Lacey?" Marco says.

"Darwin didn't know," Lacey explains. "And neither did me or Ryker. It was an honest mistake. I was in a lot of pain, and they were like my knights in shining armor, Marco. Neither one of them could bear to see me suffering." She purses her lips and preens, batting her lashes at the two men. I think the face she's making is supposed to signify gratitude. It's hard to tell though. She's had so much botox that all her expressions look the same.

"Nah. That's no excuse for what happened," Owen, who is freshly shaved and showered, makes a disgusted face and shakes his head. "Dudes can't just be whipping it out and getting into duels like that. Especially on a boat. I don't think I'll ever get that image out of my head, guys."

"To be fair," Ryker says, elbowing Darwin, "We'd tossed back a few drinks at this point. Right, Mate?"

"Yeah," Darwin nods emphatically and shoots Ryker a grateful look. "Ryker and I chose to stay on the boat and chill while the others were swimming. I was pretty lit. And I had to go real bad."

Rob waves both arms to get Marco's attention again.

"So," Marco slowly reads off the cards Rob is holding up. "You might say this was your *golden opportunity*?"

Rob gives the thumbs-up sign, and the entire cast groans. It takes a couple of seconds for Marco to translate and understand the joke in his head, but when he does, it's apparent. His eyes fly open wider.

"I didn't think I'd ever say this, but I was kind of glad to be vision-impaired at that point," Paula suddenly says, speaking in Marco's general direction. She's not turned toward any of the cameras, but one of the cameramen pivots to zoom in on her face. She's wearing a light pink satin floral minidress and a matching pair of pink, cat-eye sunglasses festooned with rhinestones.

"This must have been so scary for you," Marco says to Paula. He stands to walk to her loveseat. "What did you think? Did you know what was going on?"

"Well," Paula reaches out to feel for Marco when he sits in the empty seat beside her.

"I'm right here, Bella," Marco says, reaching out and holding her hand to his face. Paula startles but doesn't pull her hand away. Her face blooms into a smile as she explores his features with her fingertips.

"So this is what you look like," she marvels, running her fingers along his jaw and patting his lips. "I always wondered, but it was hard to know since I can't actually see the covers."

"I hope Marco lives up to your fantasy," he says.

"Your lips are very soft," she smiles, finally pulling her hand away. "High cheekbones. And your jawline is so firm. Exactly how I imagined." She sighs happily.

"Well," Marco fans himself. "It is getting warm in here, no?"

"Can I say something?" Ryker stands to speak. He's the most casually dressed cast member by far. He has shown up wearing a cartoon character tee and lounge pants that I suspect might also be his pajamas. His Australian accent seems extra pronounced tonight. "I don't think anyone should be blaming me. I was just doing what anyone would do. Darwin was way too drunk to aim. He was pissing all over the deck. Not to brag or anything, but I happen to have a precision stream. Time was of the essence. And I just wanted to get the job done properly?"

"Uggghhh! *Nobody* needed to pee on Lacey," Chloe argues. "Even the medic on board said so. He tried to stop them. That was when all hell broke loose. The medic slipped on the pee and fell, and Ryker started swinging."

Marco stands to go back to his sofa, rubbing his temples as if it's difficult to keep it all straight.

Rory holds up another card offstage. It reads: ASK ABOUT THE FIRE.

"Okay," Marco says, "but what about the fire?"

"The fire happened when the chef ran out from the kitchen to break up the fight," Lacey volunteers. "He forgot he left something on the stove."

"I was really looking forward to that bacon quesadilla," Ryker laments.

"I was really looking forward to doing more snorkeling," Owen says dejectedly. "We barely got a chance to see anything before the group date crashed and burned. Literally."

"Well, Marco sees you all have bonded over this experience. Tell me, what do you think about your choices from the other day? Would you play your cards the same way now?" Marco questions the group and proceeds to quiz the contestants individually. "Chloe, would you still choose Ryker?"

She laughs and rolls her eyes. "No way. No offense, Dude, I just don't think there's any way," she acknowledges Ryker.

"No worries. None was taken," Ryker shrugs it off. "I'd still choose Lacey if you asked me today. If she'd have me. I think I've made my intentions clear."

"What about you, Lacey? Do you still want to go on a date with Owen?" Marco says.

"Pass! Some firefighter. I didn't see him lift a finger to save me. Let alone get out his *hose*." Lacey winks at Ryker and I see Owen shudder.

Jackson nudges me with his knee and brushes my hair aside to whisper in my ear again. His hand lingers on my neck. "Check that out; it looks like your longshot choice, Ryker and Lacey, might have a chance."

"Well, guys, you know what time it is. Marco is sorry to do this to all of you. But it is time for Cupidbot to reveal the algorithm's picks for you, at which time we will perform the Shell Ceremony and decide who stays and who, if anyone, goes home.

"Ladies, you may have noticed that you each have a conch shell with your name on it. Now is the time when you will give your shell to the man you have been matched with, or, if you prefer, with another man, asking him if he will accept your offering."

"Cut!" Rob shouts. "Great work everyone! Let's get reset for the ceremony real quick. Women grab your shells, and let's lose the throne. Where's the robot?"

"Already on it!" Rory waves the controls for Cupidbot, who is rolling out onto the set playing the show's theme song.

"Ugh, I hate that song so much," Jackson says, plugging his ears.

When the robot spins around, I notice he is no longer brandishing the AI Swiper label across his digital butt.

"You got them to remove the brand name?" I ask. "How'd you do that?"

"I made that call," Jackson says. "They'll photoshop the new name in after."

"Which is? I ask.

"Let me know if you have any ideas."

Lacey and Chloe stand to retrieve their shells, but Marco grabs for Paula's. "Let me help you, Bella," he says.

**"WE'RE ROLLING AGAIN!"** Rob calls out.

"Welcome back, Friends," Macro smiles. "It is now time for the Shell Ceremony. These special conch shells have been harvested, cleaned, blessed, and painted by local craftspeople." Marco holds Paula's shell up for the camera, angling it so the camera can see the detailed painting of the sunset sky and Paula's name on the side.

The camera zooms in on Marco, caressing the shell, which he now holds to his cheek.

"By sharing and blowing on the shells, we are creating a sacred and intimate space for love to bloom.

"Paula, you will go first," Marco says, gently placing the shell in her hands. "The algorithm has made a selection for you. You must now make a decision. Will you choose to stay and pursue that recommendation, or will you choose someone else? Cupidbot, will you tell us who Paula has matched with?"

The robot rolls to Marco's side, blinking and beeping as images of all three men flash on the screen. Finally, it stops on Owen.

"Lucky Owen," Marco says, "He has matched with you, Bella Paula. What will you do?" Marco grasps her hand and Paula stands. She holds the shell aloft.

"Owen, I know we barely know each other, but if the algorithm says we are a match, I think we deserve to at least give this thing a try. Let's make the most of the rest of our time here together. What do you think? Will you accept my shell?"

"Sure, why not," Owen smiles and walks over to take the shell from her hands. "Paula, I accept this shell and want to send the message back. Do you hear my call?" He lifts the shell to his lips, and then he blows. Or rather he tries to. The sound that comes out sounds a lot like the air being let out of a wet balloon.

"Did anyone think to have these men practice blowing conch shells?" I whisper to Jackson.

"It's not that easy," Jackson acknowledges. "I had one as a kid, and I spent ages making fart sounds on that thing before I could get it to sound halfway decent."

"Maybe you need to show them how it's done," I suggest.

Jackson just shakes his head at me.

We both watch as Owen tries again, cheeks puffing out and face growing red. It sounds even worse.

"Keep rolling! We'll fix it in post," Rob shouts.

Owen takes a seat next to Paula, and Marco moves on to Lacey.

"Lacey, you have a tough choice to make," Marco gestures for her to join him with her shell at the center of the horseshoe ring. "It seems like you have two men fighting for you. Which one will you choose?"

"I don't know. What does that thing say I should do?" Lacey asks. Everyone watches the animation on Cupidbot's head flip back and forth between Ryker and Darwin, eventually stopping on a picture of Ryker. Darwin looks incredibly dejected when he sees this. But he forces himself to keep his chin up when Ryker grasps his hand. The two men lock arms, biceps bulging as they await Lacey's verdict.

Everything else pauses while the cameramen shoot several long takes of Lacey gazing at Darwin and Ryker, who are both standing tensely, hopefully staring back at her. She appears to be agonizing over the decision. The camera zooms in as her eyes fill with tears and she dramatically fans her face.

"Jesus, just get it over with. And why is she doing that hand thing?" Jackson asks.

"She probably doesn't want her mascara to run," I answer.

"She'd better pick Ryker," Jackson says.

"Patience," Isla says. "Let it ride. It will all work out."

Chloe is also starting to tear up, as she realizes that she has gone from all of the men being interested in her to none of the men being a great prospect.

"I choose," Lacey pauses dramatically. I hold my breath till she finishes the sentence, "Ryker."

"Yasss!" Ryker punches the air and skips over to Lacey, lifting her in the air and kissing her. "She's my Laceyboo!" He exclaims gleefully.

"Ryker, will you accept my shell?" Lacey thrusts the conch shell at him.

"Hells yeah, Babe," he holds it up to his lips and blows out a wet-sounding honk that reminds me of a constipated goose. "Do you hear my call?"

The camera follows Ryker carrying Lacey back to his loveseat.

"So this leaves Chloe and Darwin. It is up to you both if you stay or if you go." Marco gazes gravely at the last two in the group.

Chloe stands, head held high, maintaining her dignity.

"I think she's going to quit. Shit!" Jackson squeezes my hand.

"Shhhh...." I squeeze back. "Let it ride."

"I've never had a hard time finding dates," Chloe says. "In fact the opposite is true. I've never been skipped over like this and left all alone. I can't lie, it's been tough," she says. "But I'm not a quitter. And Darwin - we had a great time hanging out at the picnic that first day. I know I'm not the girl you're hoping for right now, but if the algorithm matched us, don't we owe it to ourselves to give this thing a shot? Darwin, will you accept my shell?"

Jackson exhales in relief beside me, still holding my hand.

"Okay, fine, whatever, you gotta be in it to win it," Darwin says, coming around the firepit to stand awkwardly beside her. He doesn't even attempt to blow the conch shell. Instead, he holds it up to his mouth making fake kazoo noises. "Doot doot doo doo - Chloe, do you hear my call?"

The whole time he's doing it, he's staring longingly in Lacey and Ryker's direction.

"Cut! That's a wrap!" Rory shouts. "Great work everyone. I know today was tough. Take tomorrow to relax. We have some fun dates planned for all three couples in the afternoon, and tomorrow night we'll be doing a karaoke takeover at the resort's pub!"

Jackson and I spill out of the tent and rush over to the gazebo to give high fives. Rob reminds us both that we need to shoot confessionals tonight, weighing in on the results of the ceremony.

"Want to grab dinner with me, first?" Jackson asks hopefully.

"Sorry, she can't." Rob slides between us, linking arms with me. "Isla is all mine tonight. We have to get right on it with planning the dates for our couples. But thanks for everything so far, Jackson, and no sweat about the logo. Just get a new one to us by the end of the week, and we'll fix everything in post. I think we only have to record a couple of pickups."

"I'm free if you want to grab something right now," Rory grabs Jackson's arm, and I feel an unfamiliar surge of possessiveness shoot through me. I don't like her touching him. It triggers such a nasty feeling when she does. Like an emotional gag reflex.

She was also awfully clingy at the pier, too.

I don't want to know, but of course I do. Her stray thoughts are like a word cloud floating above her head. A cloud filled with things like "snack," "hit that," and "shoulda waxed." Jumbled, but suggestive. I don't have to be an expert code-cracker to figure out what she's thinking about.

"Don't take too long, Rory," Rob cautions. "I know you gotta eat but I need you back here ASAP. Maybe you just fill a few plates with stuff for all of us and bring it back?"

Rory pouts. "I am not your PA, Rob. Send someone else."

"I'm happy to bring some food back if you let me know what you want. Or in Isla's case, what I want." Jackson winks at me.

After Jackson takes everyone's order and heads off towards the buffet, Rob and I take a seat back in the production tent. Rob rolls up his sleeves and leans back in his chair.

"This is where it all finally starts to come together, Isla. Let's make some magic."

# jackson

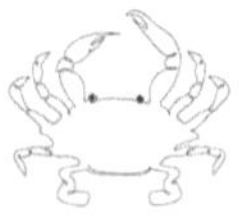

*"There's probably nothing sexier than a good sense of humor, is there? Let's hope everyone left room in their baggage for a little bit of that."*

*~Isla Fairfax, Playing With Matches Confessionals*

WHEN I GET up for my run the next morning, Isla surprises me. She's already up and dressed in white shorts and a flowy pink-and-green patterned top.

"Morning!" she tucks a small, amber glass vial in her pocket.

"Going somewhere?" I ask her.

"I thought I'd take a walk on the beach, do some meditation, and then check in with the crew to make sure the details for all the dates are coming together," Isla says. "You going for a run?"

"I was thinking about it, but honestly, I'm a little sore from windsurfing. I'd rather take a walk. Mind if I tag along?"

"Sure, I'd love that," she says.

The air is moist and fresh and pleasantly cool thanks to an early morning shower. When we get to the waterfront path, the sun bursts out from behind a cloud and the sky lights up in technicolor. Isla gasps with delight, grabs my hand, and drags me down toward the beach.

"Look - another double rainbow!" she says excitedly. "Second one in two days? It's such a good sign!"

"It's not a sign, Isla. It's an atmospheric occurrence. It's refraction. I think it happens a lot here because of ocean currents and rapidly changing weather."

"Which is *magical*," she utters sagely. "Which color is your favorite, Jackson?"

"I don't know, black?" I say, noticing we're still holding hands. I can't recall the last time I held hands with anyone as an adult. Most of my encounters with the female kind don't involve a lot of innocent hand holding. Isla laces her fingers between mine. It feels so nice. So easy. She swings our arms.

"Don't be like that. Black is not a color. And I know you know that."

"Fine," I glance around at the lush vegetation just beyond the sand. "Green. I like how green it is here. Every shade of green."

The greenery on the island puts even Washington State to shame. Everything is supersaturated, like Isla's wardrobe. It's like stepping into Oz.

"I like green, too," Isla agrees animatedly, glancing down at her top. "Especially with pink. Such a great combo, and diametric opposites on the color wheel. It creates good vibrations."

"Right," I say, raising a skeptical eyebrow. But her colorful shirt does make me smile. The little palm trees and flamingos are so cheerful. Or maybe it's just Isla.

We take the path down to the beach and stroll along the shoreline in the wet sand. The beach isn't crowded yet. In fact, there's barely anyone in sight. Early mornings here are my favorite time. I love how simple and genuine morning tasks are. There's no subterfuge in hosing down the patios and setting up the beach chairs. Nobody's faking anyone out or tricking them when they put out towels or make breakfast. It's too early for fakeness. Fakeness is a post-coffee activity.

We separate when we stop at the water's edge. We let go of each other's hands so we can kick off our shoes and walk barefoot in the sand. But the minute I let go of Isla's hand, I feel like something is missing, like someone adjusted the screen and not in a good way. The colors are duller. The sand is less velvety. The humidity seems more cloying.

Isla reaches into her pocket and pulls out the vial. She unscrews the lid, and I see that it's got a roller ball top. She rolls it on her palms and rubs her hands together. Then she stops, cups her hands, and breathes in deeply. Three times.

"What are you doing?" I ask her.

"Just a little cleansing breathing." She holds out the vial and I sniff it. "Peppermint always sets me straight. Want some?"

"No, thanks," I decline the offer, shaking out my arms and legs and bouncing on my feet. "I'm not into that stuff. There's nothing magic about essential oils."

"What are *you* doing?" she cocks her head and puts her hands on her hips.

"Just shaking it out," I say.

"So you're not into oils, but you're into somatic practice?" Isla bites her lip and reaches out her hand. "Give me your hand, Jackson,"

"No," I instinctively tuck my hands under my armpits. "What's somatic practice, now?"

"It's a way of releasing anxiety and trauma," Isla says. "By shaking it out. It's very effective, especially when done with intention."

"Don't be silly," I say, suddenly self-conscious. "I am not releasing trauma. I just do it because it feels good. Helps me focus."

"Okay," she says, the corners of her mouth tweaking into a smile. "So here's an idea. Let's do a little experiment. You try my oil, and I'll try shaking it out, and we can report back to each other. You'll have to talk me through it though. I've always been curious but I've never tried doing any kind of bodywork like that."

"You want me to talk you through shaking it out?" I ask, thinking that this is something I want to see. I want to see Isla shaking it out on the beach.

"Yes, I don't know how to do it myself."

"Okay, but you're going to have to do everything I tell you. My method only works if you follow the routine religiously," I say, with as much authority as I can while smirking inside.

"Wait. I thought you didn't even know what somatic practice is?" She says suspiciously.

"I don't. In my practice, we have always called it Kepo Key," I vamp.

"Fine. Oil first," she says. I hold out my hands and she runs the roller ball in circles on my palms. "You'll be glad to know that this also helps repel mosquitoes."

"Hey, that tickles," I complain, snatching my hands away.

"Rub your hands together, and then pretend you are holding a sacred bowl. The bowl is filled with peaceful thoughts. Place your face in the bowl and— No, don't touch your eyes, Jackson!"

"You said to place my face in the bowl!" I complain. My eyes are watering and stinging.

"I'm sorry. Place your face *above* the bowl and breathe in. Breathe in that peace and calm, imagining the contents of the bowl filling you up as you take them in."

"That's silly," I wipe my hands on my shirt. "But thanks for bug repellent." I take a deep breath and smile. The mint is refreshing and although my eyes are still watering, the humidity no longer feels so oppressive. The greens are greener again. Not that I'd ever admit that.

"Your turn," I say, rubbing my hands together in anticipation. It intensifies the smell of the mint, which I swear is now making me tingle in all my hair follicles from my scalp to my balls. How is that possible? I didn't touch my balls without realizing it, did I?

"Ready?" I say. "We can take it slow since you're new to this. Stand on your right foot."

"Like this?" She gracefully adopts a tree pose. I only know the name of this pose because of Alexis's annoying yoga phase. She tried to get the whole podcast crew to do it with her.

"No, not like tree pose," I say. "And close your eyes. Hold your left leg out in front of you. Imagine a circle drawn in the sand in front of you. Stretch your left leg into the circle."

She looks so serious. She's even pointing her toes.

"Good, good, now move it back to neutral," I walk to stand behind her, "And… back into the circle," I reach out to steady her when she wobbles, briefly putting my hands on her hips.

"When do we do the shaking part?" she asks.

"Now actually," I say. "We're almost there. I want you to repeat the motions and then at the end, you're going to shake your leg vigorously, okay? I think you're ready to speed it up and put it all together. Return to a neutral position, and then on the count of three, follow my lead, got it?"

"Okay, let's do it," she nods gravely.

"All right then," I say, launching into the song. *"You put your left foot in, you put your left foot out, you put your left foot in and you shake it all about…."*

Isla's eyes fly open. She freezes. "Kepo Key? Hokey Pokey? Very funny."

Tears are rolling down my face now, and it is not just the mint. But the mint isn't bad at all. It's lovely. As is Isla. Her face is flaming, and her eyes are shooting blue sparks. "OMG, Isla, thank you, I haven't laughed like this since my little sister–"

Isla flies at me. "I am going to kill you, Jackson Porter!" She says while tackling me and taking me down to the sand. "I will make you pay!"

Her fingers fly under my shirt, seeking out pressure points, and making me squirm.

"Are you tickle torturing me?" I gasp, underneath her. "What are you, twelve?"

"What are you? Seven? You tried to make me do the hokey pokey!"

"Stop!" I beg, not sure whether I want to laugh or moan. She is sitting on top of me, reaching her fingers into my armpit. The tips of her fragrant hair tease my face like feathers, joining the tickle campaign. But her breasts smashed against me and the way her hips are rocking?

*That's the torture right there.*

"Say Uncle," she purses her lips and sits up straight, looking down at me. I stifle the urge to buck up against her.

"Never," I retort, sitting up and grabbing her hands easily. Our palms lock and fingers interlace. Tighter this time. Both of us are exerting pressure, pushing each other. Testing our strength. Matching one another. It's just enough to maintain balance, any more or less and we'd topple over.

Her shirt has flown up, caught in the breeze and I catch a glimpse of her delicate architecture as her ribs are bared. And above that a sheer, green lacy bra, no mistaking the rosy, pebbled peaks of her nipples shining through. The best combination of pink and green that I've ever seen.

Pupils wide, heart pounding, mouth-watering, we hover like this till I'm overwhelmed by my almost vampire-like thirst to possess her. My abs are trembling. My nuts ache.

"Isla," I say her name, not even sure what I mean to say next. I ease our hands down to the sand.

"Jackson?" She arches her back, and I die a little with the need to pull her against me.

"Yes?" I say, turning my head, holding my breath, and listening. I swear I can hear her heart pounding.

Isla shifts her weight and exhales, as if she's come to a decision.

"Was there anything else you wanted to talk to me about?"

I release her hands, lift her off me, and drop back, lying flat on my back on the sand and staring at the impossibly blue sky, I take a deep breath and exhale, still smelling the peppermint oil. Isla stretches out beside me.

The mint does help clear my mind.

"I just wanted to check in to see how you were feeling about the dates. There have been too many curveballs at every stage. I don't think you understand how much I have riding on this,"

Isla sighs as she props herself up on her elbow. "I have a reputation to protect too, you know?"

"I know."

"Well, I still believe a love match is possible for everyone, despite your software's obvious issues and limitations."

"Limitations? Issues? What exactly are you talking about?" I sit up and brush the sand away.

"I'm sorry, but your app is flawed." Isla sits up too and crosses her legs. Despite looking like a wild child with tousled hair and sand stuck to her knees, she speaks with certainty and quiet authority. "If you re-collected the data and ran everyone's profiles now that they've met, you'd get different results."

"I doubt it," I scoff. "They're all adults. Their personalities are pretty well set."

"Being an adult has nothing to do with it." Isla shakes her head, looking at me with an expression somewhere between pity and wonder. "Don't you think people are capable of change?"

"In theory?" I ask. "I guess. But it's unlikely that change will stick. It's like teeth after you wear braces. Without a retainer, they tend to revert to their naturally fucked-up state."

"Maybe that's true with teeth," Isla says. "But people aren't static like that. They don't have a natural state. People are constantly changing. Your DNA is changing as we speak, and that's a factor of a million little things. The sunlight, exercise, your *libido*,…" she shrugs and pauses to look into my eyes. "Don't even get me started on chemistry. How can anyone trust an app that totally ignores that?"

"Chemistry is overrated." I fold my arms across my chest.

"No, it's not," Isla rises on her knees and scoots forward until she is kneeling between my legs. Her hands reach around to tangle in my hair. She dips her head down, aligning her cheek beside mine. She then turns her head until her lips are a fraction of an inch from mine. I can feel her breath. My heart speeds up.

"You have a surprisingly yellow aura for such a grumpy guy, Jackson," Isla traces a finger along my jawline and over my lower lip where the bite has almost fully healed.

"What color is your aura then?" I ask.

"Blue," she sighs, playing with my hair. "Do you know what happens when our auras collide?"

"Green?" I guess. And although I can't see the glow, somehow I believe her. I believe her because the moment she touches me, my favorite color seems to grow brighter.

"Mmm hmmm," she says, almost but not quite kissing me. Her lips brush mine without touching, yet close enough to feel.

"What do the colors mean?" I ask.

"Blue is about intuition. Yellow is about happiness," she murmurs.

"And green?" I whisper.

"Look it up on the internet," she smiles.

"You're a terrible tease, Isla Fairfax," I groan as I pull a strand of beach grass from her hair.

"Chemistry is *not* overrated, Jackson Porter."

"Move your shirt," I demand.

"What for?" she asks.

"Lupercalia," I tap the folded strand of beach grass against her cleavage. "Much more eco-friendly than the goat leather."

"You're crazy," Isla shakes her head at me.

"And you're beautiful," I say. I want to kiss her. I want to stay here all day. I want to forget about everything else.

"What I am is starving," Isla places her hands on my shoulders and rises to a standing position.

"Me, too. But not for breakfast," I admit.

"No, but it'll have to suffice for now," she holds out a hand to help me up. "We have a show to do."

"**HOW DO** you think the dates will go today?" I ask on the way back to the resort.

"I feel great about Ryker and Lacey," Isla says.

"That's cocky," I say.

"You don't even know what we planned for them," she pouts. "Have a little faith!"

"I know how incompatible they are," I shrug.

"Yeah, but they have *chemistry*," Isla playfully pokes me in the ribs. "Have you learned nothing this morning?"

"I think their chemistry is too explosive, and it may be all they've got. You don't make a cart move forward by lighting a stick of dynamite behind it."

"We'll see," Isla shrugs. "I have a good feeling about all the dates."

"Is that a premonition kind of feeling?" I ask.

"Not specifically," Isla frowns, considering. "I just have a strong sense that everything's going to work out for the best."

The buffet is in full swing as we get there, with a decadent spread of pancakes, waffles, fresh pastries, a juice bar, and an omelet station. My stomach rumbles. I could get used to resort living.

Isla waves cheerily to Marco who is already seated at a table. The excitement on his face as he stands and gestures to the chair for her makes my stomach churn. Eels again.

We stop at the coffee bar where Isla grabs two mugs and fills them with coffee. I grab her some creamer.

"I think I need to sit and drink this coffee before we grab our food," she says, pointing to the table where Marco is waiting. She sets the coffee down, and he stands to embrace her and smacks wet kisses on both of her cheeks. I imagine his head turning into the head of an ass. It helps. A little. I dump the creamers and lug over a chair for myself.

"Have you gentlemen thought about what you will sing at karaoke tonight?" Isla asks.

"I wasn't planning on singing tonight," I say. I'm not interested in the attention. I don't like showing off. I take a swig of the coffee. "How about you?"

"I'm totally tone deaf, trust me, nobody wants me to sing," Isla laughs.

"I beg to differ. I'm pretty sure I could scare up the karaoke version of Veruca Salt's song for you," I offer. "It doesn't require a huge vocal range."

Isla rolls her eyes at me. "We could make it a duet. You can sing the grumpy Oompa Loompa parts."

"I'm so sorry, orange is not my color," I mock apologize.

"How about you Marco?" Isla asks. She spies Rob on his way in and waves him over to the table.

"Morning, All!" Rob says. He's freshly showered and shaved and appears to be crackling with energy, as usual. "I am so happy to see my three awesome musketeers all bright and bushy-tailed and ready to rock it today! What are you chatting about here?"

"I just asked Marco if he was planning to sing at karaoke tonight," Isla says.

Rob rubs his chin, considering Marco, then he turns back to Isla. "I sure hope so! There is nothing more romantic than a man serenading a woman, is there?"

My heart quickens.

"Yes! Yes! Marco agrees," Marco bobs his head enthusiastically, as he smears butter onto a bacon slice. "Marco is trying to choose which song. I cannot decide between 'Isla Bonita' and 'Rock You Like a Hurricane.'"

He waggles his eyebrows as he says the second title, and I find myself clenching my fists under the table.

That's it. It's on for karaoke.

*Marco is going down.*

# isla

. . .

*"It's not everyone's idea of a perfect first date, but I'm partial to axe throwing. There's no need for reading the tea leaves. It's a hit or miss kind of situation."*

*~Jackson Porter, Playing with Matches Confessionals*

"OMG YOU GUYS," Rory says when we meet her at the production tent before dinner. "We got some great footage today. Hopefully, you'll both have some thoughts about the way the individual dates went. But try to save your comments for the confessionals? Rob would prefer it if we don't discuss too much amongst ourselves."

"Okay, Mom," Jackson rolls his eyes like a teenager.

"Now I'm a mom? I thought I was too young for you," Rory replies tartly. Jackson pays her no mind, but I see her watching him. I can almost feel the acidic burn of unrequited longing that's stuck in her throat. Too bad there's no antacid to cure that.

If there were, I might have to procure some of it for myself at some point soon. I want Jackson Porter so badly. But not in any kind of way that I can realistically have him.

I'm still not sure who that chemistry lesson on the beach was for. Which one of us was I testing?

I know Jackson wants me. I even know some of the *things he wants to do to me.* And, shockingly, none of them bother me. Normally when I catch a guy thinking about something naughty involving me in a fantasy, it's a complete and total turn-off. It isn't actually about me – the *person* – at all. I feel like I've clicked into an awkward porno starring the puppet version of me. I can't close that window fast enough. It's the opposite of intimate. It makes me feel objectified and dehumanized. Gross.

But when I catch a glimpse of what Jackson's thinking? It's different. I want to do the things to him that he's imagining. I want him to do those things to me. Those *exact* things. So much so that I've lost track of where his fantasies stop and mine begin. The line is fuzzy like the overlap of our auras. Green.

Green for horny, he thought. I didn't dare tell him it's the color of the heart chakra. The color of love. It would have made him bolt. Instead, I was the one to step away.

"Whose date do you want to start with?" Rory asks.

"Lacey and Ryker," Jackson says. "They are the couple that I'm the least hopeful for."

"This should be good," I clasp my hands together. "Did they enjoy going to the spa together?"

"Uh… you might say," Rory says, pulling up the footage on the computer. "We've got a few great clips. I'm not even sure what trope these two are, but it's steamy."

"Princess and Sasquatch, clearly," Jackson supplies. "It's one of the Beauty and the Beast variants." When Rory stares open-mouthed at him, he holds up his hands and shrugs. "What? I am an expert. I do a podcast about this stuff, remember?"

Rory rolls the tape. The footage on the screen shows the two of them getting a couples massage.

"We'll just leave you two here alone to *relax*," the attendant says as she leaves the candlelit room where our two contestants are oiled up and blissed out, nakedly relaxing under thin sheets.

"Oh, jeez. Do we have to watch it? I mean, did they," he uses hand gestures to try to encompass all his horror, "and did it keep recording?" Jackson turns his head sideways and squinches his eyes.

"You have a dirty mind, Jackson," Rory admonishes. "Believe it or not, they both fell asleep. Pretty boring footage. But a little after lunch there was this." She fast-forwards to the spot she is seeking. Ryker and Lacey are lounging on cushioned chaise lounges in a private courtyard, a bubbling Jacuzzi in the background. They are both wearing robes and he's feeding her strawberries. We see a bubbling flute of champagne.

"I'll just fast forward to the good part."

Lacey is straddling Ryker. Robes and towels are coming off, being flung left and right. Something lands over the camera lens, cutting off the view.

"And then after there was this." She fast forwards again.

*"I can't explain it, Ryker. There's something about you. When I'm near you, I get butterflies."*

"Oh no she didn't," Jackson's head is in his hands.

"What?" Rory and I both look at him.

"She used the 'butterflies' line." Jackson groans. "It's the third-most overused reality show phrase. Right after 'not here for the right reasons' and 'Can I grab you for a sec?' You know what's next right? The 'I think I might be falling in love with you.''

"Dude. How much reality TV do you watch?" Rory pulls a face.

"Most of the people on these shows are in it for the exposure," Jackson says. "At the risk of sounding like a cliché, I am not so sure these two are here for the right reasons."

"I have everything I need. I'm happy. They have heat," Rory says.

"Just because they were attracted to each other doesn't mean that they are a great match," Jackson says. "Lots of people are attracted to each other who maybe shouldn't be."

The space triangulates, as Jackson meets my eyes, and I look away in time to see the way Rory is looking at him and at me taking stock.

"Show us Darwin and Chloe next?" I request, doing my best to break the tension.

"Their date was super sweet," Rory zips through a bunch of footage of the two of them volunteering at the children's clinic. "I mean nothing earth-shattering or dramatic, but lots of giggling and some heartfelt moments. Especially this one."

She stops on a scene where the two contestants are helping to paint a mural on the wall. Noah's Ark? They appear to be painting a couple of goats. But suddenly Darwin is overwhelmed with emotion. He attempts to wipe the tears from his eyes and ends up streaking paint all over his face. Chloe stops what she's doing and attempts to comfort him.

*"It's okay, Darwin. You can tell me anything. I'm a nurse,"* she *says.*

*"I guess I just always had to be strong, you know. There was no room for weakness in our house. My brothers needed me. I'd like to think Gampy would be proud of me now,"* Darwin *chokes out, voice cracking.*

*"Oh Darwin, I'm sure he would,"* Chloe *takes the paintbrush from his hand and embraces him.*

The camera zooms in on the tears in Darwin's eyes. They spill over and leave a trail on his cheek.

"Poor Darwin," I say. "Who was he talking about? His grandpa?"

"His frat's mascot! Gampy the goat got taken away by animal protective services. Having him in the house was a code violation," Rory snickers.

"Oh," I say, biting my lips. "That's not good."

"I think we can make something of this footage if we cut it right," Rory judges. "It's kind of a funny tender moment. He was very attached to the goat. More than he is attached to Chloe. We also captured this key moment after," Rory says.

In the later scene, Darwin is cleaned up and the couple is seated outside the clinic, holding hands. Darwin's speaking into the camera, looking incredibly uncomfortable.

*"I dunno, Chloe. I just don't know that I'm worthy. I think you might be–"*

Rory pauses the tape. "Does anybody want to guess the end of the sentence? Jackson?"

"Too good for me?" Jackson deadpans.

"Ding ding ding! We have a winner!" Rory points at Jackson. "But also - this date is a win for me. I'm good to go with this footage. The editor will be happy; he has plenty to work with."

"What about Owen and Paula?" Jackson asks hopefully.

"I hope they had fun. We had the hardest time coming up with their date," I admit.

"Because she's blind?" Rory asks.

"No, I mean, yes… that was part of it. But I just had a hard time picturing them doing an activity that they might bond over."

"So where did you send them?" Jackson asks.

"Nowhere," I say. "They stayed here at the resort. We finally settled on a sand-sculpting lesson. They were going to create sculptures of one another, and then they were supposed to share some homemade ice cream on the beach. How'd it go?"

"Meh. *Super* awkward. Although it did get a little interesting towards the end," Rory smirks.

"The ice cream?" I ask, hopefully.

"No, turns out Paula is lactose intolerant, so we had to cancel that."

Rory pulls up the footage of Owen patting sand onto a stiff and uncomfortable Paula.

"Yiiiiikes," Jackson says. "She does *not* look happy."

She fast forwards to an equally cringeworthy peek of Paula fumbling and accidentally putting sand on Owen's face.

"Most of it was like this. They were both stressed about touching each other, like, at all."

"Oof," Jackson says. "That is not good."

"It's not ideal, but cringe has its place on reality TV, too," Rory says. "Some would say it's almost as good as the mushy stuff. Cringe is a lot of people's kink," she pauses to consider this for a moment before continuing more animatedly. "Anyways, right before they finished, *this* randomly happened."

Rory fast-forwards and rewinds till she gets to the precise clip she wants to show us. Paula is still sitting on the beach, alone this time, and Marco comes to sit next to her. The two of them talk for a bit.

"She talked to Marco?" Jackson says. "Big deal."

"No, hang on," Rory goes forward about twenty seconds, and we see Paula feeling Marco's face, in slow, elaborate, painful detail. She runs her fingers over his left eyebrow, then his right, then both, as if comparing. Eyes, nose, lips, cheek, jaw, teeth.

"He just sat there for all that?" Jackson is incredulous. "Why?"

"Marco is a sweet guy," I defend him. "I think you got the wrong impression of him."

"She said she was 'memorizing his face,'" Rory says. "And then she did this – I'll just show you the picture, it's easier." Rory pulls out her phone and shows us Paula sitting next to a beautifully detailed sand sculpture - of Marco's face. It's a perfect likeness.

"Holy shit, Paula made that?" Jackson's jaw drops.

"Yeah," Rory laughs. "Imagine how pissed off the resort's 'expert' was to discover the student was better than the teacher."

"Wow," I marvel at the likeness. "That is amazing."

"Hang on a minute? Where was Owen while all that stuff was going on?" Jackson asks Rory.

"I think he went to get something to drink. He said he was starting to feel a little lightheaded from the heat, and he took off as soon as their lesson was done. Anyways, I don't think Paula minded."

Rory turns the TV monitor off. "All in all, I think it was a good day. I don't know about long-term commitments but I think we got plenty of footage for the show."

"Well," I say to Rory. "That's great news." I turn to Jackson. "Isn't it?"

"Yeah, I guess so," Jackson says. He stands to go.

"I'll let Rob know you two watched these. If you could both stop by the confessional tent and shoot a few soundbites for us to cut in, it would be great. Jackson, maybe you could talk about why you think these couples matched. And Isla, maybe you could talk about why you chose the activities you did for them?"

"No problem," I say. "I'm just so relieved things are working out for the most part."

"Me too," Rory says, sounding less stressed. "Will I see you at karaoke later?"

"I was planning on it," I say.

"Will either of you guys be singing?" Rory asks.

"No," I smile sweetly. "But I can't wait to see who will."

# jackson

. . .

*"Sometimes I wish Jackson would step back and look at the bigger picture. You can't fix everything with logic. Nothing about falling in love makes sense. He makes me so crazy sometimes!"*

*~Isla Fairfax, Playing With Matches Confessionals*

AFTER I TAKE my turn in the confessional booth, I head straight to the pool bar. I'm relieved to see Alexis is working there, and for once, she's alone. It seems like every other time I pass by, Owen is parked at the end of the bar on one of the stools. He's been spending so much time there, the stool practically needs a plaque with his name on it.

"Can I talk to you for a minute?" I ask.

"Of course," Alexis says, looking up curiously. She's wearing a tight Peaches Resort tee that she knotted at the waist with a pair of board shorts. Her curly dark brown hair is piled on top of her head.

"How's it going here for you?" I ask, glancing around to make sure nobody's lurking. If I'm going to confide in her, I don't want anyone else to be listening. I know I can trust

Alexis, but at this point, I'm not sure if I can trust anyone else here. Even Isla. Especially Isla. Every time I'm around her, it's like everything I think I know ends up in a blender. We start conversations, and I forget what I wanted to say. Every ball I'm determined to serve ends up rolling out of bounds, and the points I'm trying to make are suddenly pointless.

"It's going okay, I guess," Alexis sighs. "I'm in paradise, barely working for a few hours a day, so what have I got to complain about, right?" She smiles as she wipes down the bar.

"Yeah," I agree, taking a seat. "Make any hot new friends here that you might want to talk about on the podcast?" I wink suggestively at her, trying to summon our usual show banter.

Alexis throws a bar rag at me. "Shut up, Jackson."

"What?" I throw the rag back at her, defending myself. "Of everyone on the podcast, I'd have thought you'd be all over the whole vacation fling thing. You're the one always telling everyone else that one-night stands are the way to go."

"Well, talking about it on the podcast is one thing. Doing it in real life is another," Alexis looks wounded. "I'd have thought you would have known that about me by now."

I consider this for a moment. I've just always assumed that there's some fact to the promiscuous act that Alexis brings to the show.

"So you're *not* into one-night stands?" I ask.

"No, Jackson. I have never had a one-night stand." A shadow crosses her face. "At least, not intentionally."

"Okay," I drum my fingers on the bar, considering this. "That's good to know. I guess I just thought…."

"It's better for the *Lit Lovers* podcast, right? You and me talking about how we're just motivated by sex? It balances out Emily and Chelsea's romanticism and primness - no offense to your sister."

"None taken," I glanced at her, smiling gently. But now I'm curious. I can't believe I had to come to the Caribbean to learn something new about someone who has been in my close friend group for years. I do my best to reframe reality. "So you're not into casual sex then? I mean, I thought we were on the same page about the whole romance thing. You aren't going to tell me you're actually into all that mushy magical BS now are you?"

Alexis fixes me with a look of disgust like I've just tried to pass off dog food as filet mignon.

"Enough with your bullshit, Jackson Porter. Everyone knows you're the biggest romantic of us all. Out of everyone on the *Lit Lovers* podcast, *you're* the sappiest one."

"Come again?"

"You heard me. I said what I said. I think it's time for an Alexis exclusive. 'Truth bomb.'" Alexis pulls out a bottle of tequila and then scrabbles in a cabinet, pulling out a bottle of absinthe. She measures two shots of each into a shaker, shakes it with some ice, and then pours the vaguely green liquid into four tiny shot glasses.

"So what did you want to talk to me about?" She shoves one of the glasses at me.

I slam the shot, which is scandalously awful. The licorice edge of the absinthe doesn't play nice with tequila at all. But it distracts me for a moment as it goes down. Much pleasanter once it gets past my tastebuds. It coats my eel-infested innards. I can't get the image of Marco serenading Isla out of my head.

"You're not fooling me or anyone else. You're the most desperate of us all to find love, only you're too chickenshit to go for it." Alexis downs her own shot and places the empty glass face down on the bar, shuddering slightly. "God, I love me a good truth bomb. Always has a kick."

"I don't know what you're talking about," I insist. I take out my trusty clicky pen and draw a quick Venn diagram on a napkin. "I'm not even sure there is such a thing as love. I believe in friendship," I label one circle, "and I believe in sex," I label the other, "and I've even been lucky enough to experience a little overlap on occasion, here in the sweet spot."

I tap the center of the diagram, which is very suggestively shaped if you ask me. Why doesn't anyone ever mention this fact about Venn diagrams? Or maybe nobody else notices. Because they aren't a big dumb, green, horndog like me. I tap the sweet spot again. "But this is just a convenient overlap, Alexis. It isn't love."

"Uh huh," Alexis nods, speaking to me like I'm a toddler. "Exactly. Having mediocre sex with your friend isn't love, Jackson. It's settling. And that is exactly what your dumb ass app is peddling. A fucking compromise."

"Relationships are all about compromise," I argue.

"Bullshit. Relationships are about passion." Alexis passes me a second shot.

"*Sex* is about passion," I say, tapping the sex circle again. I doodle devil horns on the circle and give it a flaming tail.

"I'm not just talking about the spicy parts, you idiot." Alexis does her shot, then wipes her mouth. "Though the sex part can be passionate, too."

"You sound like Isla now." I roll my eyes and knock back the second shot. Then I rub my hands together to reactivate the mint that still lingers there and inhale. It's faded too much. "Got any mint behind the bar?" I ask.

"Of course. You know my mojito game is strong," she says. Alexis hands me a few sprigs of mint leaves, and I rub them vigorously between my hands, crushing the leaves, coloring my palms with the green juice. The buzz is kicking in, making me feel warm and fuzzy.

"Is Isla what you wanted to talk to me about?" Alexis asks.

"No," I say, taking another hit of the mint.

"So what was it?" Alexis is looking over my shoulder distractedly. I turn around to see what she is looking at and realize it's Lacey and Ryker. They are leaving the confessional tent, hand in hand, laughing. I'd thought that they were the least likely of the three pairs to hit it off. But there you go. You never know.

You can lead a horse to water, but you can't make a jackass drink. It's entirely up to the asshole if he wants to stay in the sweet spot. Now that I look again, the sweet spot could also be interpreted as an asshole. I scribble all over the center of the diagram.

"You are such an idiot," Alexis sighs.

"Maybe," I reply. "But I'm an idiot who needs your help. I need you to help me pick a really good karaoke song."

# isla

. . .



*"Fate is fickle. Destiny is dodgy. How long are you supposed to wait before you take matters into your own hands? If you know what you want, you gotta go after it before someone else does. It's only logical, right? "*

*~ Jackson Porter, Playing With Matches Confessionals*

THERE'S AN OLDER man seated alone, drinking a can of Coke at one of the candlelit tables outside the English pub where we're all assembling for karaoke night. A bunch of other resort guests are gathered at the tables outside, drinking cocktails and eating the fish and chips that the pub specializes in.

"Excuse me - Isla, is it?" the man stands up and calls out to me. "Have you seen Jackson Porter?"

"Cappy!" I say, recognizing him immediately.

"That I am," he tips his hat at me in acknowledgement.

"Jackson's told me about you," I say.

"Did he now?" Cappy's brows draw together. There's something so familiar about him, "Well, what did he say then?"

"Just that you brought him here," I say, spying Rob approaching.

"Oh good, good!" Rob says. "I see you've met Cappy, our watersports consultant. I don't know what would have happened if you hadn't rescued Jackson from that storm. You're joining us for karaoke, right?"

"Well it's been a while since I've warmed up the old pipes, but don't mind if I do!" Cappy says.

"Excellent! I can't wait to hear what you've chosen to sing. Might you treat us to a rendition of *Playing with Matches*?" Rob asks hopefully. "I don't think anyone else has signed up to sing our show's theme song. It's such a karaoke classic these days."

"That old shite?" Cappy shakes his head. "No way. It's been played to death. I have something else in mind."

**THE INSIDE** of the bar is dark and crowded. A DJ sets up the karaoke equipment in the corner while a crowd of would-be singers mobs the bar to work up their courage. I glance around for Jackson, but he's nowhere to be seen.

"You looking for Jackson, too, then?" Cappy asks as Rob excuses himself to go chat with some members of the crew.

"Yeah, I don't think he's here yet," I say, trying not to let my disappointment show. I spy Marco at a table on the second level of the bar. He's sitting with Paula and Owen and waves me and Cappy over.

"Cappy, this is Marco, Paula, and Owen. Everyone, this is Cappy," I make the introductions, and everyone slides over to make room for me. Cappy pulls an extra chair over to the end of the table, turns it around backwards and sits, straddling the seat. He seems antsy.

"Have any of you seen Jackson?" Cappy asks. "I was hoping to give him something," he pats the breast pocket of the white dinner jacket he has on with his jeans.

"I saw him at the bar with Alexis earlier," Owen says.

"Okay then," Cappy says, looking extremely disappointed. "I hope I haven't missed him."

"I'm sure he'll be along soon," I reassure him.

"Who here's singing?" I ask the group.

"Marco is singing! I have prepared a special song!" Marco beams.

"You have?" I ask.

"Si! Marco is ready to serenade his Bella!" Marco leans back in his seat and smolders at all of us. He can't help it. With his hooded bedroom eyes, perfectly chiseled features, and tailored Italian wardrobe, he is objectively hot as hell.

But he's not Jackson, and this could get awkward. The room feels too close. Too many people. Too much energy. Anxiousness and excitement, anticipation, horniness, and hopefulness. Regret and resignation. There are too many messages blending, overlapping, and coming in at me all at once.

"I can't wait to hear you sing," Paula pipes up. She is sitting next to Marco and turns to smile adoringly in his direction. Marco stretches his arm out on the bench behind her, fingers lightly grazing her shoulder, a gesture that Owen, sitting on Paula's other side, totally misses. But Cappy sees.

Cappy meets my eye, nodding in their direction, and raises his brows at me. I shrug in response. It's like we've had a whole conversation, without saying a word. Cappy smiles a little and shakes his head.

"There they are!" Owen suddenly jumps up, waving at the door. "Alexis! Jackson!"

Alexis leads Jackson over, and he collapses into the chair opposite me.

"Hello, Isla," he says, slurring slightly. Then he notices Cappy. "And Cappy! You made it back for drinks! Excellent! What can I get for you?"

"I'm fine, Son," Cappy holds up his Coke. "I don't drink. But you look like you've had a few–"

"Two shots," Alexis holds up two fingers. She's talking to us, but her eyes are glued to Owen's. "Jackson's such a lightweight."

"I'm not a big drinker," Jackson agrees. "My old man was a drunk. Gotta be careful."

"Hmmph. Fair enough." Cappy studies Jackson and frowns, "Is there somewhere you need to sign up to sing?"

"Yes, you must check in over there," Marco points at the DJ stand.

"Be right back," Cappy pushes his chair back, leaving his soda behind.

"You all are in for a treat," Alexis announces to the table before she stands up. She holds a hand out to Owen. He rises beside her.

"You stay here," Alexis pokes Jackson in the chest. "Owen and I will get you signed up." The two of them head in the same direction that Cappy just went.

Suddenly it's just me, Marco, Jackson, and Paula at the table.

"You're going to sing?" I ask Jackson, surprised.

"I am," he states confidently.

"What does she mean?" Marco asks, looking from me to Jackson. "What is the treat Alexis has mentioned? Have you arranged for a special dessert for Marco?" He licks his lips.

"I can sing," Jackson rolls his eyes. "It's not a huge deal. I used to take voice lessons when I was a kid."

"You can sing?" Marco looks doubtful. "Like you surf? This I believe when I see it."

"Buckle up, Buttercup," Jackson waves Marco's comment away and turns back towards me. He smiles goofily. "Hi, Isla," he says.

"Hi," I reply. "You're drunk, aren't you?"

"Just a little," he tips his finger to the side of his nose like he's trying to share a secret. "But it's nothing serious. Just enough to take the edge off. Make me a little less chickenshit. I still know what I'm doing. And I'm doing it, Isla. We're doing this. Do you have your mint oil? Can I get a touch-up?" Jackson holds out his hands like a beggar, looking into my eyes. "Please?"

"Sure," I say, applying the mint oil to his palms.

"Oh, I love mint essential oil," Paula says, sniffing the air delicately.

"Do me, too!" Marco demands, thrusting his free hand at me.

"No!" Jackson slams his hand down on the table. "Back off. This is our thing. Mine and Isla's!" He shakes a warning finger at Marco. "Get your own thing, Buddy."

"Okay, okay," Marco holds up his hands defensively. "It's just a little mint."

"Holy fuck," Jackson whispers, rubbing his temples and holding his head in his hands. "Those truth bombs pack a punch." Almost immediately, he pulls his hands away. "Shit, I did it again!"

"Oh no. Did you touch your eyes? Can I get you anything?" I lean forward to look into his eyes, which are watering, even though he's laughing. I place a hand on his smooth cheek. He must have shaved recently. He locks eyes with me, suddenly seeming a hell of a lot more sober.

"No, Isla. I'm fine. I'm good," he takes my hand and turns it over, bringing my wrist to his mouth. Then he brushes his lips across the tender flesh of my pulse point, where surely he can feel the way my heart is hammering. "I'm better than fine."

A loud crackle of static and the buzz of microphone feedback breaks the tension as a massive black man with dreads and a tie-dyed tee steps up to the mic. When the MC speaks, his childlike voice is surprising, given his size. Just one more reminder that you cannot always judge a book by its cover.

"Testing, testing, one-two-three. Ladies and gentlemen, welcome to karaoke night at Peaches. We've got a full house tonight and a full line-up of performers. The bar is open, and we're ready to get started. Our first act is a karaoke duet! Without further ado - I present Darwin and Ryker!" Rob runs up on the stage and whispers something into the man's ear. That's when I notice that there's a cameraman in the corner. Nobody mentioned they'd be filming tonight, but of course, they're filming. Why *wouldn't* they be filming? I see one of the

PAs passing out consent forms, while another places a sign just inside the door informing onlookers that this is a live set.

"So everybody," the MC continues, "I stand corrected. What we have here is a karaoke *duel*, sung by Ryker and Darwin. And I need someone else - Lacey? Is Lacey here? I need you to come sit here in the middle."

Lacey, who has turned her injured hand into a fashion statement by wrapping a colorful silk scarf over the injury, totters over to the chair in her platform sandals. People start to clap, and she gives a little wave, bats her lashes, and pats her hair. She looks around, trying to spot the two men vying for her final shell.

Out of the corner of my eye, I see Chloe, seated at the bar with the dive instructor, rolling her eyes. Ryker and Darwin are nowhere to be seen.

"Hit it!" shouts the MC.

Suddenly lights are flashing and the music is thumping as the opening chords to a sped-up, bass-heavy version of "Don't Go Breaking My Heart" pours out of the speakers. The crowd goes wild, standing and cheering as the two men enter from opposite ends of the bar.

Cappy, Owen, and Alexis slip back into their seats at the table, angling their chairs so they can watch the show.

Lacey is lapping up her time in the spotlight. One at a time, the men pull her to her feet and spin her around. At one point Ryker dips her and behind the cameras, I see Rob and Rory high-five each other. It's all so perfectly choreographed that I have to wonder if they rehearsed it.

"Looks like they rehearsed that, don't you think?" Jackson mutters in my ear.

"There are three cameras on them. Something's up," Alexis comments.

"Mmm. Marco agrees. Something big is happening," Marco nods sagely, if a little jealously.

The song ends in a crescendo, followed by a three-way embrace, with both men kissing Lacey on the cheek, and then without any warning, locking lips with each other.

Everyone's eyes go wide except for Owen's.

"What?" he says. "You didn't see that coming? It was obvious."

"To you maybe!" Alexis swats him. "And you didn't say a word to me. That's two days of premium dishing you've cost me."

"You're off your game, Alexis," Jackson laughs. "I can't believe you didn't pick up on that."

"I can't believe your *app* didn't pick up on that," Alexis fires back. "Looks like you matched the wrong two."

"Actually, it looks like they are a three-way match," I say, suddenly getting a clear and honest sense of it. "It takes all three of them to balance each other out. That's how they work together."

"Well, that's not fair," Jackson clicks his pen. "We haven't even begun to train the AI to do poly matches."

A crackle of static from the speaker breaks the conversation up as the MC steps back onto the stage. "Ladies and Gents, next up we have Cappy, performing 'Message in a Bottle' by The Police."

"Can't believe I need to go after *that* last act," Cappy grumbles. He removes his jacket, hanging it on the back of his chair. "Watch my things?"

The mood changes immediately when Cappy takes the stage. He takes his time getting settled. He has a real presence and a beautiful, if weathered voice. He sings the song in such an evocative way that I'm instantly transported to a scene of intense desperation and longing. A sailor lost to a storm. The passage of time. Loneliness, redemption. It almost makes me want to cry.

When Cappy finishes, we all sit silently for a moment. Jackson takes my hand and squeezes. There's a tear in his eye, as well.

Then Jackson speaks.

"There's something so magical about music, the way it cuts right through all the layers, straight to the core of your emotions."

Alexis feels Jackson's forehead. "Emotions, Jackson? You feeling okay?" She asks.

"I'm fine," Jackson mugs at Alexis. "How about you?"

"Where's Cappy?" Paula asks. "I want to tell him how moving his song was to me."

"I don't know," Jackson shrugs. "Maybe he went to the bathroom."

Owen and Alexis head to the bar to get us all a round of drinks while the next few singers perform. When Rob stops by the table, we ask him if he's seen Cappy, and he tells us that Cappy took off shortly after he finished his song.

"That's odd," I say. "He asked us to watch his stuff."

"He must have forgotten it," Rob shrugs one shoulder dismissively. "Give it here. We've got his contact info. I'll see that it gets back to him."

"Marco is next!" Marco claps his hands excitedly. "Let's go. You must make sure the camera is ready for Marco's performance."

"You know what, I could use some fresh air. I'm just going to go have a look around outside and see if Cappy's still here," Jackson says, standing as well. "I'll be right back."

As the current set ends and Marco and Rob stand to go, Owen wishes him luck.

"Marco does not need luck. Marco has *charisma*," Marco says, swaggering down to the mic, Rob beside him.

"Good Lord, what do you think he's going to sing?" Alexis says as they get everything set up. It's taking twice as long because of the cameramen.

*Please don't let it be "Isla Bonita."*

"I don't know," I say nervously, wishing Jackson would come back. I map an escape route to the door. Cameras or no cameras, I don't want to be trapped if I have to make a speedy exit.

"Look, Alexis," I whisper to Jackson's friend. "I might have to get out of here real quick. Can you cover for me if I need to dash?"

"What's the matter? Eat something funny?" she asks sympathetically.

"No. I just don't know what Marco's going to–"

I recognize the song Marco has chosen the minute I hear the first three notes. It's not either of the two he has mentioned. Instead, he's chosen "Jesse's Girl."

I heave a sigh of relief.

Somewhere, somehow, someone has scared up a fog machine, and Marco bursts through the front door of the pub, wearing a cape, a Zorro mask, what appears to be a Speedo swimsuit, and little more. He is also brandishing a massive sword.

I have no idea what the cosplay is about, but the crowd goes wild as he does some faux fencing moves.

"Is Marco wearing a costume?" Paula asks. She is leaning forward, listening intently, but obviously, she can't see what's happening.

"Yeah," Owen is sitting up straighter now, taking it all in. "Marco is wearing the hell out of that cape and swimsuit," he says.

"I hear it swishing. I can picture it," Paula grins.

And then Marco launches into the song, except he subs in the name of the rival lover. Instead of "Jessie," he sings "Owen."

"Shut. The. Front. Door." Alexis exclaims.

Marco continues to belt it out, overenunciating everything and mispronouncing every third word as he acts the song out in melodramatic pantomime. As he sings, Paula sways back and forth. Her smile is beatific. Spontaneously, the entire crowd in the bar starts clapping to the beat, and several people sing along. For the grand finale, Marco stands on a chair, leaps onto our table, and falls to his knees in front of me and Paula.

The crowd goes wild. Even wilder than they did for Ryker and Darwin. Marco takes Paula's hand and smothers it with kisses.

"Thank you, mi amore, Bella Paula," he says. "For helping me understand the true nature of love."

Marco leaps down and takes a bow, clearly enjoying the clapping and cheering. He mugs for the camera and does one last flourish, waving his cape before heading to the restroom to change back into his clothes.

"I think I'm just going to hit the hay," Paula says, once he's gone. She wiggles out of her seat and reaches for her cane, motioning for us to remain where we are. "Don't get up, I'll be fine. I'll have someone get me a golf cart to get back to the room."

We all freeze.

"Are you sure?" Owen asks. "I could walk you back."

"No, Owen. You stay here," Paula insists. "I'll see you at the final ceremony tomorrow night. You stay. Enjoy the rest of your night."

"You sure?" Owen asks

"Totally sure," Paula insists.

We all watch as she makes her way across the bar. Marco, still wearing his cape, meets her by the door, and the two of them slip out together.

"Well, well, well," Alexis whistles. "I hate to tell you, Owen, but I think you may have just been dumped."

"Yeah," Owen says, "about that… I think I'm gonna be okay." He threads his fingers through Alexis's and pulls her closer, kissing her on the neck. She colors and looks around.

"Owen! Aren't you afraid they're going to kick you off the show?"

"What do I care if they do?" Owen laughs. "I came here to meet someone special, and I did. As far as I'm concerned, it's all good." He pulls Alexis in for a passionate kiss, and it's completely apparent that it isn't the first one. I can see from the way he's stroking her and she's practically purring that this has been going on for a little while already. My mouth drops open. How have I missed this?

I clear my throat.

"What about Paula?" I ask Owen a little pointedly. "Looks like you've been playing a little shell game."

*Pun intended.*

Of all the contestants, Owen was probably the last one I would have expected to be cheating.

"I swear I wanted to end things yesterday at the Shell Ceremony, but Alexis wouldn't let me."

"Isla, can you imagine if he'd dumped a blind girl?" Alexis asked. "The whole country would hate him. Not only would we both have been sent home immediately, but he'd have a hard time finding a job."

"But now she's the one dumping me," Owen grins. "I think we'll all be fine. Just fine. And on that note, what say we get out of here, Alexis?" His hand is already halfway up her shirt.

"OMG, I *hate* karaoke," Alexis says. "You don't have to ask me twice."

"Me too, my spicy cocktail, me too," Owen says, pulling her to her feet.

"Wait a minute!" I call out. "You're all just going to leave me? Don't you want to stick around for Jackson?"

But they aren't listening to me. They're out the door so fast I think I see a vapor trail in their wake.

Marco and Paula? Owen and Alexis? Lacey, Darwin, *and* Ryker?

Most of our mis-matched group has already departed the bar. Only Chloe and the dive instructor are still here - looking chummy at a table over in the corner. They don't look like they'd appreciate my company.

I sit alone through one more set, listening to a woman from upstate New York belting out show tunes from Annie. There's no sign of Jackson. I wait for Little Orphan Annie to finish her song before collecting my things to leave.

"Jackson Porter?" The MC calls out his name. "You're up."

There's a hush as everyone looks around expectantly. "Jackson? Has anyone seen that dude? Did he get stage fright?" the MC jokes.

"Nope," a familiar voice booms through the mic as Jackson steps onto the stage and takes it from the MC. "I'm right here." Jackson pulls a chair to the middle of the stage. "But I can't do this alone. I need you to come over here, Ms. Fairfax." He points at the chair, "Would you please sit your exquisite British bum down here so I can serenade you?"

"Jackson," my heart is thumping like it's trying to get out of my chest."You don't have to–"

"I know," he says, pointing at the seat again.

*"Sit!"*

*"Sit down!"*

*"Sit down in the chair already, Honey!"*

People are starting to chant for me to sit. But I can't move. My legs are frozen, glued to the spot where I'm standing.

"Shhhh!" Jackson holds up a finger. "Don't pressure her. Give her a second." He walks to my side and takes my hand, leading me gently to the center of the stage. "You don't have to say or do anything. All you have to do is take a seat. Let me sing to you."

I look down at the chair.

"Please?" Jackson says.

*There's a lump in my throat. Why is there such a big lump in my throat?*

I bend my knees and sink into the seat as the music starts. A few people clap and whistle as the drum taps out a steady rhythm with Jackson's foot tapping along, keeping perfect time. It's the same impatient tapping I've noticed him doing again and again, ever since the first time I met him. At times, I've thought it was aimed at me.

But as soon as I see his foot tapping out the beat to Bruce Springsteen's "I'm on Fire," I recognize that beat for the quiet frustration it really is.

And then his foot stops tapping, and he sings.

From the moment he opens his mouth and the first low, growly note comes pouring out, the entire bar is struck silent. The longing in his voice. The rawness. The pain. The desire.

He sings to me like a man whose rib cage has been split open. He reaches out to touch me like I'm a butterfly he's afraid to bleed out on. His touch ignites me. It lights me up from the inside like a buzzing string of lanterns made entirely out of fireflies.

I'm pretty sure if he doesn't touch me again, I'll dissolve. The fireflies will fly away. There will be nothing left of me.

Why is Jackson Porter a data guy? Why is anyone with a voice like this not a singer?

The whole world disappears. It's just the two of us, floating in a candlelit hollow. He howls the last note. Such a short song.

Or maybe it was long. I'm not sure. I just know I'm not ready for the shock of it ending.

When the song ends and the lights come up, the world comes crashing in with a landslide of gaping jaws and wolf-whistles. It invades my space with camera lenses and furry microphones scurrying around me like mechanical rats.

Jackson is still holding the mic. The music has stopped, but the earth hasn't stopped shaking. He's still bleeding emotion. And I'm still buzzing like a power line.

And I'm crying. I realize I'm crying. Fat tears are rolling down my face. I'm holding my breath because I don't know what will happen when I try to swallow the lump in my throat. I may explode.

"I'm sorry," I say. "I'm so sorry."

And then I bolt.

I hear the mic clatter to the floor behind me as Jackson follows. But I keep going. I run past the swimming pools full of starlight and the fountains full of wishes. I run till I reach the beach, and then I keep running till I get to the water's edge and wade right in.

The whole time I'm running, I know without looking that he's there, too. Right behind me. I know he could easily overtake me. But he doesn't. He just follows me, hanging back, saying nothing, keeping his distance, until I get to the water. Only then does he come to my side, wading in beside me, pushing past the moonlit waves.

When we're both waist-deep, Jackson silently takes my hand.

"Stop," he says, preventing me from pulling away.

"I can't," I shake my head.

"Then at least let me come in with you," he says, pulling me toward him. I am about to lose my footing, but he lifts me before I can fall and holds me close, bobbing against him in the waves. His lips brush against mine, and I taste salt, the ocean, the tip of his tongue, and the tang of my own overwhelming desire.

"You knew this was going to happen, didn't you?" he says. "You saw it. Tell me the truth?"

"I knew I wanted you," I admit. "But I didn't think you –," I break off searching for the words. "I thought you just wanted to have sex with me to prove a point."

"The point being?"

"That you were right about relationships. That it's all ones and zeros. Sex and friendship and occasionally sex with friends."

Jackson runs his hands under my clothes and puts his thumbs on the tips of my breasts.

"Isla, I swear to God, when I put my hands on your body, I can feel it in my soul. If you told me right now that you were making the clouds move and the stars twinkle, I would believe you."

He rests his lips in the hollow of my throat and presses a quick kiss before continuing. "I want to give you an epic hickey. I want to claim you, and I want you to claim me. "

"I'm scared," I admit.

"Shall I sing to you some more?"

"Absolutely. All day, every day. No more speaking. From now on, you only sing."

"If I sing again, will you come back to the room with me?" Jackson hums.

"Quickly," I agree fervently. "Before I burn up."

WE TUMBLE into bed nearly naked, clothing shed and strewn in a trail behind us.

The tangled sheets, salty skin – I've seen this.

"I didn't think I was going to be able to wait," I breathe against his ribs as I make my way down the length of his torso, touching and exploring him with my tongue.

He moans.

I tug at his damp boxers. "Have you ever made love in the ocean before?"

"No, I've never had sex in the ocean," Jackson admits.

"Me either," I say, feeling an excited surge of victory as my hand brushes the apparent evidence of his arousal. I straddle him. His skin is hot, pulsing against me.

"But I already feel like I'm out to sea when I'm with you," Jackson says. "Like I might drown if I'm not careful. You're rocking my world, Isla Fairfax." Jackson holds my hips still, pulling off his shorts and flinging them to the ground. His erection strains against my lacey undergarments.

With one hand he pushes the crotch of my panties aside. He slips a long finger deep inside me. Now it's my turn to moan.

"I need to be inside of you, and I need that *now*," he says, his voice low and tearing. And with one swift movement, he pulls the lace aside and spears me, thrusting so hard and deep that the pleasure feels like stars in the sky are rushing to meet me.

"Lean back, let yourself float," Jackson says, gripping my hips. "I won't let you go."

In a flash I see myself as he sees me, bathed in the bluish-white light with the moonlight spilling across my breasts. It's me, but not me. Even though my hair is a mess, I love the way I look. I love the gift of seeing myself through him.

"Did you wear this bra for me?" Jackson's voice is husky, as he nuzzles one breast, then the other through the sheer lace.

"No, I wore it for me," I say. "I wanted to feel sexy. I wanted to at least have that power over you."

"You have all kinds of power over me," he scoops my breasts out from their lace cage and kisses them before laying me back. My hair fans out around me.

"This is happening, it's not a fever dream?" I say.

"It's happening," Jackson says firmly, thrusting again. Harder, and faster.

"Do you hear the ocean?" I ask.

"I do." He pins my hands above my head, our fingers intertwined. "It wants us back."

"It wants to swallow us whole," I agree.

"Maybe we should let it then," he lowers his lips to mine, kissing my top lip, then the bottom before pressing his whole mouth against mine and splitting my mouth open with his silken tongue.

The waves are coming faster and larger now. He pulls me up and against him at the last moment, wrapping his arms around me so tight that it's almost impossible to see where either of us ends or begins as we both give in to the inevitable tide.

# jackson

. . .



*"I'm not sure what's going to happen in the finale. But I'm hoping for the best. Better than that, actually."*

*~ Isla Fairfax*

"WHAT THE HELL were you thinking, Jackson?" My VC is usually calm, cool, and collected. But not this morning.

I'm pacing in my boxer shorts on the balcony. I don't want Geoff's diatribe to wake Isla. We didn't get much sleep last night. Most of what Geoff is saying doesn't register. I'm too amped up on pheromones and dopamine to care. I think about the night we had, and it comes back in abstract waves of sensation and emotion.

"Jackson!" Geoff growls. "Are you even listening to me?"

"How bad could the video be?" I ask.

"Well, you said you use apps, primarily your own competitor's apps, to get laid whenever you want."

"What's so terrible about that? My app isn't about getting *laid*," I say.

"Maybe it's all a game for you, Jackson, but it isn't for your investors. We're real people. With wives and families. I put a lot of money into this. And it's one thing if you're doing your best to bring a product to market and it has a few hiccups. But if you don't even believe in it, and you're yanking everyone's chain? Then you're a whole other level of asshole."

I flinch at the dressing down.

"Watch the video. I just texted it to you," Geoff says.

In the video, I'm at the beach bar with Alexis. Marco's sliding a flaming cocktail down the bar in the background. "I am perfectly capable of getting laid any time I want to get laid," I say, practically spitting with disgust. "There are plenty of other apps I like to use for that."

The caption: "Asswipe: AI Swiper founder Jackson Porter admits he doesn't use his own products for booty calls."

"Fuuuuuuck," I say. "I didn't realize anyone was filming me."

"Well, surprise! They were. What were you thinking? Are any of the couples you matched even getting together?"

"Does it count if it's a three-way situation?" I ask, hopefully.

"That is not funny, Jackson!"

He's right. I owe it to them to make things right. "I'll think of something," I say. "I'll find a way to fix it. What's the latest word on the re-brand? Do we have the new name yet?"

"We're keeping the name," Geoff says.

"Are you kidding me? How can you even say that, now that that video has gone viral?"

Geoff bursts into laughter. For a moment I wonder if he's lost it.

"You lucky bastard, Jackson. Do you know how many downloads we've had in the last twenty-four hours? Turns out that stupid video is the *best* thing that's ever happened for the app, Jackson! People are making reaction videos discussing how happy they are to find an app that isn't just for hookups. We've had requests from people who want to use our system to find platonic friends and an inquiry from a large HR firm that thinks the compatibility analysis might aid in job placement. Things are looking up!"

"You're kidding me," I heave a massive sigh of relief.

"I shit you not," Geoff says.

"So people don't hate me?" I ask, hopefully.

"No, they think you're a total asswipe. But they love the product."

"And the name? You're sure about it?"

"It's memorable. Asswiper, AI Swiper... The point is that people remember it. I hate to admit it, but you really are a fucking genius."

As I end the call, I peer in through the sliding glass door at Isla. She's still sleeping soundly. Nakedly. I want to wake her with kisses and a plate of fruit and bacon. I sneak back in to get dressed and bring some food back to the suite before she wakes.

**ROB AND RORY** are eating their breakfast on the patio outside the buffet. Rory has a set of flashcards with the cast members' photos on one side and the show logo on the other. She's laid them out in a grid and she's flipping them over like it's a kid's game.

"Jackson!" Rob looks up. "Your performance last night was incredible! Brains *and* talent? Game over!" He shakes his hand like he's putting out a match.

"You forgot to mention my dashing good looks," I say, dragging a metal patio chair over to their table.

"So humble, too." Rory snorts.

"How'd it go with Isla after?" Rob asks. "Did you catch up to her?"

"I did," I smile goofily.

"That smile tells me all I need to know," Rob bursts into a grin. "Oh, Jackson, Dude. I am so happy for you. There's nothing like it, right?"

"Nothing like what? Getting laid?" Rory rolls her eyes and flips the cards back over for another round of the game.

"Don't be crass, Rory," Rob frowns at his assistant producer. "It's obvious that it's more than that. It looks like the matchmaker has matched himself. Jackson here is in love."

"You got all that from my smile?" I ask, a little incredulous.

"I have a sixth sense about these things," Rob asserts confidently. "What are you going to do about it? Have you told her?"

"Not yet," I admit. Rory's matching game doesn't seem to be going well. She keeps messing up the matches and sweeps the cards back into a pile, frustrated.

"Ugh. Looks like you two may be the only ones leaving here together," Rory taps the deck into a neat stack and tucks it into her front pocket.

"Nevermind about that now!" Rob waves her concerns away. "Have you thought about the big reveal?" Rob waves his hands in front of his face for emphasis. "You couldn't ask for a more romantic place for it. Go big, or go home. Amiright?" he elbows Rory and winks at her conspiratorially.

"Yeah sure," she agrees. "Everyone loves a grand gesture. It makes for a good story. You do that podcast, Jackson. You know the drill."

"I don't know how to tell her," I admit. "I mean I'd love it to be special, but I'm not good at planning this sort of thing."

"Well, my friend," Rob smiles delightedly and claps me on the back. "You've come to the right place. Lucky for you I *am* pretty good at this stuff."

Rory and Rob exchange a look, and then Rory nods at Rob and pushes her seat back.

"Okay, I'm gonna let you dudes talk this one out. We've got a lot to do to get ready for the finale tonight."

"Is that cooler on the boat?" Rob asks.

"Yep. All loaded up and good to go."

Rob checks his watch, "Listen, I have to head out on a boat in fifteen minutes. We're shooting some quick B-roll of the wildlife at the nearby nature preserve. Great stuff for color. Why don't you come along for the ride, and we'll brainstorm some ideas, okay?"

"I was planning to bring back breakfast for Isla," I start to say.

"We won't be long. It's barely eight. I'll text Rory to bring something over and let her know."

"You think?" I look doubtfully over my shoulder.

"Absolutely," Rob says with assurance. "She probably won't even be up yet by the time we get back."

"WHERE'S THE CAMERA CREW?" I ask. The speedboat driver cuts the engine as we glide toward the simple wooden dock jutting out from a wide, barren stretch of white sand. The small island is uninhabited by humans, although I can see a radio tower of some sort up on the peak. Dense mangroves line the shoreline, and I am delighted to see a giant egret take flight.

"Great snorkeling around here," Rob says. "We're not far from where we took the cast out the other day."

Rob and I have barely exchanged three words since we left the buffet. The motor was too loud and the sea too rough for us to talk very much on the quick, exhilarating trip over.

"The crew got here before us. They're probably over there by the shelter, setting up." Rob points at a small lean-to, facing away from the beach and passes a large blue cooler to me. "Why don't you hop out and bring them this cooler? I'm just gonna be a sec," he holds up one finger as he gets his phone out. "I have to make a quick call. I have some solid ideas for you, though."

I glance warily at the floating dock where a small lizard suns himself without a care in the world. Then I squint at the empty horizon. Nothing but water for miles.

"You going?" Rob asks. "I thought you were in a hurry?"

"Fine," I say. "Just a sec." I clap loudly like Isla did and the little demon skitters back towards the beach.

*Phew.*

I hold out an arm to steady myself, and I climb out with the cooler. Once I'm on the dock, I take a few careful steps, scanning the beach for any sign of the crew. "Are you sure they're already here?"

The beach is empty and peaceful. Too peaceful. And there are no footsteps. No *human* footsteps. The sand is littered with skittery footprints.

"Hey, Rob, what did you say this island was called?" I ask, vaguely remembering something.

I turn back to the boat, where Rob is pocketing his phone.

"Reptile Isle," he says. "The webcam feed of the iguanas is super popular. There are thousands of them here."

He steps up onto the side of the boat, holding onto the boat's awning, almost as if he's about to step onto the dock with me. But then the boat driver fires up the engine.

"Sorry, Jackson," he calls out as the boat backs away. "But you'll be fine, I swear. You'll survive. There's water, bug spray, sunscreen, and some power bars in the cooler. Oh, and a radio. You might try calling Cappy. I have a feeling he'll be back in the area. He left a packet of stuff at the bar last night. I think he actually might have meant it for you."

*Cappy?*

"What the fuck, Rob?!" I shout as the boat backs away. "What the actual fuck?!"

"Patience, Jackson! I swear it will all work out! Worst case scenario, there's a tour group coming tomorrow. Of course Isla will be gone by then," he pauses thoughtfully. "It'd be better if you made it back before we finish filming the final Shell Ceremony." Rob waves as the boat stops reversing, then it turns and motors away.

# isla

"I'm just hoping I haven't (bleeped) everything up. There's a lot of things I still need to say."

~ Jackson Porter, *Playing With Matches, Confessionals*

A LOUD KNOCK on my door awakens me from a deep slumber. I stretch and pat the bed beside me, feeling for Jackson, but the sheets are cool. There's no sign of him.

By the time I get to the door, the knocker is gone but there is a basket full of pastries and coffee with a note.

*Jackson asked that we send this over for you before he took off. Call time to shoot the final episode is 4 pm. See you at the gazebo.*
*~Rory*

Jackson asked Rory to send me food before he *took off*. To where? And without saying a word to me? Why? It doesn't seem right.

I wait patiently in the room until noon for him to come back before getting dressed and seeking answers. "Has anyone seen Jackson?" I ask the crew at the confessional tent. They all shake their heads. I can't picture where he might be.

"No. He hasn't checked in yet today. If you see him, please send him our way?"

"How about Rob?" I ask.

"Oh yeah, he's around here somewhere. He was headed to the pool bar for a pre-finale toast with the whole cast," one of the grips says. "I'd check there."

"Thanks, I say," backing out of the stuffy tent and heading toward the pool.

Sure enough, the entire cast, including Marco, is assembled at the bar. Owen is behind the counter, assisting Alexis. Darwin and Ryker are holding hands, and Chloe and Paula are giggling about something. When everyone sees me, they all start clapping.

"Somebody sure slept in this morning. Late night?" Lacey winks suggestively at me.

"There she is!" shouts Ryker, patting the empty stool beside him. "Get in here. We can't do a proper toast without you and Jackson, can we?"

"Oh good, there you are, Bella Isla!" Marco is sitting next to Paula with his hand on the small of her back. He stands to hug me, looking around baffled. "But, where is Jackson? I want to congratulate him. No more virgin, eh?"

Alexis rolls her eyes.

"I was going to ask you all if you saw him."

"No," Marco looks concerned. "I have not seen him, but never mind. I must talk to you, Bella. Everyone, do you mind if I grab Isla for a moment?" He's speaking to everyone but looking at Paula.

"Not at all, Amore. Go, go," Paula smiles and waves us away.

*I already know what this is about.*

"I see that you've formed quite an attachment to Paula," I say to Marco.

"I am so sorry, Bella. Marco thought he was in love with you," he apologizes. "But now Marco knows the difference. I just hope I can convince her I am worthy."

"Of course, you are, Marco. Why would you even say that?" I give him a quick hug.

"All the other women, they look at me. But Paula, she sees me. Nobody else has ever *seen* me before."

His eyes are full of tears. "I am so in love with her, Isla. And it is all because of you. You and your magic, I am sure of it. You bring us together. You are like the good witch of romance. You will write a book about us, no?" He smiles.

"Maybe," I hedge but I can't help smiling back.

"Good. Then Marco will finally grace the cover of one of your books," he crows, satisfied. "But what about your AI Swiper?" he says, taking extra pains to enunciate the A and the I. "Where is Jackson?"

"That's what I was wondering, too," I say.

"There is Rob. Maybe he knows?" Marco points back toward the pool area where I see Rob and Rory threading their way around chaise lounges with a cameraman in tow, headed towards the crowd at the bar.

**"I WOULDN'T WORRY TOO MUCH,"** Rob shrugs. "I'm sure he'll be back by later tonight."

"Back from where?" I ask.

"Last time I saw him was on a boat," Rob says. "He seemed pretty agitated actually."

"What?" Alexis looks dubious. "This is not like him. He wouldn't just leave."

"Who knows," Rob examines his cuticles. "Perhaps he just felt like his work here was done. I mean, I'm assuming he got what he came for." Rob looks up at me for the briefest instant.

"Orrrrrr," Rory pulls out her phone and scrolls, "maybe it has something to do with this? This video has been all over the internet this morning. You're in it, too," she points at Alexis.

Alexis's eyes bug out. "Hand that here," she snatches for the phone, unsuccessfully. Rory holds it up high so everyone can see and hits play.

*"I am perfectly capable of getting laid any time I want to get laid!"* Jackson's voice rings out, loud and clear. *"There are plenty of other apps I like to use for that."*

"Oof," Rory says. "That's gotta make you question everything about the guy, huh?"

# jackson

· · ·

*"We all play with the hand we're dealt, I suppose. Bluffing will only get you so far. Eventually, you have to show your hand. Tonight's going to be hard."*

*~Isla Fairfax, Playing with Matches Confessionals*

I PICK my way across the sand warily, watching for lizards. The problem, of course, is their uncanny ability to blend in with the background. You don't know they're there till they leap out at you. And by then it's too late.

I start to sweat at the very thought of scaly scurrying. Is there anything more horrible than a lizard? Their tails keep moving for ages after they get cut off, and then they *grow back*. They're worse than zombies. No wonder I had nightmares about them as a child.

I shudder.

*Think of Isla. Think of all the things I still want to say to her. If I survive.*

But of course, I will survive. I don't think Rob was lying about the tour group headed here tomorrow - the resort had a full rack of ecotour brochures. Brochures I raced past thanks to the giant photos of sunning iguanas on their cover. Worst case, I just have to make it till tomorrow morning. There's no way I'll be getting any sleep with thousands of those prehistoric monstrosities waiting to devour me the instant I nod off.

Tomorrow seems like a very, very long time away. By then, the final episode of the show will have wrapped and most of the cast and crew will already be making their way home.

*Surely, Isla will wonder where I am?*

I set the cooler down in the shade of the lean-to and grab myself a water bottle from the cool interior compartment. At least I won't be dehydrated. Slamming the lid shut, I take a seat and resume my vigil. I'd rather not be sitting on the ground if I spy a furfuraceous land beast.

I check the battery on my phone. Ten percent. Of course, I forgot to charge it last night. Charging my phone was not the number one thing on my mind. And I didn't worry about it when I had that long Facetime call with Geoff. I just thought I'd charge it later when I got back with breakfast.

*Stupid, Jackson.*

Not that a phone will do me a lot of good without any cell signal. I should have realized something was up the minute Rob said he was making a call. I've barely got one bar here.

*Stupid, stupid, Jackson.*

But there's wifi on the island. I'm sure of it. I can see the faint signal. It's coming from the rocky hilltop area where the tower is.

*Webcams. Rob mentioned that the webcams were popular.*

I gaze up at the outcrop. If I were a cold-blooded crawler, that peak would probably look like the perfect place to sunbathe and survey my domain. I can feel their tiny little dragon eyes all staring back at me.

*If I climb up there, I can probably use my hacked phone to get on the wifi.*

No. No. No. *There is no way.* I jump up and shake it out, wishing I had some of Isla's peppermint oil to clear my head. Does peppermint repel reptiles? Maybe bug spray does? I stand up, open the cooler and survey the contents. Three power bars, which I decide to save for later. Three liters of water, which should be plenty. One GoPro camera with a sticky note attached that says "In case you want to film a confessional while you're here." *As if.* I take the camera out and chuck it as far as I can.

There's also a manila envelope with a few loose items and what feels like a handheld radio and one bottle of herbal bug spray, which I apply liberally. It does smell a little minty, which makes me miss Isla even more. What must she be thinking? Where will Rob say I am?

A horrifying thought occurs to me.

*What if Isla sees that video without me there to explain?*

She'll think I'm full of shit. That I played her. Who could blame her? Why hadn't I just told her the way that I feel about her last night?

*What if she leaves before I get back?*

The wind picks up, rustling the vegetation, and I jump at the burst of movement in my peripheral vision. But it's only a bird. An innocuous, little bird. I'm being ridiculous. Godzilla isn't coming to get me. Godzilla isn't even real. They're just lizards. Little harmless lizards. Not even poisonous. I'm not a little kid anymore. They're probably more afraid of me than I am of them. I take a deep cleansing breath as I try to refocus.

And then a tiny lizard darts out of the bushes and *runs over my foot*.

I produce a sound reminiscent of the screech my little sister did when I used to put fake snakes in her cereal boxes. I don't even care. There's nobody here to hear me scream.

I'm so busy freaking out that I don't immediately notice the six-foot iguana that's calmly watching me from his sunbathing spot on the beach. My stomach clenches, and I feel my sweat glands kicking into overdrive. I must get off this island. Now!

Radio. There's a radio. I have no idea how it works, but I will figure it out.

I fling the cooler open and tear into the bulky manila envelope. I have no idea whether Cappy will actually be in the area but it's worth a try. If he's not in radio distance, maybe someone else will hear my call. But there's something strangely fitting about reaching out to Cappy. The salty sea captain saved me once, so maybe he can do it again? I'd gladly don a plastic tarp if it means I can get away from Don Iguana over there.

I'd never had a chance to tell Cappy how much I'd enjoyed his song last night. I'd gone outside to look for him, and he was nowhere to be found. He'd just vanished.

I reach into the envelope to pull out the radio, and a token of some sort falls out. Like a poker chip. But not a poker chip. Reaching for it and turning it over in my palm, I recognize the writing on it. It's a sobriety chip. Fifteen years. That's a long time. A good run. Good for Cappy. I'm pretty surprised he left it behind at the bar though. Seems like the sort of thing you'd want to hang onto.

And then the faded and cracked dog collar falls out of the torn envelope, and I drop the chip in the sand. A round silver registration tag with a dog license number and a heart-shaped enamel pendant exactly like the one that my sister made in grade school are both still attached

Frantically I grab the thing up out of the sand, running my finger over the number. I hold it up to the green tag that's hanging around my neck, matching the sizes. Hands shaking, I remove the necklace. There's a number on the back. A number I've memorized over the years I've been wearing this thing. I use a backward version as my password. I already know the numbers match. But I have to see them, side by side.

My eyes fill with tears as I flip the dog's tag back over and read the worn engraving. *Murphy Porter. Goodest Good Boy.*

We'd buried him without his collar. His name tag had randomly fallen off the day before.

Nobody knew why the old dog got in the car with our dad. Nobody knew where they'd been going. Not even my dad. He couldn't remember anything. He was lucky to survive the crash. Murphy wasn't as lucky.

After that, my dad had gone to rehab. And he'd relapsed a few times. And then he disappeared.

*Jesus, Jackson.*

Why hadn't I recognized my own damned father? Why hadn't I put it together sooner? I'd been looking at that Uber driver in LA for a sign. But it never even occurred to me that the bushy-bearded old man with the half-open fly who rescued me from the storm might be *my* old man.

"I hate you!" I shout at the lizard. "You stupid fucking asshole!" He blinks his evil eye at me. Cold and inhuman. Like a monster. Like a nightmare.

One time when I was about seven or so and I'd just watched Godzilla, my dad came home drunk. He was stomping all over the place and wrecking stuff. My mom called him that. She called him Godzilla. And when I went back to sleep, I dreamed my beloved dad turned into a scary, tough-skinned lizard man. His eyes went cold. He didn't care if I cried. He wrecked all my stuff. He wrecked me.

I pick up the chip and pocket it, checking back in the envelope for a letter. There isn't one. Just a small business card with "Captain James Porter" in an old-fashioned script. Below this, it says "Available for Private Tours, Parasailing, and Sportfishing."

I flip the card over. On the back he's written;

*I'm sorry, Son. I don't expect to be forgiven. Glad you're okay.*

Am I okay? Am I really?

I wipe away a tear and yell at the iguana again. "Fuck off! I don't want to hear it from you!"

There's only one thing to be done. I've got to climb up that hill, find the lizard webcam, and hack my way onto the wifi so I can call someone for help.

*I'll be damned if I'm calling my fucking father.*

AS I CLIMB up the small hill, I'm glad for the bug spray. The flies are thick, and the mosquitoes are large. A couple of them get me, despite the spray.

When I reach the edge of the rocky platform, I get my first glimpse at the situation. Which is lizardy. *So lizardy.* Wall-to-wall carpet of lizards. Of course, the webcam is positioned smack in the middle of all that would-be wallet leather.

"Here goes," I say to nobody in particular. The lizards could give a shit. A twisted branch I've scavenged from the beach comes in handy to clear my path. I swing it back and forth in wide swathes. But the lizards are not afraid of me. I swear they're mocking me. They look at me with their deadpan stares and slow unblinking eyes like something out of a Wes Anderson film. I can see the captions:

Somewhere in the Caribbean

Reptile Isle

1 pm

Some of the bigger guys don't seem to want to get out of my way. One of the macho ones glares and hisses at me.

"How about I sing you guys a song?" I offer. "Any requests?"

They just blink at me so I start singing the first thing that comes to mind. "Puff the Magic Dragon."

*They seem to like it.*

They let me pass and their eyes go all sleepy and unthreatening. I change the name of the little boy in the song to "Jackie Porter," automatically, the same as my dad used to do when he sang me to sleep when I was little. When he wasn't being the dragon. When he wasn't Godzilla.

I'd forgotten about that, too. Yet somehow, I still know all the words to the song.

Finally, I reach the tower with the webcam. There's some kind of repeater that's getting enough juice to the camera to run the live stream. I just need to tap into it. Piece of cake. Except my phone is down to six percent. I pull up the network settings to see what I'm working with. My phone searches for the signal, spinner spinning as I come to the end of my song.

I swear the reptiles get pissed the minute I finish. Their eyes pop open and they start hissing again.

"Okay, okay, assholes. You like show tunes?" I launch into a rendition of "Popular" from the show *Wicked*. Chelsea had played that song on repeat when the show first came out. With any luck, this will be my last tune.

But I can't seem to hack in. Three percent.

"No. No, no!" I shake my phone like the friction will somehow activate a few extra minutes of battery life. Two percent.

Finally, when my phone is down to one percent, I connect to the network. I don't even bother pulling up my contacts. I just press the side button and tell Siri to call Isla. If I've only got one call, I'm gonna make it count.

Miraculously the call connects and goes right through. I almost cheer when I hear the phone ringing.

*Pick up Isla! Pick up fast!*

One ring. Two rings. Three rings. Four. Finally, she picks up on the fifth ring.

"Hello?"

And then my phone dies.

# isla

. . .

*"My favorite color is green. All shades of green. Except the lizardy ones. Not a fan of the reptiles."*

*~Jackson Porter, Playing with Matches Confessionals*

I PACK UP ALL my things before heading back to the beach to film the final episode of *Playing with Matches* later this afternoon. I've already done my last confessional. I have nothing left to say. My flight is leaving early tomorrow morning.

With each passing hour, I grow more concerned about Jackson's unexplained absence. My intuition tells me something is wrong. I just can't put my finger on it. Why would he just leave? Was he freaking out about what happened between us? Had he not meant the things he said? Had I just imagined the way he seemed to feel and convinced myself that there was something there because I wanted it so badly?

I wanted him so badly. I still want him so badly. I don't buy Rob's suggestion that he simply left. He wouldn't have left his things here if he had. Nothing in his room has been touched. His clothes from last night are hanging on the line in the bathroom, still damp and salty with ocean water. His clothes are still all tidily folded in the drawers.

When I fluff the pillows, I can smell his shampoo on the sheets. I pick up one of the pillows and hold it to my face, embracing it like a lover. Inhaling him.

*Where are you, Jackson?*

His clothes are one thing, but the laptop is another. He might leave here without his clothes, but not his laptop! Both of our passports are still in the safe. Rory and Rob seem so unconcerned. Do they know something that I don't know?

I try Jackson's phone one more time. Straight to voicemail.

What if Jackson decided to go for a swim and something happened? Unlikely, given that his swimsuit is still here. Or what if he was kidnapped? That happens to rich tech CEOs. Angry investors, jealous ex-lovers, government spies. My mind races through one ridiculous scenario after another.

Then, my mum calls.

"Isla, Darling! Did you see the pics of the ponies I posted on Instagram? We dressed them up like the Kardashians."

"No, Mummy. I thought I told you we've had to stay off social media."

"Really? Even Facebook and Instagram?"

"Especially Facebook and Instagram," I sigh.

"Well, that's no fun," my mum says. "Anyways, I wanted to let you know that Daddy fixed the pipes, so you don't have to call a plumber."

"*Daddy* fixed the plumbing?" I ask, shocked.

"I know. Can you believe it? Thirty-five years I have known this man and he's barely picked up a screwdriver. But lately, he's been on this whole YouTube tutorial kick, and he's turning into a regular Mr. Fixit."

"Daddy is watching YouTube tutorials on home repair?" I ask, finding it hard to fathom.

"Yes, Darling, and the best part about it is that I was so turned on after he serviced the pipes, that I asked him to service my pipes, and oh my! I'm going to ask him to pound some nails into the wall next. I know just what I'm going to wear!"

"Mum!" I object. "I cannot unhear that. I told you I didn't want to talk about that stuff."

"No, Isla, you told me you didn't want to talk about *your* sexual health. You didn't say I couldn't talk about mine."

"Let's not talk about anyone's sexual health, Mum?" I beg.

"Fine. But I still think you should have a fling before you leave. What about that American tech entrepreneur? He came up in my feed this morning. He seems like he might be amenable to a hook-up."

"I gotta go, Mum," I say. "Don't forget I'll be there next week."

I find Rob down on the beach with the crew. They're prepping the gazebo and tweaking the seating arrangements for the final ceremony. Cameramen are capturing B-roll of the tiki torches, firepits, floral garlands, and conch shells.

"Isla, you look luminous. Have you done your confessional already?" He points me back toward the pool area where the confessional tent is still set up. I see Owen and Alexis coming out. "Better hurry up. We're wrapping that up in an hour or so."

"I'm good," I say. "Do you have a minute?" I see a flicker of something across his usually cheerful and impassive face.

Impatience? He glances around, removes his headset, and waves to the crew.

"I'm taking five," he shouts - holding up five fingers. "Okay, Isla, what can I do for you? You have three minutes. I kinda need the other two to take a leak." He smiles apologetically.

I get right to the point.

"I'm worried that nobody's heard from Jackson," I say. "I've called him several times, and he's not picking up. His phone is going straight to voicemail."

"I'm sorry to ask, but is it possible he's blocked you?" Rob says. He seems relieved to see Cappy strolling up the beach. The old sea captain is all cleaned up. His beard is combed, and his clothes are pressed. "Let me go talk to Cappy; maybe he's seen him."

"I'm coming, too," I say.

"No, no, I'm sorry, Isla. I have some other private biz I need to chat with Cappy about. Stuff for tonight's episode. I'm worried, too, though. If we don't hear from Jackson by the time we're done taping, I say we get the authorities involved. I just don't think they'd be willing to do anything just yet though."

Rob turns to go, and I feel my phone buzzing in my pocket. I'm so overwhelmed with relief to see the call is from Jackson. In my haste to answer, I clumsily drop the phone on the sand. Snatching it up again, I swipe at the screen hurriedly.

"Hello?" I say. "Jackson? Are you okay?"

There's nobody there. When I look at the screen again the call has disconnected.

# jackson

. . .

*"Miracles happen. People change. They learn to speak new love languages. There's a YouTube tutorial for everything these days."*

*~Isla Fairfax, Playing With Matches Confessionals*

MOTHERFU-

I'm so busy cursing at my useless phone that I slip on some iguana shit and nearly wipe out right next to the big daddy hisser. At this point, we're starting to get to know one another, and I'd like to think we have formed an uneasy alliance. He bloats his grotesque throat balloon at me and thrashes his tail.

"It's not funny. And you'll have to be a bit nicer if you want me to sing to you some more," I say. Another iguana turns toward me and clicks nervously, like he's saying *"You can't speak to the boss like that, Dude. He'll fuck you up."* The clicking sounds a bit like my trusty pen. I find it soothing.

"Fine. FINE," I say. "Hope you like late 80s hits." Then I launch into "Playing With Matches," totally belting it out.

> We're a love inferno, with no escape,
> Blazing emotions that we just can't shake,
> We're playing with fire, got nowhere to go,
> Destined to burn, in this twisted show.

It's a great song. There's a reason it was a hit. Catchy tune, with a great theme. It's been used in a few movies.

My voice sounds like my dad's did. That's one thing I inherited from him. Chelsea was jealous of me for getting Dad's voice. She wanted to be in all the high school musicals, but she couldn't sing for shit. That's how she ended up backstage with Dean.

I was never grateful for getting blessed with the voice. It only highlighted how many other things I might have inherited. His temper, his selfishness, and his ability to abandon his family. There were plenty of things I didn't want.

I rattle the dog tags and the sobriety chip in my pocket. Murphy had been an old dog when he died. But he'd been in decent shape. He was my best friend.

I sing the song a second time before I make it back to the bottom of the rock. The big hissy bloke follows after me like maybe I have some food. *Or maybe I am food.*

"Don't you follow me," I scold. "You stay here with your friends. They need you. You're their leader." The lizard thrashes his tail again, does a few pushups, as if to say, *"Damn straight I'm the man!"* and then he scurries nimbly back up to his sunny patch at the top of the rock.

The cooler is still there, right where I left it in the shade of the lean-to.

I tear open a Power Bar and drink down half the second bottle of water. In my pocket, I turn the sobriety chip over. I run my thumb over Murphy's tags, rubbing the two discs together.

*I don't expect you to forgive me.*

The handheld radio reminds me of the walkie-talkies my friends and I played with as kids. We pretended to be spies and outlaws. We crept around barns in dirt lots and hid in sheds. I stayed out way too late. I was always the last one to be called home. There were times when I wondered how long it would take for anyone to realize it if I didn't come home at all.

I have two options left. I can spend the night here and miss the chance to see Isla again before she leaves, OR I can man up and use the radio to call Cappy.

There's no question what I'm going to do. I can't let Isla leave the island without telling her how I feel about her.

The radio comes alive with a crackle of static and fuzz that reminds me of time travel. You don't hear these sorts of sounds anymore. Who still uses VHF radios? Everything is satellite.

"This is Jackson Porter on Reptile Isle requesting help. Cappy, you there? Anyone? Can you read me?" I say.

The only reply is the crackle of more static and a noise like rushing air. I consider changing the channel but I'm assuming there's a reason why the dial is duct-taped in place.

"Hello? Can anyone hear me? I'm stuck on Reptile Isle."

"Jackson?" The voice is echo-y and distant like he's speaking into a tin can attached to a wire on the other side of the universe.

"Dad?" I say, voice cracking. "I mean Cappy? Is that you?"

"Hang tight, Son. I'll be there in ten minutes. Rob told me where he left you. I don't think he knew about your lizard thing. Think you can make it out to the dock?"

# isla

. . .

*"Don't think I won't kill you, Mother(BLEEP). I need to get back to the island so I can tell Isla how I feel about her. You're gonna need a bigger army of dragons if you want to stop me."*

*~Jackson Porter, Playing With Matches Reptile Isle Webcam Footage*

SITTING in the cramped tent and watching the final episode being taped from behind the scenes, isn't the same without Jackson. The sun is just starting to set, and my heart is aching.

*He isn't back.*

I thought I knew how much he wanted me when he sang to me. I thought I knew *why*. When he made love to me last night, I knew exactly what I wanted and not just for one night. I allowed myself to hope that the family curse was lifted. I thought that somehow I'd have a chance, too.

I already knew. I knew I was falling in love. And the premonition blurred the lines between past, present, and future for me. It tints every memory and infuses me with a certainty I've never felt before. I am in love with him. It feels like I've always been in love with him.

I should have known not to start something when the moon was full. The pull of the tides was too strong. The tug of his teeth against my lower lip. The way he carried me to the bed and dropped me there, then just stood there over me, staring at me. Drinking me up. I'm never going to forget last night.

*Is it because I was too much? Or not enough?*

It always comes down to that.

"Welcome back to the pavilion," Marco greets the three couples. The couples are all arranged on the loveseats in the same pairings that we ended the last episode on. Before the dates. It seems like that was ages ago.

"So you have all gone on your individual dates by now and spent time together here at the beautiful Peaches Resort. And what I am dying to know is, what do you think? Did the algorithm pick the right person for you? Were your dates magical? Tonight we will be learning which of our couples will leave together, and which ones will continue playing with matches. I just hope nobody gets burned!"

"Cut!" Rob yells. "Two minutes everyone. I just want to reset to make sure we're getting that glorious sunset in the background as we go into the final Shell Ceremony."

"Knock, knock," Alexis says quietly, waving the tent flap. "Permission to enter?" The crew member nods, and I wave her to the empty chair next to mine.

"Please come join me," I say.

"He's still not back?" Alexis looks concerned.

"Nope, and nobody's heard from him," I shake my head, unable to dispel the tightness in my throat. "You're good friends with him; is this normal for him?"

"No," Alexis shakes her head. "I can't think of any reason, unless…"

"Unless what?"

"What happened last night, Isla?" Alexa looks at me intently. "After Jackson sang to you?"

I wrap my arms around myself, close my eyes, and shake my head. I can't. I can't do this now. The fabric walls of the tent feel like they're sucking into the center towards me, suffocating me. A moth flaps hopelessly against one of the monitors.

"Nothing," I say. "I mean, we had a nice night."

Alexis glances around the tent at the tech crew in their oversized headphones. They are all completely engrossed in what they are doing. The crew has resettled everyone, and they're getting ready to film from another angle.

"Do you want to get out of here?" Alexis asks.

"Yes," I say with enthusiasm. "It's a little stuffy. I think I'd rather watch outside."

"Let's go then," Alexis holds out her hand to help me up, and we walk into the night. "I'm sure he's fine, wherever he is. Jackson's not a risk-taker. At least not with his physical self," she rolls her eyes. "Did he do the Bruce Springsteen song?"

"He did," I smile at the memory.

"I'm sorry I missed that." Alexis's eyes are shining, and I see where she's looking. She's gazing at Owen and Paula. Someone is checking Owen's mic. We settle ourselves on a bench, close enough to watch and far enough to be out of the shot.

"Okay, everyone, we're ready to roll again. Nice job on the backdrop, Mother Nature!" Rob says. "Quiet on the set!"

Marco is back. He's wearing a pale, untucked linen shirt with his designer jeans. He's a little less perfectly coiffed than other times I've seen him. His hair is a little tousled and uneven, and he's not wearing any make-up. He seems relaxed. Happy even. Somehow, this natural look only makes him seem more handsome. He glances at Paula quickly before launching into his monologue.

"This is the moment we are waiting for. The moment where we see who will be leaving as a couple and who will be going home alone."

Alexis squeezes my hand and sits up straighter.

"We will begin with Paula and Owen. Paula and Owen had a beautiful date learning sand sculpture techniques. But was it enough to cement their bond? Paula?" Marco places her shell gently in her hands. "The shell is in your hands," Marco says. "What will you do?" I think he's holding his breath.

Alexis grips me tighter.

"I'm so sorry, Owen," Paula says. "You are a lovely man. Truly a sweetheart. But I just can't see us moving forward," she smiles apologetically. "And what I mean when I say seeing it, is seeing it here." She pats her breastbone. "I'm going to go with my heart and continue to play with fire, Owen. I don't think you're my match."

"Well, this means you'll both be going home, Owen and Paula. Please take a moment to say goodbye to everyone." Marco says. Owen is biting his cheeks, trying not to smile as he fist-bumps the rest of the cast.

Marco waits to hug Paula last, trailing his fingers over her bare back, off camera, before a PA leads her away.

Alexis exhales. "Thank God that's over," she whispers.

"Lacey?" Marco picks up Lacey's shell and hands it to her. She stands for a moment, gazing between Ryker and Darwin, biting her lip and twirling the end of a long dark strand of hair indecisively.

"Is there a problem, Lacey?" Marco asks. He's holding another shell behind his back.

"Yes, Marco," Lacey pouts. "I guess I've always been a little extra. And now I need to ask you for a favor."

"We had a feeling this might happen. So we took the liberty of making this for you." Marco holds up the second shell. Lacey smiles broadly and takes it in her other hand.

"Ryker? Darwin?" She holds the shells aloft, one in each hand. "Will you boys accept my shells?

"We will!" Darwin jumps to his feet, waiting for Ryker to come to his side. They take the shells from her.

"Lacey?" Darwin asks, nodding at Ryker. The two men link arms, each holding a shell to their lips.

"Do you hear our call?" Ryker smiles at her.

And then they blow.

"Good Lord!" Alexis doubles over laughing. "What would you call that?"

"Flatulent goat," I state with conviction. "And on that note," I say, "I think I'm going to call it a day and head back to the room." I give Alexis a quick hug and turn to go.

"Try it again, Guys," Rob says. "Otherwise we'll fix it in post. Let me count you down. Three... Two..."

But before he gets to one, I hear it. A loud, clear note cutting through the air, coming from the direction of the water.

It sounds like a low, sonorous horn, piercing the night.

The set goes silent as everyone strains to listen. There's a second sound now, too, a low mechanical hum that sounds like a boat motor. And then the horn sounds again. Closer this time.

"Did you hear that?" I turn back to Alexis. We are all looking out to sea now. Her eyes are wide, too.

"Hells yes," she says. "Was that a conch shell? I mean a conch shell the way it's *supposed* to sound?"

# jackson

. . .

*"I'm not sure what's next for me. Things feel a bit up in the air. Has anyone heard from Jackson?"*

*~ Isla Fairfax, Playing with Matches Confessionals*

"SO," my father asks as I climb aboard his boat, "How's it going, Jackson?"

"Seriously?" I ask. "It's gone better."

"Yeah," he agrees. "But it could be worse. It sure is great to see you, Son."

"How'd Rob get you here?" I ask.

"Well," Dad says, staring at the horizon. "He told me he was a huge fan - that's why he named the show after my hit song. He wanted me to be a part of the show somehow. And then he spun a tale about how his own dad was a drunk and died before they had a chance to reconcile. Said that he'd never forgive himself if he didn't at least try to make things right between us."

"Did he now?" I say. "Did his dad pass before or after he met his fiance, using my app?"

"Huh," my father shakes the seaspray off his hat and repositions it. He smiles wryly.

"Do you think any of it's true?" I ask.

"What's the difference? He didn't get me to do anything that I didn't want to do. I've been dying to reach out to you and your sister for years. I was just too chickenshit."

"What did he tell you about us?" I ask.

"He told me your sister's getting married, to someone he knows. We got to talking, and he asked if I knew about your app, which I did not. And then he told me how your company's been struggling. He thought that maybe you've been struggling a bit, too."

I consider this. "So you thought, what? You'd just show up and try to fix me and all would be forgiven?"

"I don't expect you to forgive me," Dad echoes the sentiment from the card he left in the envelope. "But I was hoping that maybe we could stay in touch. And maybe over time, if you feel okay with it, you and your sister could let me back into your lives. Just a little. On a trial basis."

The boat bucks, jumping over a wave, and I sit down hard, reaching for a rail to hold onto. Dad barely budges. It's like his feet are glued to the deck. He was always like that, on surfboards and on boats. Steady on the water and tipsy on the ground. It's like he wasn't made to navigate life on land.

"Okay," I say.

"Okay?" he looks surprised. "Just like that?"

"I can't speak for Chelsea, Dad. It's not like either of us can erase the past. But I'd like to stay in touch more." I reach into my pocket for the sobriety chip. "And you should probably keep this. It's a big accomplishment."

"Thank you." Cappy pockets the chip and sizes me up. We sit in silence for a few minutes before he speaks again.

"Tell me about your matchmaking app," he says.

"We analyze several factors to create a predictive long-term compatibility model," I sum it up with my elevator pitch.

"Crunchy vs smooth peanut butter? Regular or delicate underwear loads? This is your idea of love?" Cappy looks at me with disgust and spits into the passing water.

"It may sound trivial, but these are all critical factors when it comes to assessing long-term compatibility."

"Bullshit," My father laughs. "Your mother and I had absolutely nothing in common. And look what happened?"

"Umm, what happened with you and Mom is pretty much the reason I created the app," I say. "The two of you were a total trainwreck. I wouldn't wish that on anyone."

"We weren't a trainwreck because of a lack of love or compatibility, Jackson," my dad says. "We were a trainwreck because I'm an alcoholic. And let me tell you, if your mom and I hadn't loved each other and you kids so much, it probably would have ended way worse. For sure I'd be dead. What happened to our family was my fault. But it had nothing to do with love." He takes off and shakes his cap again, but it's clear he's just using this as an excuse to wipe his eyes. "I'm sorry it affected you this way."

"What way?" I say defensively, "In the make-a-success-of-myself way? The make-life-better-for-other-people-instead-of-making-it-a-living-hell way?"

"No, the dumbass, pigheaded, chickenshit, afraid-of-love way," Cappy kicks the boat into a higher gear, and we pick up speed, going faster each time we slap down over the waves. "You're what, thirty-four? Thirty-five? Tell me about your last serious relationship."

"I don't do those," I fold my arms around myself, shivering.

"Why not?" my father reaches for a beach towel and tosses it at me. "Wrap yourself up in that. It's clean."

"I just don't. I'm not interested in that kind of thing," I say automatically, only realizing when the words are already halfway out that it's not how I feel.

"Really?" Dad says. "Then you won't mind if we do a spot of fishing before you get back? I hear the snappers are biting." He cuts the engine.

"I'd rather get back," I clench my teeth.

"Oh yeah, why's that? What's your hurry, Son?" My father opens a cabinet and pulls out a tackle box.

"I have some important work to do," I say.

"Oh, come on. Work can wait. We've got over a decade of catching up to do."

He knows I'm lying. He could always read me. And he always called me on my shit.

*My old man can be such an asshole.*

"Fine. If you must know, I need to talk to Isla. I'm sure she's worried about me. After we spent last night together, I snuck out to grab us breakfast and disappeared for the whole day."

"I saw her earlier," Dad says. "That must be why she looked so sad. Rob said he was worried she might leave early. I don't even know if she'll still be there. Oh, well. Easy come, easy go. Right?"

"What?" I stand up. "Turn the boat back on right now. I gotta get back there."

"Or what?" Dad blocks me as I try to reach the controls.

"Or she might leave without my talking to her and telling her something important," I say, trying a second time, unsuccessfully, to start the boat.

"I'm not that old, Jackson. I just look it. I'm in good shape. You're not gonna get me to hand over the helm of my boat," my father says. "So you may as well fess up, so we can get back in a timely fashion."

"Fess up about what?" I say.

"How you feel about that funny red-headed British girl."

"I have no idea what you're talking about," I argue pointlessly. I don't know how he knows. But I don't want to let him have the victory.

"Oh come on, Son. I saw the way you looked at her, and I heard you singing to her last night. Please tell me you're not the kind of asshole who uses your talent just to get laid?"

"Isla's the only woman I've ever sung to," I admit.

"But she's just a friend," my dad says, giving me a pointed look as he leans back against the steering wheel column, arms folded. "Or what do you call that friends with benefits deal? Fuckbuddy? Fess up already, you dolt." He raises a contrary eyebrow at me, and it's infuriatingly similar to looking in a mirror. Is this how my sister feels when I give her a hard time?

"Jesus, Dad, did it ever occur to you that I might want to say it to her before I say it to you!?" I groan. "Can we please just go back now?"

"Close enough," my father capitulates, starting the engine. "Although you might want to practice your delivery with me. You only get to tell someone you love them for the first time once. You want to make it special."

"Thanks, but no," I shake my head. "I'm good. And I'm in a hurry."

"Right then," my father kicks the boat into a gear that we haven't accessed yet, and I'm thrown back into my seat.

I can see the resort in the distance, and the lights of the film crew filming the final ceremony at the gazebo on the beachfront. I just hope I'm not too late.

A few hundred yards more, and I can make out individual cast members through my father's binoculars. I see Ryker and Darwin engaged in some sort of weird, stand-up arm wrestling contest.

Scanning the area around the gazebo, I spy the tent with the monitors. Is Isla in there without me? I do a visual sweep of the beach. That's when I see her. A flash of bright red hair against a plain white dress. She's hugging Alexis.

"Shit! I think she's leaving!" I put the binoculars down, frustrated. "Can we go any faster?"

"We're almost there," Dad pats my shoulder.

"But what if she leaves? What if I'm too late?" I panic.

"Tell you what," my father reaches back into the cabinet beneath the steering wheel and pulls out a large polished conch shell. "You still remember how to blow one of these like I taught you?"

# isla

*"I love you, Isla Fairfax. And if for some reason I don't survive this ordeal, I hope this webcam footage will serve as a testament. I'm going to go back down to the beach now and call Cappy. Who happens to be my father, by the way. But I'll explain about that later."*

*~ Jackson Porter, Playing With Matches Reptile Isle Webcam Footage*

"IT'S JACKSON." Alexis shouts, staring at the horizon "I know it's him!" She uses her phone like a telescope, zooming in and snapping a photo. "That crazy bastard. What's he up to?"

We watch as a small craft bypasses the pier traveling parallel to the beach. It heads straight towards the stretch of sand in front of the gazebo where we are filming.

"Right on time," Rory mumbles as she rushes past on her way down to the water's edge.

"What's right on time?" Alexis asks. But Rory ignores her. Alexis grabs my hand. "Come on," she tugs me after her. "Let's go see what's going on."

I look back at the gazebo where the cameraman seems dumbfounded about what to do. The camera is still pointed at Darwin, Ryker, and Lacey. Rob snaps his fingers impatiently at the guy.

"Don't stop shooting now. Keep rolling! Follow Isla down to the beach!"

As the rest of the cast trails down to the beach and the colors in the sky start to fade from orange to purple, the crew scrambles to set up lights.

"This is so exciting!" Marco narrates loudly. He has Paula's shell tucked under his arm as he guides her down the beach. "Nobody knows where Jackson has been all day! And now he is arriving at the beach on a small boat, *blowing a shell*. What can it mean?"

I kick off my shoes and race to the water's edge. As the boat draws closer I make out the two people on board. Jackson is waving and the other man is… Cappy? Is that Cappy driving the boat?

Suddenly Jackson stands up on the bow of the boat and dives into the water, swimming for the shore. Lacey gasps.

"Oh my God!" Marco says, continuing to narrate. I'm not sure whether he's still doing it for Paula's sake or if it's still for the show. "Now the AI Swiper is diving into the water and swimming for the shore. We do not know where he has been or why he is here now or what this can mean for him and Isla."

"Yesss!" Paula pumps a fist. "Go Jackson!"

I look around for Rob and finally spot the producer a short way down the beach. He's standing with the dive instructor who is holding a pair of binoculars and a flotation belt. Rory is also waiting nearby holding a stack of towels. It's almost like they knew someone would be swimming to shore.

*What is going on here?*

Jackson is almost at the beach now, and the cast and crew are all cheering and clapping. When he's close enough to stand in the water, he strides toward us through the surf, like some sort of glowering sea demon. His shirt clings to him, and his silhouette is sharp and perfectly cut, backlit by the boat's lights. "Rob?" I turn toward the producer, just before Jackson reaches the shore. "What have you done?"

"He needed a grand gesture, and I needed a grand finale." Rob shrugs and holds out his hands, palms up. "It's a win-win." And then Jackson decks him.

Cappy flashes the boat's lights twice.

"Maybe I had that coming," Rob calls from the ground. He spits out some sand. "But if we producers have offended, please forgive me, Jackson? I didn't force anyone to come here. The world is the stage. I've merely assembled the cast, and what great luck to get you all here together like this! If you ask me to not air any of this, I won't. I consider you a friend."

Rob holds out his hand hopefully, and after a moment's hesitation, Jackson begrudgingly helps him up.

"I think," Rob continues, carefully, "if we can all calm down and embrace the serendipity of this moment, we have the opportunity to make both great TV *and* amends."

Jackson snatches a towel from Rory and roughly dries his hair with it.

"Keep rolling!" Rob cautiously gives the cameraman the thumbs up.

"The AI Swiper is very angry. He has made it to shore, and he punched the producer!" Marco's accent is getting more pronounced as he continues to provide the blow-by-blow account.

Jackson turns and glares at Marco, who visibly cowers.

"Also Jackson is very handsome, and when he storms the beach like this, how can any woman resist?" Marco adds, speaking in a conciliatory fashion.

"I don't understand what's going on here," I say. *Why are Ryker and Darwin helping the crew members drag the shell-encrusted, tiled throne toward me?* "What about the finale?"

"Turns out the finale of the show isn't about all these people, Isla. I think it's about you and me." Jackson says. He is pacing in front of me.

My heart is pounding. I pan across the strange scene, trying to take it all in. I feel cornered. Cappy is jogging towards us from the pier. I take a few steps back.

*Everyone is looking at me.*

Jackson has stopped pacing.

"I'm so glad I got back here in time. There's something I need to say to you, Isla. Will you hear me out?" Jackson asks, imploringly.

"I think you should sit down in the mermaid chair," Alexis has appeared at my side, and she gives me a little nudge.

Cappy nods encouragingly. "Hear him out."

Tentatively I sit down. I'm so relieved to see Jackson. I'd been so worried. Where was he?

*And why do I keep picturing dragons?*

Jackson kneels in front of me.

I'm not used to being the center of attention. It feels very strange to have so many people looking at us. I try to paint them all out as I focus on the man in front of me.

Jackson takes my hand. His hands are shaking.

"You scare the shit out of me, Isla Fairfax. But I'm tired of being scared. I don't want to be friends or friends with benefits. I don't want to settle into some safe, tidy, sweet spot. I want more than that. I want to love you. And I want you to love me, even if it's messy and terrifying. I would fight dragons for you. I am in love with you. You were right about everything. Especially the chemistry part. Ones and zeros are not nearly enough for me. I want infinity."

Tears are streaming down my face. This feels like a dream. I almost wish someone would pinch me.

"I love you, too," I say. "I think I have since the moment you brought up Lupercalia. I wanted to wring your neck. But that's not all I wanted to do to you."

"I'm so sorry I was such a jerk to you." Jackson takes my hand and lifts me to my feet. He wipes my tears away and kisses me gently on the lips.

"Ahem," Marco coughs. "I think that Cappy here has something that he wants to give to you?"

"I do," Cappy steps forward, holding the most enormous polished conch shell I've ever seen. He hands it to me and winks. "Here you go, Isla."

I turn the shell over in my hands, marveling at the glossy pink and white opening. And then I hold it to my ear, listening for the sound of the ocean and hearing so much more. Children laughing. Corks popping. Champagne fizzing. Glasses clinking. Fireworks bursting, Sleigh bells ringing, and mini-Shetland ponies neighing. A symphony of happy sounds. A lifetime of them. All inside the rushing waters.

"Jackson," I hold out the shell in front of me. "Will you accept my shell?"

"I will," he grins, holding it up to his lips. "And Isla, do you hear my call?"

He lifts the shell and blows it loud and clear enough to split the night sky. A few night birds scatter, and the stars start to twinkle like someone just flipped the on switch.

"Did you two hear Jackson blow that shell?" Lacey looks critically at her beaus. "*That* is how it's done, Boys."

"And that," Rob says with a triumphant grin, "is a wrap!"

# epilogue: isla

*Six Months Later*

I'm back at home in Rome. It's a typically brisk February day, but the sun is shining and there's a line forming outside the bookshop for the book signing event for the final book in *The Mystic Matchmaker* series. People are excited to get their hands on an autographed copy. The ticketed event is sold out.

"Are you ready to do this?" Emily asks.

"I am," I smile. "Remember the last time we were here?"

"How could I forget?" She laughs, glancing back at her fiancé Blaze, who's happily ensconced in an armchair in the back corner of the cozy bookstore reading a book. "I don't think he minds being back here and not having to sign any books."

"It was nice of the two of you to be here for my book signing," I sigh.

"We're just glad the timing worked out so well. I'm so glad I could get here a little early and see my family and help you get ready!"

Epilogue: Isla

I want to tell Emily that she is like a sister to me. The sister I never had. But I already know she feels the same way. She squeezes my hand.

Suddenly the door bursts open, and a shockingly handsome man in a pirate-style shirt and a cape enters, gently leading a petite brunette in a laced-up corset over a velvet gown.

There's a bit of screaming going on outside the door. The security guard that we hired for the event is earning his keep. I have to wonder who the crowd is really here to see, him or me.

"Marco is here!" the man tosses back his long curly hair.

"And Paula is here, too!" the woman beside him announces.

I rush to hug them both and introduce them to Blaze and Emily. And then we all admire the cover of the final book of *The Mystic Matchmaker* series which features Marco, front, center, and shirtless on the cover.

"Now this is a bestseller!" Marco exclaims, tapping the book emphatically and admiring the image of himself.

"Fourth week in a row at the top of the charts," I smile with pride.

"Marco tells you, I make the books sell!"

"Where's Jackson?" Paula asks, tilting her head as if she's listening for him. She's so perceptive that it's easy to forget how little she can see. "Isn't he here?"

"He was supposed to be here an hour ago," I sigh. "He went to pick up his sister at the airport but her flight must have been delayed. He texted us a while ago that they were running late. He'd better get here soon. He's bringing the coffee and pastries!"

"Oh, no!" Paula frowns worriedly. "I hope that they get here soon." Then she smiles. "Jackson is good at the dramatic last-minute arrivals."

"I'm sure he'll be here soon," Emily assures everyone. "I'm just going to finish getting everything set up while we wait. How many books did you want on the table?" she asks me. "Nice costumes, by the way," she admires Marco and Paula's outfits.

"Thank you," Paula beams. "I made them myself. A love for cosplay is just one of the many things Marco and I have in common. I am so grateful to Isla and Jackson for bringing us together."

"It was fate," I say.

If you'd asked me whether the two of them would stay together when we left the island, I would have given them fifty-fifty odds. Not that I doubted Marco's affection for Paula. I just questioned whether it would stick. He's notoriously fickle.

But the two have not left each other's side for a moment since we left the Peaches Resort. After introducing Paula to his family, Marco proposed.

"I'm here, I'm here!" The bell on the door announces Jackson, followed by Chelsea and – much to my surprise – Alexis and then a pretty jet-haired petite woman in a fabulous furry coat. She has an infant swaddled in a front carrier. She looks tired but happy to be here.

"Oh my God! Georgia! I can't believe you're here with little Joanie!" Emily rushes to take the baby.

"What's going on?" I ask, utterly gobsmacked to see the whole *Lit Lovers* crew and then some, suddenly assembled on my turf. "When did you all get here?"

"She's surprised!" Alexis cheers. "I knew we could do it!" She high-fives Emily and introduces me to Georgia who has her hands full with the fussing baby.

"Owen, Hudson, and Dean should be here any minute with the coffee. I can't wait for you to meet Dean and Hudson!" Jackson is practically bouncing.

"I've heard so much about them that they already feel like family," I smile.

"Let Auntie Em do her thing, Georgia. Hand that baby over here!" Emily, who is unfazed by the infant's fussing and takes the baby from her.

"Do you know how hard it was to surprise you?" Jackson takes his coat off and wraps his arms around me. His body is still warm from the wool overcoat, and I lean into his sunny glow. "It doesn't take much to pull the wool over my eyes, but you're another story. The lengths these people went to!"

"How long have you all been planning this?" I ask. I am dumbfounded, too. It's not like me to be this blindsided. I usually get a feeling, but this time – nothing. "Seriously, Jackson, you must have known if you planned it?"

"That's just it! I didn't plan a thing," Jackson exclaims, releasing me. "I had no idea who else I was picking up at the airport besides Chelsea. That's why it took so long. We had to figure out all the cars."

"Your face when we all got off the flight!" Chelsea laughs. "That alone is worth the jet lag. Not that it's too bad. We had those lay flat seats in business class. I slept like a baby!"

I turn to Emily, who is now bouncing the baby and cooing at her. Blaze has also come over to greet everyone. Upon seeing him, Marco drops the stack of books emblazoned with his image that he was hauling to the signing tables. He rushes straight over to give Blaze a huge bear hug.

"Dottore Amore!" he addresses Blaze by the nickname the Italian press has for him. "You must meet my bella amore, Paula!"

Once the intros are over, I raise an eyebrow at Emily. "Surely you knew about this?"

"I had no clue," she swears. "I wish I could have pulled off keeping it all a secret, but I'm too much of an open book. You've read me before, Isla." She tilts her head towards Blaze. "You knew what I was thinking before I knew."

"So whose idea was all this?" I ask as the harried security guard lets in Dean, Owen, and Hudson. Dean and Owen are carrying large cardboard carafes of coffee, and Hudson is pushing a pram full of bagged pastries from my favorite bakery around the corner.

The shopkeeper and her assistants rush over to take the items from them, rapidly getting them set up on a table in the back of the bookshop.

For a moment, Jackson just stands there grinning at his two best friends. "We decided to do this so last minute. I can't believe you guys all came. I can't believe you're actually here."

"I'd like to take all the credit, but Rob Goodfellow organized all the plane tickets," Dean says. "But we would have found a way regardless. Rob sends his well wishes for the wedding, by the way. He said he's sorry he can't be here. He's shooting something in Tierra Del Fuego."

"We wouldn't miss this for the world," Hudson chimes in. "I can't wait to see what a Lupercalia-themed wedding is like. I just hope it's okay that we've come a day early and crashed your book signing."

The bookstore owner looks at our large entourage and frowns. She taps her watch impatiently, pointing to the crowd outside. A couple of paparazzi are circling out front like sharks.

"It's time. We can't keep them waiting any longer," Jackson says. "They seem quite anxious to get their hands on your book, Isla."

"There's just one thing," I remember. "I need a pen!"

"I got you, take mine. " Jackson pulls his trusty clicky pen from his pocket. He clicks it a few times and waves it with a flourish. "You know I'd brave dragons for you."

"I know," I laugh, "I've seen the webcam footage."

"I'd run naked through the streets of Rome for you, too," Jackson whispers in my ear, pulling me in for one more kiss before the shopkeeper opens the door.

"I don't think that will be necessary," I say.

"Well, maybe I could run naked through the apartment later?" He looks hopeful.

"I'm counting on it," I laugh, reaching for the pen. Jackson holds it just out of my reach, smiling mischievously.

"Give it!" I poke him in the ribs.

"Not until you say the magic words," his eyes flash.

"Okay then, you depraved fiend," I whisper so only he can hear, growling slightly in his ear. "I want it NOW!"

# about the author

Ciara lives in Southern California with her husband, four fantastic children, and an odd-eyed cat. She enjoys traveling, crafting, and taking naps on cruise ships.

For news about Ciara's upcoming releases, bonus material & newsletter subscription info please visit:

linktr.ee/ciarablumeauthor